50
Mysteries

Selected By
Isaac Asimov,
Martin H. Greenberg.
And Joseph D. Olander

GP

GOODWILL PUBLISHING HOUSE™

B-3, RATTAN JYOTI, 18, RAJENDRA PLACE, NEW DELHI-110008 (INDIA)
TEL.: 25750801, 25755519, 25820556 FAX : 91-11-25763428

This special low priced Indian reprint is published by arrangement with Sterling Publishing Company, Inc. New York, U.S.A.

Published in India by
GOODWILL PUBLISHING HOUSE™
B-3 Rattan Jyoti,18 Rajendra Place
New Delhi-110008 (INDIA)
Tel. : 25750801, 25755519, 25820556
Fax : 91-11-25763428
E-mail : goodwillpub@vsnl.net
website : www.goodwillpublishinghouse.com

Printed at :-
Kumar offset
New Delhi

CONTENTS

Snacks

by Isaac Asimov

As a man who constantly battles the upward-edging scale, I am perfectly ready (even delighted) to admit that nothing beats a nice roast duck dinner—or filet mignon—or brook trout—with, of course, all the fixings.

Yet even the best trenchermen among us will admit that there are times during the light-hearted conviviality of a successful cocktail party when nothing beats a carrot stick dipped into something garlicky, the cracker on which a bit of chopped liver or smoked salmon rests, the shrimp dipped in a tangy sauce.

There are, in other words, times for the full dinner and times for the snacks.

And so it is in literature. What is better than a long and exciting mystery novel when we have a day of leisure in which to track down the clues and follow the intricate play of action?

But suppose we need something for just those few minutes before dropping off, or for some minutes of comfort over a sandwich or while waiting for a train? In that case, how about all the excitement, thrills, and surprise of a mystery novel compressed into two thousand words or less? A snack, in other words.

If there's nothing like a snack at the right time, then here in this book are an even fifty of them, every one of them guaranteed by your humble anthologists. (And pray notice that even the introduction is snack-sized)

P.S. This anthology was inspired by the fact that I had done three previously on short-short science fiction, and I felt the same could be done for mysteries. It is hard, however, to do anything in the realm of the mystery anthology that the master, Ellery Queen, has not already done. In 1969 he published *Mini-Mysteries,* a collection of seventy stories, and this anthology follows in the tradition.

Six Words

by Lew Gillis

The editor looked up in annoyance. There, standing before him, having somehow penetrated to the heart of his cozy editorial sanctum, was—of all things—an author.

Automatically the editor's eyes flicked over the piles of manuscripts on his desk. Perhaps, he thought, this was some outraged author come to claim a treasured story submitted long ago and still grinding—slowly—through the mill of the gods.

But no, this author had come equipped with a manuscript of his own, which he now unceremoniously thrust into the face of the startled editor.

"Publish this!" he said peremptorily.

"Is *that* all?" the editor replied, recovering quickly. "May I remind you, my dear sir—"

"Publish this!" the author repeated, this time more menacingly. He was a large lumpy man with an untidy beard, and he looked as though he meant business.

The editor smiled expansively, playing for time. "There are, of course, many ways," he began, "to get a story published, Mr. . . . Mr. . . . ?"

"Gillis," the author stated. "Lew Gillis." He still stood with his manuscript thrust at the editor. "I am aware of the many ways to get a story published," he said flatly. "During the last several years I have had occasion to try them all."

"Really?" the editor rejoined brightly. He was growing bored.

"Without success," said Lew Gillis.

"Ah!" Things were becoming clearer. The man was obviously a disappointed author.

"I have, for example," Lew Gillis said, "submitted my

stories with covering letters calling attention to my previous literary successes." He shrugged. "To no avail."

"Perhaps," the editor suggested, "had these previous literary successes not been figments of your—"

"I have ignominiously scraped acquaintance with published authors, poor wretches of little or no talent, for the sole purpose of using their barely recognizable names to get past secretaries and into the presence of editors," Gillis continued.

"But this device, too," the editor completed the thought, "availed you nothing." He smiled wearily. "And not surprising either, when you consider that editors abhor—"

"Finally," the author went on, "I hit upon a scheme which, during the last year, has brought me considerable success."

In spite of himself the editor was interested. "A scheme?" he repeated.

"An extremely simple scheme," said the author. "Nowadays when I have a story to sell I merely choose an editor, find a way to elude his secretary, hold my manuscript out to him, as I am doing with you now, and speak six words."

"And those six words are . . .?" The editor felt some resentment at having to supply all the straight lines.

"And this six words are"—the burly author paused mischievously—"potent. Yes, yes, certainly potent."

"I imagine they would have to be," the editor acknowledged with ill-concealed sarcasm, "to achieve such remarkable results. Still, I don't understand—"

"The first response to them is invariably derisive," the author admitted, "as yours will no doubt be. Editors, as a class, are preternaturally contemptuous of authors. I would even feel justified in calling them monomaniacally arrogant."

"Surely," replied the editor, "that's a bit of an overstate- —"

"In the end, however, I have managed to convince most of them of the seriousness of my intentions. Those few I have not—" he shrugged. "Well, you would no doubt recognize their names at once. I could easily supply documentation."

"All this is very interesting, Mr. . . . . Mr. . . .?"

"Gillis," the author stated again. "Lew Gillis."

"But I'm afraid I must tell you, sir," the editor continued, probing with his foot as unobtrusively as possible for the emergency alarm button beneath his desk, "that there are no circumstances I can think of, no combination whatever of six words I can imagine, that could force me to publish a story, by you or by anyone else, that I did not expressly choose to publish."

For a moment the bearded author made no reply. Then once more, without warning, he thrust his manuscript, its title and author's name—SIX WORDS by Lew Gillis—now clearly visible, into the face of the editor.

"Publish this," he began, with an air of once and for all concluding the business.

"Or—?" the editor inquired.

Gillis grinned savagely. "That," he said, "is the third word."

The Little Things

by Isaac Asimov

Mrs. Clara Bernstein was somewhat past fifty and the temperature outside was somewhat past ninety. The air-conditioning was working, but though it removed the fact of heat it didn't remove the *idea* of heat.

Mrs. Hester Gold, who was visiting the 21st floor from her own place in 4-C, said, "It's cooler down on my floor." She was over fifty, too, and had blonde hair that didn't remove a single year from her age.

Clara said, "It's the little things, really. I can stand the heat. It's the dripping I can't stand. Don't you hear it?"

"No," said Hester, "but I know what you mean. My boy, Joe, has a button off his blazer. Seventy-two dollars, and without the button it's nothing. A fancy brass button on the sleeve and he doesn't have it to sew back on."

"So what's the problem? Take one off the other sleeve also."

"Not the same. The blazer just won't look good. If a button is loose, don't wait, get it sewed. Twenty-two years old and he still doesn't understand. He goes off, he doesn't tell me when he'll be back—"

Clara said impatiently, "Listen. How can you say you don't hear the dripping? Come with me to the bathroom. If I tell you it's dripping, it's dripping."

Hester followed and assumed an attitude of listening. In the silence it could be heard—drip—drip—drip—

Clara said, "Like water torture. You hear it all night. Three nights now."

Hester adjusted her large faintly tinted glasses, as though that would make her hear better, and cocked her head. She said, "Probably the shower dripping upstairs, in 22-G. It's Mrs. Maclaren's place. I know her. Listen, she's a good-hearted person. Knock on her door and tell her. She won't bite your head off."

Clara said, "I'm not afraid of her. I banged on her door five times already. No one answers. I phoned her. No one answers."

"So she's away," said Hester. "It's summertime. People go away."

"And if she's away for the whole summer, do I have to listen to the dripping a whole summer?"

"Tell the super."

"That idiot. He doesn't have the key to her special lock and he won't break in for a drip. Besides, she's not away. I know her automobile and it's downstairs in the garage right now."

Hester said uneasily. "She could go away in someone else's car."

Clara sniffed. "That I'm sure of. *Mrs.* Maclaren."

Hester frowned, "So she's divorced. It's not so terrible. And she's still maybe thirty—thirty-five—and she dresses fancy. Also not so terrible."

"If you want my opinion, Hester," said Clara, "what she's doing up there I wouldn't like to say. I hear things."

"What do you hear?"

"Footsteps. Sounds. Listen, she's right above and I know where her bedroom is."

Hester said tartly, "Don't be so old-fashioned. What she does is her business."

"All right. But she uses the bathroom a lot, so why does she leave it dripping? I wish she *would* answer the door. I'll bet anything she's got a décor in her apartment like a French I-don't-know-what."

"You're wrong, if you want to know. You're plain wrong. She's got regular furniture and lots of houseplants."

"And how do you know that?"

Hester looked uncomfortable. "I water the plants when she's not home. She's a single woman. She goes on trips, so I help her out."

"Oh? Then you would *know* if she was out of town. Did she tell you she'd be out of town?"

"No, she didn't."

Clara leaned back and folded her arms. "And you have the keys to her place then?"

Hester said, "Yes, but I can't just go in."

"Why not? She could be away. So you have to water her plants."

"She didn't tell me to."

Clara said, "For all you know she's sick in bed and can't answer the door."

"She'd have to be pretty sick not to use the phone when it's right near the bed."

"Maybe she had a heart attack. Listen, maybe she's dead and that's why she doesn't shut off the drip."

"She's a young woman. She wouldn't have a heart attack."

"You can't be sure. With the life she lives—maybe a boyfriend killed her. We've *got* to go in."

"That's breaking and entering," said Hester.

"With a *key*? If she's away you can't leave the plants to die. You water them and I'll shut off the drip. What harm? —And if she's dead, do you want her to lay there till who knows when?"

"She's not dead," said Hester, but she went downstairs to the fourth floor for Mrs. Maclaren's keys.

"No one in the hall," whispered Clara. "Anyone could break in anywhere anytime."

"Sh," whispered Hester. "What if she's inside and says 'Who's there'?"

"So say you came to water the plants and I'll ask her to shut off the drip."

The key to one lock and then the key to the other turned smoothly and with only the tiniest click at the end. Hester took a deep breath and opened the door a crack. She knocked.

"There's no answer," whispered Clara impatiently. She pushed the door wide open.

"The air conditioner isn't even on. It's legitimate. You want to water the plants."

The door closed behind them. Clara said, "It smells stuffy, in here. Feels like a damp oven."

They walked softly down the corridor. Empty utility room on the right, empty bathroom—

Clara looked in. "No drip. It's in the master bedroom."

At the end of the corridor there was the living room on the left, with its plants.

"They need water," said Clara. "I'll go into the master bath—"

She opened the bedroom door and stopped. No motion. No sound. Her mouth opened wide.

Hester was at her side. The smell was stifling. "What—"

"Oh, my God," said Clara, but without breath to scream.

The bed coverings were in total disarray. Mrs. Maclaren's head lolled off the bed, her long brown hair brushing the floor, her neck bruised, one arm dangling on the floor, hand open, palm up.

"The police," said Clara. "We've got to call the police."

Hester, gasping, moved forward.

"You mustn't touch anything," said Clara.

The glint of brass in the open hand—

Hester had found her son's missing button.

A Matter of Life and Death
by Bill Pronzini and Barry N. Malzberg

Letter from Herman Skolnick to the Committee for the Divine, Bay City, California:

I have perruzed your recent advertisement in *Astounding Spirits* with great interest. It is absolutely vital that I know the answer to the following question: is there a Life After Death? Please reply by return mail (my address is % General Delivery, Bay City).

P.S. I am quite serious. I must know the answer to this question immediately.

Letter from the Committee for the Divine to Herman Skolnick:

You will find the answer to your question, and many others, in our Course on Celestial Metaphysics, brochures on which are being released to you in conjunction with this letter. Payment of the full enrollment fee is due upon your signing up for the course, but there will be no further charges of any sort.

Letter from Herman Skolnick to the Committee for the Divine:

I do not think you understand the seriousness of my intent, or the necessity of my need for the answer to my question. I am desperate and I have neither the time nor the funds to enroll in your Course. I beg you to answer: is there a Life After Death?

Letter from the Committee for the Divine to Herman Skolnick:

As a result of certain laws of publications and information, regulating our use of the mails for our services, we are unable to reply to your question, the answer to which, as was stated in previous correspondence, will be found in our course on Celestial Metaphysics. We will allow a ten percent (10%) reduction in the price of the Course for immediate enrollment and will guarantee to refund your money promptly if you are not satisfied with the results.

Letter from Herman Skolnick to Elsa Wiggins, The Helping Hand Mission, Bay City, California:
I have heard many good things about the work you've been doing, and am writing to you because I urgently need your help. Please tell me (% General Delivery, Bay City): is there a Life After Death?

Letter from Elsa Wiggins to Herman Skolnick:
Thank you, brother, for your expression of faith in the community service which we at The Helping Hand Mission are so unselfishly performing in offering Hope for the lost, the intemperate, and the mis-directed among us. From your letter, we know that you too are one of those lost souls—but we cannot begin to offer you the proper guidance through correspondence. Won't you come in and see us?

(Our free lunch is served every day at noon; dinner at six p.m. Soup and coffee available at all hours. Liquor and tobacco prohibited. Donations always welcome, large or small.)

Letter from Herman Skolnick to Miss Dorinda, % the Miss Dorinda Answers column, Bay City Express, *Bay City, California:*
I am desperate to know the answer to this question: is there a Life After Death? No one seems willing to help me. Please, please, won't you tell me the answer (my address is % General Delivery, Bay City).

Letter from Miss Dorinda to Herman Skolnick:
I detected a genuine note of soulful desperation in your recent letter, Mr. Skolnick, and so I'm rushing this reply to you right away (we do have to be careful, you know, since many misguided individuals seem to take great pleasure in playing cruel and heartless practical jokes on selfless servants of the human condition such as myself).

The question of whether or not there is Life After Death is one which has bothered every profound person at one time or another during the course of his life. But to some questions, Mr. Skolnick, there are simply no answers. Can it be you seek guidance in this matter because of some crushing personal crisis? Such as a storm on the bittersweet sea of matrimony? If so, perhaps my new book, *Miss Dorinda Answers: Crises in Marriage,* which was recently published by Nabob Press at $6.95, might contain valuable insights.

I cannot help you otherwise, Mr. Skolnick, unless you confide in me the reasons for your desperate need to know if there is a Life After Death. But I do want to help you, very much, and if you will write to me again, outlining the nature of your personal crisis, I will do everything in my power to re-establish emotional harmony in your life.

Letter from Herman Skolnick to Doctor Franklin Powers, % The Magazine of Psychic Phenomenon, New York City:

I have perruzed your recent column in *The Magazine of Psychic Phenomenon,* in which you offered to respond to any questions from readers on topics of profound significance. I have such a question, Doctor, and I must have the answer as soon as possible. My address is % General Delivery, Bay City, California, and I assure you that I am asking your help with all the earnestness I possess. Help me! I am desperate!

Is there a Life After Death?

Letter from Doctor Franklin Powers to Herman Skolnick:

Thank you for your recent inquiry, Mr. Skolnick.

Ordinarily, I would not undertake to set forth such an opinion as you request; however, I do have definite feelings on the subject, being, if I may modestly say so, an eminently qualified authority on spiritual matters through my close association with Madame Zelda and other recognized mediums. Simply stated, my opinion then is thus: yes, Mr. Skolnick, there is a Life After Death—although even my dear departed aunt, with whom I have had several illuminating conversations through Madame Zelda, is unable to tell me its exact nature.

I hope you will find this response to be of some use, and I would like to hear from you again should you feel inclined.

Just why do you wish so desperately to know if there is a Life After Death?

Suicide note found near the body of Herman Skolnick:

I have feared for my sanity for some time now, and cannot face the prospect of another tomorrow. I would have drunk the ratsbane preparation long ago if I had not been disturbed about the question of Life After Death. I have now obtained sufficient proof, however, that there *is* a Life After Death and thus the final obstacle to the taking of my own life has been removed. I am sorry for all the trouble and inconvenience my death will cause my fiancée, my acquaintances, and of course the police, but I must selfishly think of myself at this moment. I simply cannot go on any longer.

Statement of the Foreman of the Jury at the Coroner's Inquest into the death of Herman Skolnick:

In view of the statements of investigating officers and of the strange nature of the correspondence found in the deceased's possession, we the jury of this inquest are of uniform agreement that Herman Skolnick was mentally disturbed and died by his own hand.

Letter from Robert Claverly to Miss Francine Allard, Bay City:

I realize this is a poor time to attempt to re-establish our once deeply-meaningful relationship, Francie, but you know how I feel about you. I'll be here and waiting whenever you need me. Perhaps, once time has begun to heal your grief and shock at the death of your fiancé, Herman Skolnick, and you have had the opportunity to carefully perruze our relationship in your mind, you will realize that I am and always have been the only man who could ever make you truly happy, and that I stand ready to do anything—anything at all—so that we might always be together. . .

Perfect Pigeon

by Carroll Mayers

At first I didn't favor the idea. I mean, all the odds have to be on your side for a successful bank hit. But Frankie kept pressing me. Like: "It'll be a piece of cake, Joe."

"You've checked them all?" I asked.

"Every bank in the city. Security Savings is our best bet."

"Because of one character." I made it a statement, not a question.

"Exactly," Frankie said. "I've been practically in his pocket for a week. He's Casper Milquetoast in person."

"Even a worm can turn."

"Not this worm. I *know* him, I tell you."

You've read accounts in the papers where a lone bandit tries to heist a bank by passing the teller a note threatening bodily harm, or maybe death, if he or she doesn't give with a jackpot of cash. Sometimes the bandit scores. Usually he doesn't. Usually the teller is only momentarily taken aback, then manages either to cry out or press an alarm button. Perhaps both. Whatever, it's a fiasco for the heister.

Frankie had in mind the note-passing gambit. The thing was, he had a refinement. He meant to be particular about the teller he passed that note *to*.

I couldn't fault Frankie's basic reasoning. If he could tab a teller, male or female, a real Nervous Nellie who'd be too scared, too paralyzed, to take any physical action other than complete compliance, Frankie would be home free—"a piece of cake."

That was where Frankie's "survey" came in. Checking the personnel (first by general appearance, then by discreet, in-depth, after-work surveillance) of every bank in the city, Frankie had come up with the perfect pigeon.

One Homer Jennings.

Homer was a teller at Security Savings, and the exact type Frankie wanted. Why Homer hadn't been put out to pasture long ago was a mystery. Certainly crowding mandatory retirement, Homer had a physique like Twiggy's and eyesight comparable to Mr. Magoo's. A lifetime bachelor, he lived alone behind triple-bolted doors and seldom went out after dark. More important, he frequently wrote letters to the newspapers deploring "crime in the streets."

Unbelievable? Not really. And he was definitely our man.

However, I still wasn't completely sold. "There's an alarm at Security Savings, isn't there?"

"Sure. A button on the floor at each teller's station."

"And you're saying Homer will be so terrified he'll simply freeze, do nothing but hand over the money? Won't even shift one foot to that button?"

"He won't risk it, Joe. He'll be scared witless, believe me."

It sounded good the way Frankie spelled it out. Also, I'd be going along just for the ride, so to speak. Because I wouldn't be *in* the bank at the moment of truth. I'd be outside, behind the wheel of a souped-up jalopy, ready to do my specialty as a crack wheel-man. Which was why Frankie had latched onto me in the first place.

I finally agreed. "Okay, deal me in," I told him. "You've got a gun to flash along with that note?"

He grinned. "I'll pick up a plastic model at the five-and-dime. With Homer that'll be enough."

But Frankie didn't stop with Homer. For three days before our hit he diligently checked traffic in the bank, determining busy and slack periods. He settled on one-thirty in the afternoon, after the luncheon rush and before the closing surge. He also surveyed the traffic on the streets at that hour and set up my best route to take off when he scooted out with the cash.

So there it was. A real easy score, right?

Wrong. We never racked it up. I managed to wheel clear when the alarm clanged, but Frankie never got out of the bank. An alerted guard's shot shattered his shoulder.

I have to admit poor Frankie had Homer Jennings pegged one hundred percent. The old gaffer *was* terrified—so terrified that when Frankie gave him a glimpse of the toy gun to reinforce the note, Homer fainted dead away and his body collapsed on the alarm button, kicking it off just as neatly as if he'd nudged it with his foot.

The Cop Who Loved Flowers

by Henry Slesar

Spring comes resolutely, even to police stations, and once again Captain Don Flammer felt the familiar, pleasant twitching of his senses. Flammer loved the springtime—the green yielding of the earth, the flourishing trees, and most of all, the flowers. He liked being a country cop, and the petunia border around the Haleyville Police Headquarters was his own idea and special project.

But by the time June arrived, it was plain that there was something different about Captain Flammer this spring. Flammer wasn't himself. He frowned too much; he neglected the garden; he spent too much time indoors. His friends on the force were concerned, but not mystified. They knew Flammer's trouble: he was still thinking about Mrs. McVey.

It was love of flowers that had introduced them. Mrs. McVey and her husband had moved into the small two-story house on Arden Road, and the woman had waved a magic green wand over the scraggly garden she had inherited. Roses began to climb in wild profusion; massive pink hydrangea bloomed beside the porch; giant pansies, mums, peonies showed their faces; violets and bluebells crept among the rocks; and petunias, more velvety than the Captain's, invaded the terrace.

One day the Captain had stopped his car and walked red-faced to the fence where Mrs. McVey was training ivy.

Flammer was a bachelor, in his forties, and not at ease with women. Mrs. McVey was a few years younger, a bit too thin for prettiness, but with a smile as warming as the sunshine.

"I just wanted to say," he told her heavily, "that you have the nicest garden in Haleyville." Then he frowned as if he had just arrested her, and stomped back to his car.

It wasn't the most auspicious beginning for a friendship, but it was a beginning. Flammer stopped his car in the McVey driveway at least one afternoon a week, and Mrs. McVey made it clear, with smiles, hot tea, and homemade cookies, that she welcomed his visits.

The first time he met Mr. McVey, he didn't like him. McVey was a sharp-featured man with a mouth that looked as if it were perpetually sucking a lemon. When Flammer spoke to him of flowers, the sour mouth twisted in contempt.

"Joe doesn't care for the garden," Mrs. McVey said. "But he knows how much it means to me, especially because he travels so much."

It wasn't a romance, of course. Everybody knew that— even the town gossips. Flammer was a cop, and cops were notoriously stolid. And Mrs. McVey wasn't pretty enough to fit the role.

So nobody in Haleyville gossiped, or giggled behind their backs. Mrs. McVey and the Captain met, week after week, right out in the open where the whole town could see them. But he was in love with her before the autumn came, and she was in love with him; yet they never talked about it.

She did talk about her husband. Little by little, learning to trust Flammer, inspired by her feelings for him, she told him about Joe.

"I'm worried because I think he's sick," she said. "Sick in a way no ordinary doctor can tell. There's such bitterness in him. He grew up expecting so much from life and he got so little."

"Not so little," Flammer said bluntly.

"He hates coming home from his trips. He never says that in so many words, but I know. He can't wait to be off again."

"Do you think he's—" Flammer blushed at the question forming in his own mind.

"I don't accuse him of anything," Mrs. McVey said. "I

never ask him any questions, and he hates to be prodded. There are times when—well, I'm a little afraid of Joe."

Flammer looked from the porch at the pink hydrangea bush, still full-bloomed at summer's end, and thought about how much he would enjoy holding Mrs. McVey's earth-stained hand. Instead, he took a sip of her tea.

On September 19th Mrs. McVey was shot with a .32 revolver. The sound exploded in the night, and woke the neighbors on both sides of the McVey house.

It was some time before the neighbors heard the feeble cries for help that followed the report of the gun, and called the Haleyville police. Captain Flammer never quite forgave the officer on duty that night for not calling him at home when the shooting occurred. He had to wait until morning to learn that Mrs. McVey was dead.

No one on the scene saw anything more in Captain Flammer's face than the concern of a conscientious police-man. He went about his job with all the necessary detach-ment. He questioned Mr. McVey and made no comment on his story.

"It was about two in the morning," McVey said. "Grace woke up and said she thought she heard a noise downstairs. She was always hearing noises, so I told her to go back to sleep. Only she didn't; she put on a kimono and went down to look for herself. She was right for a change—it was a burglar—and he must have got scared and shot her the minute he saw her . . . I came out when I heard the noise, and I saw him running away.

"What did he look like?"

"Like two feet running," Joe McVey said. "That was all I saw of him. But you can see what he was doing here."

Flammer looked around—at the living-room debris, the opened drawers, the scattered contents, the flagrant evi-dence of burglary, so easy to create, or fabricate.

The physical investigation went forward promptly. House and grounds were searched, without result—no meaningful fingerprints or footprints were found, no weapon turned up—indeed, they found no clue of any kind to the murderous burglar of Arden Road. Then they searched for answers to other questions: Was there really a burglar at all? Or had Joe McVey killed his wife?

Captain Flammer conducted his calm inquiry into the case, and nobody knew of his tightened throat, of the painful constriction in his heart, of the hot moisture that burned behind his eyes.

But when he was through, he had discovered nothing to change the verdict at the coroner's inquest: Death at the hands of person or persons unknown. He didn't agree with that verdict, but he lacked an iota of proof to change it. He knew who the Unknown Person was; he saw his hateful, sour-mouthed face in his dreams.

Joe McVey disposed of the two-story house less than a month after his wife's death—sold it at a bargain price to a couple with a grown daughter. Joe McVey then left Haleyville—went to Chicago, some said—and Captain Flammer no longer looked forward to spring, and the coming of the flowers, with joyful expectation.

But spring came again, resolutely as always, and despite the Captain's mood of sorrow and resentment at his own inadequacy, his senses began to twitch. He began driving out into the countryside. And one day he stopped his car in front of the former McVey house.

The woman who stood on the porch, framed by clumps of blue hydrangea, lifted her arm and waved. If a heart can somersault, Flammer's did. He almost said Grace's name aloud, even after he realized that the woman was only a girl, plumpish, not yet twenty.

"Hello," she said, looking at the police car in the driveway. "Beautiful day, isn't it?"

"Yes," Flammer said dully. "Are the Mitchells at home?"

"No, they're out. I'm their daughter Angela." She smiled uncertainly. "You're not here on anything official, I hope?"

"No," Flammer said.

"Of course, I know all about this house, about what happened here last year—the murder and everything." She lowered her voice. "You never caught that burglar, did you?"

"No, we never did."

"She must have been a very nice woman—Mrs. McVey, I mean. She certainly loved flowers, didn't she? I don't think I ever saw a garden as beautiful as this one."

"Yes," Captain Flammer said. "She loved flowers very much."

Sadly, he touched a blue blossom on the hydrangea bush, and started back toward his car. He found that his eyes were filling up, and yet they had seen things clearly.

For suddenly he stopped and said, "Blue?"

The young woman watched him quizzically.

"Blue," he said again, returning and staring at the flowering hydrangea bush. "It was pink last year—I know it was. And now it's blue."

"What are you talking about?"

"Hydrangea," Flammer said. "Do you know about hydrangea?"

"I don't know a thing about flowers. As long as they're pretty—"

"They're pretty when they're pink," Flammer said. "But when there's alum in the soil—or iron—they come up blue. Blue like this."

"But what's the difference?" the girl said. "Pink or blue, what difference? So there's iron in the soil—"

"Yes," Captain Flammer said. "There must be iron in the soil. And now, Miss Mitchell, I'll ask you to please fetch me a shovel."

She looked bewildered, but then she got him the shovel. There was no triumph on Flammer's face when he dug up the revolver at the base of the hydrangea bush, its barrel rusted, its trigger stiff.

He didn't rejoice even when the gun had been identified, as both the weapon that had killed Grace McVey and as the property of Joe McVey. He didn't rejoice when the killer had been brought back to face justice. But while he felt no sense of victory, Captain Flammer admitted one thing: there was a great deal of satisfaction to be derived from the love of flowers.

Trick or Treat

by Judith Garner

I was sitting with my American friend Bambi in our basement kitchen when the front doorbell rang. As the caretaker, I immediately rose to answer it, not for the first time cursing the necessity of taking on this job for the rent-free quarters.

It was October 30, and Mrs. Adams, my niggardly employer, had forbidden fires so early in the season. But already the chill and damp promised a fierce winter. I opened the street door to a grotesque little figure outlined against the yellow fog.

It was a small girl, about eight or nine years old, dressed as a witch in a long black university gown and pointed Welsh hat. She was not one of the tenants of our service flats, but I vaguely thought I had seen her playing in the Gardens with her Nanny and a pram. I had an idea she was an American, that her father had something to do with the Embassy. Not a pretty child, she had an old-fashioned rubber doll in a very dilapidated push-chair.

"Trick or treat?" she asked.

"Treat," I said firmly, thinking I was being offered a choice.

She looked at me expectantly, but when I made no move, she inquired, "Well, where is it then?"

"What?"

"My treat," she said patiently. "If you don't give me a treat, I'll play a trick on you."

"You be off now," I said crossly. "Why, it's extortion! You Americans are all gangsters at heart!"

I closed the door in her hostile little face and went down

to the basement, where Bambi was lighting yet another of her cigarettes.

"Trick or treat," I explained.

"Oh!" she exclaimed. "I didn't know you had that custom in England."

"We don't. What is it, American?"

"Yes, indeed. We always used to go out in costumes trick-or-treating in New York."

"What kind of trick can I expect?"

"Well, my mother used to let us take a sockful of flour. If you hit it against the door it leaves a lovely mark."

"I thought I heard some sort of thud as I came downstairs," I said, "but it didn't sound like a sockful of flour, more like a kick."

"Well, they say things are very unpleasant in the States at Halloween nowadays. How gangs will break your windows or slash your tires if you don't give them at least a dollar."

I thought the custom simply encouraged hooliganism and I said so. "Anyhow, Halloween isn't until tomorrow."

Bambi looked put out at my unfriendliness about her national customs. "Good lord!" she said. "I've been giving away pennies for the Guy for the last month. I do think Guy Fawkes is just as peculiar. Fancy burning a human figure!"

I couldn't see it that way, but I held my tongue. Tonight I resented Bambi; poor though she was personally, I envied her the affluence of her background. Besides, I had always wanted to travel myself.

I poured her another cup of tea, and she reverted to her show-business anecdotes. Then Ron, my husband, joined us, and we played dominoes with the gas money until eleven.

I was up at six the next morning, bringing Ron his tea and stoking up the boiler for the hot water. At 7:30 I went up to the ground floor for the milk. The milkman was just leaving.

"Curious decorations you have around here," he said, gesturing at our front door. It certainly was odd. Nailed to the door was a doll's hand. It had a rubber skin filled with cotton; the stuffing was coming out. It looked ugly and perverted.

"If I'd seen that in Brixton or Camden Town," the man

said, "you know what I would have thought? That someone was practicing voodoo. But you don't get that sort of thing around here. Not in Gloucester Road, you don't."

I pulled the dirty thing off the door and chucked it into an open dustbin. "It's all up and down the Gardens," he continued. "Bits of a doll, nailed to the doors."

Not being superstitious, I just shrugged and went upstairs to distribute the milk. Later, having got my son off to school, I began cleaning the flats and the halls.

I did not associate the mutilated doll with my small visitor of the previous evening until, Mrs. Adams having sent me out shopping, I saw the torso just being removed from Professor Newton's door.

"Creepy, isn't it?" I greeted him.

"It's that wretched Halloween child who did it. Trick or treat indeed! Something disturbing about that family. Too much sibling rivalry is my diagnosis. I shall make a formal protest to the parents. Better yet, I shall write a letter to the *Times*, protesting about the importing of foreign customs—noxious foreign customs!" Having with some difficulty removed the nails, the Professor took the grisly souvenir into the house with him and indignantly slammed the door.

The head of the doll was impaled on the railings at the corner. There I found Lady Arthwaite studying it with interest. "I wonder what the poor thing has done to be decapitated," she murmured to me as I passed. "Positively medieval, isn't it? Or, to be precise, it's—well, I haven't seen a doll like that since before the war. The skin texture is so much more lifelike than this disgusting plastic you get nowadays. I would have liked one like it for my little granddaughter."

But as it was chilly I could not wait around. Nevertheless, her homely words took something of the horror out of the incident. I did my shopping, and made Mrs. Adams' lunch. I worked until it became dark, which was very early.

A storm was brewing. The sky was very dark and threatening. My son got home from school just in time, but I made him a nice cup of hot cocoa anyhow, in case the chill had entered his bones. He is a delicate boy.

The rain came pelting down just after five. Ron was

drenched when he came in half an hour later. "Halloween," he said. "I need a drink." I mixed the whiskey and hot lemonade the way he liked it.

He sat crouching over the newly stoked boiler in his second-hand smoking jacket. I began preparing the dinner—chops, chips, and peas, with fruit salad and custard for dessert.

We began to eat. Suddenly the front doorbell sounded again. Muttering angrily, I climbed the stairs.

The little American stood there, dressed like a pirate this time.

"Trick or treat?" she said.

This time she had her baby brother in the push-chair.

Twice Around the Block

by Lawrence Treat

At an hour after midnight, only a handful of people got off at the subway station that served the huge, sprawling, small-homes development called Sunny Hills. Harry, big and handsome and blustery, was by intention the last one out.

He had the cap, the glove, and the knife, well concealed under his coat. He was never without them, for he did not know just when his chance would come. Maybe tonight, maybe not for two or three weeks. It would come when he was able to walk past the night watchman's shack without being seen.

Although Harry's plans had been perfected for some time, he was smart enough not to push them. He'd stood Mary for three years, he could wait a little longer. Besides, she had a part-time job in a department store, and she handed him her pay envelope every week.

Mary did it meekly, pleased that they were finally building up a savings account. He'd always made good money, but he spent it all on himself. He had flash and style to him, although he hadn't realized how exceptional he was in that respect until Velma moved in next door.

He never could understand why a woman like Velma had landed in Sunny Hills, where even the small, neat houses were so monotonously alike that you could hardly tell them apart. But she spoke vaguely of some trouble she'd been in, and he gathered that she'd been forced to quit her job in the night club where she'd had the hat-check concession.

From the moment they saw each other, they sparked like a pair of high tension wires, and neither of them had tried to resist. Shortly after the first crackle, Harry had managed to get himself transferred to the night shift so that he could see her during the day—without frustrating complications.

But it wasn't satisfying. The nights were what depressed him, going back to the house where he no longer belonged, to the woman he didn't want, the woman he had grown to hate.

"Kitten," he had said to Velma once. "If something would only happen to her. If she could meet with an accident—"

"You could make it seem like an accident," Velma had said in her low, torchy voice.

"If I do, you're going to be part of it."

"Well?"

"Maybe it would be smarter to try and get a divorce."

"You'd have to pay alimony. There wouldn't be much left."

"You like money, don't you?" he'd said. And her black eyes, lifting slowly, practically singed him.

After that, he began his preparations. He bought the roll of film and kept it at home—just in case. He always took the rear car of the subway and was the last one out. Also just in case. And he checked the subway schedule and found out that the night trains ran exactly fifteen minutes apart, and every evening he set his watch by the subway clock. Just in case.

Tonight was no different from the other nights. He came out of the subway exit and looked around to make sure that nobody had noticed him. Except for one cab, with the driver dozing over the steering wheel, the street was deserted.

He crossed the roadway and strode down the long block, and for the hundredth time he thought it over. He put his hand in his pocket and touched the knife. He'd found it in a public lavatory. There was no conceivable way of tracing it and no one except Mary had ever glimpsed it.

As he approached the night watchman's booth he walked fast, the tempo of his pulse lifting. Then he was alongside the cubicle, and his heart gave a sharp, convulsive jerk. Mike Hogan wasn't there. This was it—the one unbelievable chance.

Harry didn't panic. He sidled stealthily over to the shadows, beyond the ornamental gateway to Sunny Hills. He put the cap on, pulling it low, and he raised his coat collar. He left the sidewalk and slunk across the front yards, keeping close to the houses. If anybody saw him, they'd take him for a prowler.

All right. Let them see him, let them tell the police later on that a man had sneaked across the lawns. Wake up, you fools, and take a quick look. Quick, but not careful.

At the corner of his block, he turned and glanced behind him. Stay calm now, make sure. When he'd convinced himself that the coast was clear he started running—quietly, with a low, scuttling stoop. He was chuckling to himself, in silent excitement, buoyed up by the certainty that everything would go right.

He put his key in the door and stepped inside. He was glad it was pitch dark. He might have hesitated and drawn back if he'd seen Mary's face. He wasn't a cruel man, he told himself. He was merely a man who faced facts.

He took out the knife and snapped it open. His palm was wet, but he gripped the rough handle firmly. He flexed his arm once, his features hardening.

He walked swiftly and soundlessly down the familiar hall. He ascended the one step, and opened the door to the right. Her bed was directly behind it.

He struck savagely and repeatedly. This was the part he'd dreaded, but it was soon over, cleanly, effectively. Her breath caught and she moaned, but she didn't even wake up.

He wheeled and went out, circled the house and stopped in front of the bedroom window. He put on the thick, heavy glove and punched once at the glass. There was a brittle, crackling sound—and that was all.

When he came into the room again, later, he'd have time to raise the sash, and the evidence of a marauding burglar would be clinched as far as the police were concerned.

He glanced at his watch again. He was surprised that it had taken him only six minutes, and the precision of his timing gave him added confidence.

He returned to the street and began the long circle of the block, back to the subway station. He ran openly now, deliberately keeping to the concrete sidewalk so that his steps thudded audibly. That was part of the plan. He was willing to be seen, at a distance, to establish the presence of somebody running away.

He took the shortcut through the field and stopped at the rubbish pile, where he discarded the glove and the cap. Squinting in the darkness, he took out his keys. If the police should suspect him—if they should make more than a cursory investigation—he didn't want them to find he had a key to Velma's house. He threw the key away.

He put his key-ring back in his pocket, set his hat firmly on his head, and marched briskly towards the subway exit. He got there with a couple of minutes to spare, and stood for a moment in the shadows of the adjoining newsstand. He took long, slow, deep breaths, and thought it through again—detail by detail.

He'd forgotten nothing; he'd made no mistakes. He could trust Velma not to talk. She had good reason to stay silent, but if she did break, there was no proof. No witnesses—and no overheard quarrels with Mary. No guilt-pointing link between him and the knife.

He heard the rumble of the subway, and two or three passengers came up the steps. He waited a few seconds, then stepped into the light. The lone cab was still there, the driver awake now. Harry waved to him and continued on his way.

He headed for the watchman's shack. Hogan would have to go home with him and be present when he discovered the body. That was vitally important. But Harry had laid the background long ago. He'd stopped here night after night for the past month, not missing a single night.

Hogan stepped out of his shelter, recognized Harry, and grinned. "Evening, Harry," he said. "On the dot, as usual."

Harry smiled. "Sure, right on schedule. And Mike—that roll of film I told you about. I got it at home for you. It won't cost you a cent, either."

"That's damn nice of you, Harry."

"Come on back with me, and I'll give it to you now."

"Thanks," said Hogan. He fell into step with Harry and began grumbling endlessly about his camera problems. Harry hardly listened.

As they rounded the corner of his block, Harry took out his keys. He stopped in front of his house—number forty-eight.

"Come in," he said. "I got them in the bedroom. It won't take me a minute."

He put the key in the lock and tried to turn it. It stuck, and he pulled it out to examine it.

"What's the matter?" said Hogan pleasantly. "Got the wrong key?"

Harry gave him a look of terror and rammed the key back in the lock. The wrong key?

Then the door swung open. Mary, hugging her robe tight around her shoulders, said, "Oh, I'm so glad you're back. I'm so relieved."

Harry straightened up, and stared unbelievingly at his wife. A quick, hard lump seemed to rip at his stomach, and he grabbed the doorway for support—the doorway that was identical with Velma's.

Mary's voice seemed to come from a great distance. "I heard glass break; it woke me," she said. "I'm sure something happened to that woman next door. And I was so scared. Just think—it might have been me."

An Easy Score

by Al Nussbaum

It's impossible to say exactly why the two men chose old Mrs. Hartman for their victim. Perhaps it was her obvious age and frailty. Perhaps it was the fact that she had come out of the bank only minutes before. Perhaps they had been attracted by the oversized shoulder bag she clutched protectively, or the fact that she walked only a block before leaving the busy thoroughfare and strolling along a quiet and deserted side street.

Any combination, or all of these factors, may have influenced them. In any case, they had seen her and marked her an easy score. They had come up behind her and then separated, one going to either side. The one on her left had tripped her and, at the same instant, the other man cut the strap on her shoulder bag and tried to take it away from her. Instead of throwing her hands out to block her fall, as they had expected her to do, the gray-haired old woman grabbed the bag with both hands and gripped it tightly. She fell to the pavement, and there was the sound of an old bone snapping, but she didn't give up her hold on the bag.

One man wrapped the dangling end of the shoulder strap around his hand and tried to wrench the bag free, while the other man kicked the old woman with his square-toed boots. There were no cries for help, no screams. The only sounds were the shuffle of feet and the men's heavy breathing as they tried to force Mrs. Hartman to release her bag. The men were determined to have the bag. Every tug on the strap was accompanied by several kicks to loosen her hold; but her tightly clamped jaws and frantic grip were evidence that she was just as determined not to have it taken from her.

Unfortunately, the woman wasn't a match for even one man, let alone two. It was only seconds before she had been thrust into unconsciousness by pain and exhaustion. They tore the bag from her limp fingers and ran away, leaving her sprawled across the sidewalk.

No one saw the attack and robbery. It was almost fifteen minutes before Mrs. Hartman was discovered by another pedestrian. The police and an ambulance arrived simultaneously, but by then the two men were miles away.

She regained consciousness for a few moments as she was being carried to the ambulance on a stretcher. She turned her pain-filled eyes toward a uniformed policeman who was standing nearby, looking down at her. "My money," she said in a tone so weak he almost missed it. "They stole my purse, and it had all my money in it."

"How much was taken, ma'am?" the officer asked.

She paused a moment, then managed to reply, "Thirty-three thousand dollars," before losing consciousness again.

She hadn't been able to say much, but it was enough to raise the mugging from the level of a relatively minor offense, as such things go, and give it the stature of a major crime. Four detectives were dispatched to the hospital emergency ward to be on hand when she could speak again; and an equal number of newspaper reporters and television newsmen converged upon the hospital, too.

When she was wheeled from the treatment room, Mrs. Hartman looked like a mummy. Both of her arms and one leg were in heavy casts and her head was swathed in bandages. She was awake, though, and able to answer a few more questions. Detective Sergeant Kendris, a burly man in his forties, did all the talking. The people from the news media had to make do with what they were able to overhear and the photos they could take.

"Mrs. Hartman, can you hear me all right?" Kendris asked.

"Yes," the woman replied weakly.

"You told the officer where you were found that you had been robbed of thirty-three thousand dollars. Is that right?"

"Yes . . ."

"How did you happen to have so much cash with you?"

Mrs. Hartman hesitated, as though seeking the right words. Then she confessed, "I'm . . . I'm a foolish old woman. I don't always show good sense. Once every year, and sometimes twice, I draw all my savings from the bank. I keep the money at home for a few days, to look at it and touch it, then put it back in the bank. This time . . ." her voice trailed off weakly " . . . I lost it all."

"Did you recognize the thief?"

"There were two of them, but I'd never seen them before. And I'm not sure I'd know them if I saw them again. It all happened so very fast . . ."

At that point the sedative the doctor had administered took hold and she went to sleep.

"If you have any more questions, Sergeant Kendris," the nurse said, "you'll have to come back tomorrow."

The next afternoon, Kendris stormed into the hospital, looking like an angry bear, but he didn't get to speak to Mrs. Hartman. She slept all day, and the doctor refused to allow Kendris to awaken her.

The following day, Kendris returned again. He had calmed somewhat, but he was still visibly angry. Mrs. Hartman was propped up in bed and a high-school-age hospital volunteer was reading to her from the newspaper. Kendris asked the girl to wait outside while he talked to Mrs. Hartman.

"All right," he demanded once they were alone, "what was the idea of lying to me?"

"I . . . I don't know what you mean," she answered.

"Come off it! You know what I'm talking about—your imaginary thirty-three thousand dollars. The robbery was all over the newspapers and television, but when I went to the bank to see if they had a record of the serial numbers on the money, I learned you've never had an account there. The only time they see you is when, like the day before yesterday, you stop in to cash your Social Security check. Why did you lie?"

The injured woman's hands opened and closed and opened again in a gesture of helplessness. "I didn't want the thieves to get away with it. I . . . I wanted them to pay for what they did to me."

"But you *didn't* have to lie," Kendris persisted. "Don't you know we'd have worked just as hard, made exactly the same effort, to recover your Social Security pension as we did for the larger amount?"

When she didn't reply immediately, Kendris had time to examine what he'd just said and to see how ridiculous it was. As long as it had been believed that thirty-three thousand dollars had been stolen, there had been four detectives assigned to the case, and reporters to record their every move; but now he was the only one officially assigned, and that would last only until he returned to the office and put his report in the Unsolved File. At least he had the grace to be embarrassed.

"Oh, that isn't what I meant! I'm sure the police do their best regardless of the amount lost," Mrs. Hartman said, but to Kendris' ears the words had a hollow ring. It made him all the more ashamed to have this beaten-up old woman show more concern for his feelings than he'd shown for hers.

"Look," he said, cutting the interview short, "let's just forget the whole thing." He began moving toward the door. "If anything turns up, you'll be notified," he said, and then he was gone from the room.

The young hospital volunteer returned. She picked up the newspaper she'd set aside when Kendris arrived, and sat beside the bed.

"Would you like me to read some more?" she asked.

"Yes, please," Mrs. Hartman answered. "Read the part about the murders again."

"But I've already read it four times," the girl protested.

"I know, but please read it again."

The girl cleared her throat and then began. "Police investigated a disturbance in an apartment at 895 Seventh Avenue at about ten last night and found two men, William White and Jesse Bolt, who shared the apartment, dead on the living room floor, the result of a knife fight. Neighbors said the men had been arguing and fighting most of the day, each accusing the other of cheating him out of an undisclosed amount of money. The knife fight in which they killed one another was the climax of the day-long confrontation. Both men had long arrest records. Police are continuing their investigation."

Mrs. Hartman smiled behind her bruised lips. "Please, read it again," she said softly.

The Good Lord Will Provide

by Lawrence Treat and Charles M. Plotz

April 3

Dear Judy,

It's been a whole year now, a whole long year without you. But I been a real good prisoner staying out of trouble like a cat stays away from water. They all say I'll get my parole next April, plenty of time to put in a crop. So hang on, you and Uncle Ike. The only thing bothering me is I ain't heard from you in so long. Why? What's happening?

Judy, it's not like I done anything wrong. All I did was drive that car. I didn't know they had guns and itchy fingers, I didn't even know them good. They was just a couple of city fellas hanging around a bar and I got chinning with them and happened to let drop I was the champeen stock car racer of Hadley County. I done a little bragging maybe. I musta told them I could just about drive a car up the side of a wall and down the other side and if they wanted to see how good I was, why come on out and look. Which they did.

Maybe I was a little stupid but when they allowed they'd pay me right then and there to take them to the bank next day and then on out to the back hills where there was no roads, which they said they wanted to do just for the hell of it—well all I did was ask how much. And when they told me I plumb near keeled over. Because it was almost as much as we needed for that mortgage payment. I figured money was money and if they were taking a lot of it out of the bank, why wouldn't they be generous? What I didn't know was they didn't have no account there.

So I reckon I was real stupid. But stupid or not I sure was lucky because if I'd stayed with that pair much longer I'da got killed too. But they paid me to get them out of town and up into the hills and after I done that I took off and come straight back to you.

When Ike heard the news on the radio he knowed right off it was me at the wheel of the car. Nobody else could have outdrove and outsmarted the cops and I bet I could have got clear off to Mexico or maybe China if I'da wanted to. And if the airplanes hadn't spotted me like they did that pair. But I done what I was paid for, so I come back where I belonged. And if they took fifty thousand like the papers said or a million I wouldn't know. I was waiting out in the car and all the money I ever seen was what I give you. And like I said, I got it the day before and it wasn't stolen from the bank. Not that bank anyhow.

The sheriff kept asking me where the stolen money was. After all the two bank robbers was dead with no trace of the money and all the sheriff had was me. Just a poor dumb farmer with a knack for handling a car.

But I don't want to worry you with all this. I'm real lonesome for you like I said. So when are you coming up here to visit me? And how are you and how's Ike and the farm?

Your loving husband
Walt

R.F.D. 2, Hadley

April 10

Dear Walt

I got your letter and the reason I ain't come to see you is that I just don't have the money for the trip. Besides I got to do all the chores now. Uncle Ike's down with the rhumatiz again and Doc Saunders says he won't be up and around until the warm spring weather sets in and that's not liable to happen until May. And when Ike's feeling puny he wants me around all the time and all he does is complain and tell me everybody's out to take the skin off me. He even tried to chase George off the place when George came around in his new car to ask me out for a ride. And I sure needed to get away from the farm for awhile.

George was real nice to me too. He wanted to know how I was getting along without you and if I missed you much. Well I said it was kind of lonesome, there was things a girl needed sometimes and who was around except Ike? Seems George got my meaning wrong but I straightened him out real good. Afterwards I told him right out that we was liable to lose the farm unless we got that mortgage installment paid and how could I pay it until I got a crop in? And I said that what with George getting promoted to be vice president of the bank he could maybe do something. He said he'd see what he could manage and that was about as far as we got. Anyhow it was nice getting away from Ike for awhile, specially when George took me to dinner at that new place in town.

Walt, I wish you was a banker too.

Your loving wife
Judy

STATE PENITENTIARY

April 15

Dear Judy,

I know it's hard on you and with Ike to take care of it's even worse. He's tetchy enough when he feels good but when he's got the aches he's enough to try the patience of a saint. But the good Lord will provide, Judy, and I know what I'm saying.

About George and the bank holding off—you want to get it writ down. So next time you see him you want to ask him about Ruthie Watkins which I found out about from a guy up here named Ernie Taylor. Ernie, his business is selling letters. And like he says, if I got a cow or a bushel of wheat I can sell them, can't I? So why can't he sell letters?

Ernie and me get along fine because the both of us we're

innocent men and we shouldn't ought to be here. But as long as we are we talk about things and Ernie happened to mention some letters he got hold of which George writ to this Ruthie Watkins. So maybe you better mention them to George next time you see him.

Your loving husband
Walt

R.F.D. 2, Hadley

April 22

Dear Walt,

George took me out to dinner again and we talked about a lot of things. And like you told me to I just happened to mention Ruthie Watkins and then I said about the mortgage and how it ought to be writ down. And the very next day I got a letter from the bank promising to hold off until autumn but I don't know what good it's going to do. Because next time I was out with George, Ike got hold of some of that while mule stuff and after that he got the idea he ought to go riding in the tractor. Which he did, as far as that big ditch on the west side. Ike didn't get hurt bad, just a bruise or two that he's relaxing from, but you ought to see what's left of that tractor. So how do I make that mortgage payment in the fall with no crop coming in? And if I don't pay up we got no farm.

I'm tired, Walt. I'm plumb tired and just about at the end of my tether. You said the good Lord will provide—but how? How?

Your loving wife
Judy

STATE PENITENTIARY

April 28

Dear Judy,

You got to be patient like I said and if you're real patient the Lord *will* provide. Because He come to me in a dream and He said that there was something buried in the south field that would take care of us. So you tell Ike to get over that rhumatiz of his. Tell him I only got a year to go and then I'm going to dig up that something in the south field and after that everything's going to be all right.

Your loving husband
Walt

R.F.D. 2, Hadley

May 4

Dear Walt,

I don't know just how to tell you this but I guess I'll just set it down the way it happened.

You know how Ike hates the law ever since they come around and took you away. So when the sheriff and six deputies showed up the day before yesterday Ike tried to chase them away. He got up out of bed and ran all over the place looking for his shotgun, only I had it hid. Then he yelled at them and called them all kinds of names and they finally grabbed him and tied him up for a spell, so he never did see what they done. He's spry again, all that running after the deputies loosened him up and now he's as good as ever. But I don't rightly know what the sheriff come for and you'll never tumble to what those deputies of his done.

Walt, they went down to that south field and the six of them spent the whole day digging and then they come back the next day and kept on until they dug up just about every inch of that field. And I never did see any six men look so tired and they sure was mad. I asked them lots of questions and one of them—I think he come all the way down from the prison—he allowed as how all your mail gets read. Walter, what did he say that for?

Your loving wife
Judy

May 7

Dear Judy,
  Now plant.

Your loving husband
Walt

Boomerang

by Harold Q. Masur

The thin man on the witness stand fumbled with the edge of his necktie. He had been Raynor's secretary and one of the two men present in the district attorney's house the night he'd been murdered.

I asked him: "The day Raynor was killed, didn't he tell you he had enough on the defendant to hang him?"

"Objection!" Sam Lubock, the defense lawyer, had leaped to his feet, thick-jowled face flooded with color.

"Sustained," snapped Judge Martin. He said it without even glancing at me.

That's how it had been all through the trial—Lubock making objections, the judge sustaining them. And this was supposed to be a court of justice. The lady outside, weighing scales in her hand, must have been laughing in her stone throat. Only there was nothing funny about it.

Lubock grinned and sat down beside his client.

I looked at the defendant, and a white sheet of fury blazed through me. There was no doubt in my mind that he had murdered my chief, District Attorney Raynor, the one man I had worshiped and respected.

Judged by certain standards, Frank Hauser was a success. He had made and kept three fortunes, had done it over the sweat and toil and blood of a hundred men. Night clubs, clip joints, slot machines, numbers, protective societies—anything that paid big dividends.

He was a slender man, smooth and oily, cold and deadly as a rattlesnake. He sat there, smiling contemptuously, a stain on the community. Any time he pulled the strings, a couple of politicians danced.

And then, quite suddenly, two months ago, a reform ticket had placed Dan Raynor in the district attorney's office. Dan Raynor was not for sale. Nobody had that kind of money. Alone, Raynor was not dangerous. But teamed with his special investigator, Tom Gahagan, they menaced the organization, the very existence of Hauser's machine.

Gahagan was all cop. Ploddingly, meticulously, he'd piled up the evidence against Hauser, enough to send the man to the gallows, and some half dozen big shots with him.

So of course Raynor had to go. The evidence had to be blown out of the safe. And Gahagan—well, that was the question. Where was Gahagan? The only man who could tie Hauser to this rap.

At the bottom of the river? Bought off? Hiding? I didn't know, and it probably wouldn't do much good if I did.

Because this was one murder case that was fixed. Good and tight. Hauser was going to go scot free.

The jurors had been bought and paid for. I'd known that since the second day of the trial. What's more, Hauser was the man who'd hoisted Martin to the bench. And the judge was going to protect him even if he had to rewrite the rules of evidence. With Gahagan missing there wasn't anything I could do.

What I really wanted though, was to get Gahagan up there on the witness stand. I wanted him to shout his testimony until the bailiffs dragged him from the chair. Sure, it wouldn't hang Hauser, but the spectators would hear it, the reporters would hear it, and maybe the world would learn what was going on in this beautiful city of ours.

You see, Gahagan had been in the district attorney's home that night Raynor was killed. He had been in another room, but at the sound of the shot he'd caught a fleeting glimpse of the car as it rocketed away down the street. He had recognized it as Hauser's.

But—Gahagan—was—missing—

I clenched my fists. Fifty grand! A hundred grand! That kind of money was chicken feed to Hauser. But it might turn the head of even a man like Gahagan.

I know. It had been offered to me. I was still weak from temptation. But if I'd ever accepted a bribe from Raynor's killer, it wouldn't have been much fun living with myself.

The weapon that had smoked down Raynor had been tossed through the window of his study. It was an old Colt army automatic, millions of which had been manufactured, practically impossible to trace. It had already been introduced into evidence. I picked it up and showed it to the thin man on the witness stand.

"When you heard the shot and ran into the deceased's study, where did you find this gun?"

Raynor's secretary wet his lips, his eyes wandered to the floor. He said: "Mr. Raynor was holding it in his hand."

For a brief instant I was shocked into immobility. I just stood there, staring at him, completely stunned. A whisper rippled through the courtroom.

It had happened. They'd bought off Raynor's secretary. They were trying to show that the D.A. must have committed suicide. My own witness had boomeranged. And I was bound by his answers.

I guess what happened then was absolutely unprecedented. I saw red. My face was burning. I took a single step forward and sent my fist crashing full into his face.

Hell broke loose. Judge Martin started banging with his gavel. Sam Lubock was on his feet shouting. Two bailiffs were dragging me back. Hauser's mouth was warped by a thin smile. If I could have got my hands on him at that moment, I would've choked the life out of him.

I waited for the judge to finish his scalding comments. I didn't apologize. I didn't say anything. I just stood there, licked, beaten, ready to give up the fight. And then, suddenly, there was a flurry in the rear of the courtroom.

I turned and the pulse started hammering against my temples. A tall figure, his hands pressed tightly against his sides, was walking in stiff-legged, jerky steps down the aisle.

Tom Gahagan . . .

He didn't look at me. He didn't look at anybody. He went straight to the witness chair, gripped the arms and eased himself into it. His eyes were narrowed, his lips grim and colorless. He seemed tired, almost exhausted. Then his eyes found mine, and I saw a thin sheen of oily perspiration standing out over his whole face.

Lubock vented an audible gasp. Hauser was staring pop-eyed. Both men looked dumbfounded, as if they'd paid Gahagan to go to Africa and were suddenly amazed to find him here. I knew then that they had never expected him to show up.

Excitement quickened my blood. Here was a chance to do something. If only Judge Martin didn't order the bailiffs to throw us both into the clink for contempt of court. I asked Gahagan a few preliminary questions and he answered them in short cryptic sentences. Then I picked up the old Colt army automatic and handed it to him.

"This is the People's exhibit one," I said. "Do you recognize it?"

He turned it over slowly in his hands. You could hear a watch ticking in the courtroom. All eyes were focused upon him. He opened it, peered into the empty chamber, then held it loosely in his lap. He looked up.

"Yes. This is the gun that killed Mr. Raynor."

"Where were you when the shot was fired?"

Gahagan's eyes met mine in a steady look. "I had just opened the door to Mr. Raynor's study."

That was a lie! I sucked in a sharp breath, waiting for Lubock's objection. Gahagan hadn't been near the study. But Lubock was biding his time. I knew then what was going through Gahagan's mind. Probably he felt that if all the other witnesses were perjuring themselves for the defense, he could lie for the prosecution.

A thought struck me and suddenly my hands were clammy, like two lumps of cold dough. What if Gahagan had sold himself? What if he testified that he had seen Raynor commit suicide? Scarcely breathing, I asked my next question.

"What did you see?"

Lubock and Hauser were both leaning tensely forward,

watching Gahagan. Judge Martin sat stiffly at the bench. Gahagan's eyes traveled along the counsel table and came to rest on Hauser. He said in a low voice:

"I saw Hauser standing at the window holding this gun in his hand, pointing it at Raynor, like this—"

And he lifted the gun, sighting along the dull barrel directly at the defendant. Hauser's mouth sagged loosely and he stiffened in his chair. For once in his life I could see that Lubock was speechless. But his neck muscles were taut and he was getting ready to jump up. For the moment, Gahagan's play had caught everyone by surprise.

His eyes were opaque, like blank empty windows. A vein bulged in a blue diagonal across his forehead. His voice came out clearly, almost ringing:

"Hauser pulled the trigger—like—this—"

A shot exploded in the courtroom. And as I watched, a raw red-lipped hole suddenly jumped into the temple above the bridge of Hauser's nose. A split-second of unbelief rioted across his face, then he toppled forward over the defense table.

A woman screamed, high and shrill. Spectators ducked under their seats. The jurymen cowered back against the rear of the jury box. Judge Martin held his gavel poised in midair. Lubock held a horror-stricken look upon his client.

Gahagan dropped the gun. It clattered to the floor. His face, the color of wax, was lighted by a smile, a strange triumphant smile. Unseen, he had slipped a shell into the automatic. I grabbed his arm and dug my fingers into it.

"They didn't want me to testify," he said in a dull voice. "They were holding me in a warehouse."

"Good Lord, man! This is murder. You didn't really see Hauser kill the D.A."

Gahagan coughed. "No, but I saw him kill somebody else down in that warehouse this morning."

I stared at him. "Who?"

"Me," Gahagan whispered hoarsely.

And then he tumbled forward out of the witness chair in a half turn, sprawling to the floor on his back. He didn't say anything more. I didn't expect him to. For his coat had pulled open and in stark crimson relief against the white of his shirt was the jagged tear of a bullet hole.

The Way It's Supposed To Be

by Elsin Ann Graffam

We had so much fun. I don't remember about when I was *real* little, but I'm ten now and I know we had a good time, just the two of us, ever since my father went away.

Mom had his picture on the mantel and she talked about him all the time—how he loved me so much and what he was like and stuff. My Dad was a great guy, on the football team at college and everything. Then he was a stockbroker and married to Mom. Mom was glad he bought stocks for us because that meant she didn't have to go out to work and leave me when he went away.

I was three when he went away and I don't remember him. I tried to when I was little, but I just couldn't. But it was okay. He was sort of alive to me in the picture. Mom would say, "Daddy would be so proud to know you had all A's on your report card," and I'd look at his picture there on the mantel, and he'd be smiling, happy for me. I bet you didn't know that pictures could smile, did you? Well, they can.

People called Mom a widow and I didn't find out until last year what that meant. Dad was an old man. He's got gray hair in the picture and that means you're old. Mom doesn't have gray hair. She's young. And pretty. She's got a lot of fluffy blonde hair around her face and big blue eyes. She's the most beautiful lady in the whole world.

I'll never leave my mother. The other guys, you know, they say they're going down to Florida and dig for treasure or go overseas and look for monsters in some lake. They can't wait to leave home. But not me.

I can't tell them that. I told Billy Earle once that I'd never leave Mom and he laughed at me. But they can't understand. They don't have a Mom like mine. All their mothers have lines between their eyes. That means they frown a lot. My mother never frowns. She's the nicest person on earth. I'll never leave her. I told that to Dad a year ago and he looked down at me from the mantel and said, "You're a good boy, Glenn."

Maybe the guys don't understand, but Dad does.

Everything was real neat until Mr. Knott came along. One night last summer I woke up because I thought the TV was on too loud. I went into the living room to tell Mom to turn it down, and there was a man sitting on the sofa. Mom jumped when she saw me.

"Is anything wrong?" I asked her.

"No, everything is wonderful," she said.

I didn't like Mr. Knott. He was old and he had a big nose.

"Who is he?" I asked her.

She said, "This is Mr. Knott and he's my friend."

I went back to bed but I couldn't sleep. I thought I was the only friend Mom had. I hoped with all my might that Mom would never see him again. But she did. He was over a lot. Mom would say, "Come on, Glenn, just say hello to Mr. Knott."

When my tenth birthday came last October, I shut my eyes real tight when I blew out the candles, and I wished that Mr. Knott would go away and never come back. But it didn't work.

After a while the lady down the street came to babysit me. Mom would go out with Mr. Knott. I'd lie down on my bed the whole time they were away, thinking maybe I'd die of sadness and then Mom would be sorry for what she did. But I never died and Mom kept on seeing Mr. Knott.

Once they were away for a whole weekend. Mom kissed me good-bye that Saturday morning and hugged me real tight. But I didn't care—nothing mattered any more, not after that rotten old man came along. I wanted more than anything else for it to stay that way, just the two of us, Mom and me. The way it's supposed to be.

"Surprise!" Mr. Knott said to me that Sunday night when he and Mom got home. "Your mother and I were married yesterday morning," he said.

Mom said, "That's right, Glenn. I didn't want to tell because we were afraid you wouldn't understand. We're going to be so happy!"

We, we, we! Only the "we" wasn't Mom and me, it was Mom and that old man.

You don't die from crying, or I'd be dead now. I never said a word to him, or looked at him. Mom and he would talk and I'd feel like I was in a deep dark hole. The more days that went by, the deeper and darker that hole got. It was blacker than night there.

Dad didn't like it any more than I did. Sometimes I'd stand in front of the fireplace and look at his picture on the mantel, and you know what? He was *crying*. Big tears came down the glass in the frame. They made a puddle on the mantel.

One night when I was talking to Dad, the puddle ran over and made spots on the rug. Mom came in the room just then and asked me what I was doing.

"Look!" I said. "Dad's crying because you married that man! See?"

She looked at me funny and left the room. Right after that I heard Mom and Mr. Knott arguing. It was the first time in my life I ever heard my mother yell.

The next day I got home from school and threw my books on the sofa. Something was wrong. I looked around the room. Then I saw it. Or, I mean, I didn't see it. There was a blank space where Dad's picture should have been.

"Mom!" I yelled. "Where is it?!"

"Where is what?" she asked. As if she didn't know!

"My Dad's picture is gone!"

And she said, "Well, Mr. Knott thought it was a good idea to put it away since he is your father now."

I banged my head against the mantel and yelled that Mr. Knott was not my father, I had only one real father and he was the man in the picture.

Mom said, "Glenn, you're old enough to realize that a lady needs a husband. Your father has been dead for six and a half years. I was all alone. Now I have somebody to love me. Mr. Knott is my husband and the sooner you accept that the better off we'll all be!"

And she had frown marks between her eyes.

That night the babysitter came over. Mom and Mr. Knott went to the movies. I was glad they were gone. I snuck into Mom's room and opened the top drawer of her dresser. I knew it would be there. I was right.

I took it out and looked at it. In the little bit of light from the hall, Dad's face was more alive than ever. His eyes looked right into mine and he told me exactly what to do.

That was five days ago. I'm out of that dark hole now. Things are fine again. It's just Mom and me, the way it's supposed to be.

Some cops came and talked to me after they took the body away. Mom was crying. "Don't worry," the biggest cop said to her. "They can't touch the boy. He's too young to know what he did."

Mom shook her head until her hair was flying and she said something I don't understand to the cop.

"That's exactly," she cried, "what they told me six and a half years ago!"

Thank You, Mr. Thurston

by Ed Dumonte

They all told me, "Mr. Thurston can help you." When I took my pictures to dealers or collectors or to other artists they all said, "See Mr. Thurston—he will know what to do."

But how could I? Alone and friendless in the city, I had no influence, no channel of communication, to a man of Mr. Thurston's stature and importance. I understand this now. But I wasted many weeks sitting in the anteroom of Mr. Thurston's office. Each morning I rolled up several of my best canvases and went to Mr. Thurston's office to wait.

"Mr. Thurston sees no one without an appointment," the

girl would tell me. Or "Mr. Thurston will be in conference all day."

All the mornings and all the afternoons of all the days I waited patiently, hopefully, and I never got so much as a glimpse of Mr. Thurston. At last my money ran out and I had to take my paintings into the streets again—to display on fences and trees.

But I didn't stop trying to get Mr. Thurston's attention. Everybody knows that an artist has no chance of getting a showing or any critical attention unless he can win the patronage of some great man. Perhaps, I reasoned, if I couldn't speak for my paintings, my paintings could speak for me.

Among my best works were scenes of the city, done soon after I arrived, while the city was still fresh and beautiful to me. One of my impressions was a skyline of vertical lines and planes done in shades of gray. Another, painted at the waterfront, interpreted the warehouses as cubes of dingy brown, the river as a parallelogram of polluted blue, the whole surmounted and spanned by arches of rust. These were two of the pictures I rolled into a tube and mailed to Mr. Thurston.

After a week my paintings were returned . . . unopened. Stuffed into the wrapping was a note: "Mr. Thurston does not examine unsolicited artwork."

I was almost angered by the note. But when I thought about it, I decided it was reasonable. Mr. Thurston was a great and influential man, his name on every tongue. He must receive thousands of requests for help every week, hundreds of paintings from daubers and Sunday artists. He could hardly be expected to give his valuable time to every unknown artist who called on him.

For a time I puzzled over ways and means of getting to see Mr. Thurston. My problem was solved, I thought, by a prosperous-looking gentleman who one afternoon stopped and examined my street display.

He liked my pictures. They showed depth and feeling, he said. Excellent composition, striking colors. When he asked why I didn't have a dealer to represent me or a gallery to hang my pictures, I told him, and he understood.

Although he had no influence himself, he said, he had a friend who would be most interested in seeing my work.

And he wrote me a letter of introduction to Mr. Thurston.

Was it to be that easy, then?

The next day I brushed my suit, applied a bit of black paint to my shoes, and with two paintings under my arm I went back to Mr. Thurston's office. I interrupted one of the familiar excuses to give the secretary my letter. She disappeared into the inner office, returned after a few moments, and handed the letter back to me.

"Mr. Thurston has asked me to tell you that he is acquainted with the writer of this letter, and that his personal distaste for the man is exceeded only by his abhorrence for his judgment of art. Under no circumstances would Mr. Thurston consider sponsoring a piece of work recommended by that man."

As she spoke I flushed with anger; but my anger changed, as I realized what had happened, to my embarrassment and shame. I had been duped, tricked by one of Mr. Thurston's enemies, cruelly used as a pawn in some hideous joke. I fled from the office and ran blindly back to my room.

I lay for hours on my cot, moaning with anguish as the consequences of what I had done became all too clear to me. Foolishly I had let my name be associated with a man whom Mr. Thurston despised, and forever afterward, though innocent of any offense, my name and my work would be attacked by Mr. Thurston as if I too were his enemy.

All that was left to me was to leave the city, leave my oils and brushes, leave my paintings for the janitor's boilers, and try to endure somehow the living-death of the world of non-art. But I was not yet free to go.

If I were ever to know peace I must find *some* way to apologize to Mr. Thurston. Not that he would accept it, for he was a great and important man, and I had offended him beyond endurance. And, too, there was so little I could do. A public apology from a nonentity has no significance. I would gladly have cut off my ear and sent it to him, but he would probably return the package unopened.

The answer came to me in a flash of inspiration. I would do a portrait of Mr. Thurston!—a portrait that would express more clearly than words the respect and admiration I felt for him. A portrait of feeling and sincerity beyond any doubt or question . . .

I immediately started to work, searching newspaper and

magazine files for pictures of Mr. Thurston, rereading his famous articles of criticism and opinion. From these fundamentals of likeness and character I made sketches—ten of fifteen sketches to capture the arch of an eyebrow or the shading of a cheekbone. Forty or fifty sketches to find the proper angle of the head and express the character of the chin. Hundreds of sketches to re-create for all the world to see the soul of this great and influential man.

At last I was satisfied with the sketches, and then slowly, painstakingly, I began to commit to canvas the image I had conceived. For days, without food or rest, I fought with mass and color to put a living man into oil—the massive brow illuminated from within by a brilliant intelligence, the eyes that saw beneath the flat surface of canvas to the heart and soul that gave a painting life, the thin lip that curved into an almost cruel disdain for shoddiness or incompetence, the sweeping line of jaw and chin that bespoke the sensitivity of a true critic and connoisseur . . .

When the painting was finished, I carried it to Mr. Thurston's office and left it propped against a chair. Then, wrung dry by exhaustion and the passion of my work, I returned to my room and collapsed into unconsciousness.

I don't know how much later it was or how it came about, but my next memory is of Mr. Thurston himself standing over me, shaking the portrait in my face and shouting at me.

"I am accustomed to being hounded by every inconsequential dauber in the city," he said. "If you have been the most persistent, I reasoned that it must be because you were the least talented. When I found this—this atrocity—in my anteroom I saw that I was right.

"I do not make a practice of offering constructive criticism for every smear of paint I see. But since to do so in your case may save me the further annoyance of being exposed to your work, I shall make this exception. My critical opinion is: stop painting! If you must paint, study under the proper teachers and you may one day be capable of designing wallpaper. You will certainly never rise above that level.

"Use your eyes and whatever sense you may have and you will see the truth of what I say. Compare this—this portrait!—with its subject, for example. Do the frontal lobes of my brain really peep through a gap in my forehead? Do my eyes indeed dangle out of their sockets? Have I somehow missed seeing in my mirror what is apparently a third eye? Are the bones of my jaw as badly broken and dislocated as this—this execrable—this heinous—this shocking—"

Mr. Thurston went on. And on and on. But I was no longer capable of understanding what he said. The very core and fiber of my being had been torn apart and shredded, as by some mighty internal explosion. With excruciating pain and blinding light the truth of all that Mr. Thurston said burst upon me.

It was futile to try to express thoughts and emotions with abstract forms, as I had been doing. My pictures had to look like the objects they represented. It was really so simple . . .

It goes without saying that it was Mr. Thurston's wise and generous criticism that made my paintings the success they are today. A reporter was with the policemen who broke open the door of my room and his newspaper printed photographs of Mr. Thurston lying beside his portrait. Other reporters, too, were kind in describing the likeness as "uncanny," "startling," "an incredible similarity." Art dealers and collectors have been clamoring for more of my work ever since.

Unfortunately the light here is bad and I am kept too busy shuttling between the courtroom and the doctor's examinations to continue my painting. So the portrait of Mr. Thurston will probably be my last painting. That's the opinion of the lawyer assigned to me by the judge; he believes I have only another six weeks or two months left, and I'm too exhausted to complete a major work in that time.

But that's all right. The portrait is my masterpiece.

Thank you, Mr. Thurston.

Funeral Music

by Francis M. Nevins, Jr.

As he wrote the confession he could hear the laughter of children playing in a distant meadow.

Hydrangea bushes, deep blue and soft white, swayed in the light summer breeze outside the study windows. He bent over the steel typing table and tapped out the confession with slow precision, using only the middle finger of his right hand. From the stereo speakers mounted on wall brackets above the desk came the softly haunting strains of the Baudelin *String Suite No. 2* as the words slowly filled the sheets of cream bond paper under the printed heading: H. JOSHUA HAWES.

"Before I take my life I must write this. Paul Baudelin's second wife did not die by her own hand but by mine.

"I will not repeat at length what I established in my book, *The Life and Music of Baudelin,* and what has been confirmed for me each day of the seven years I have lived with the Master as his business manager, biographer, and shield against the blows of everyday existence. Before his first marriage he was simply one of many competent young composers in a milieu dominated by his betters—Stravinsky, Shostakovich, Hindemith, Poulenc, Milhaud.

"Then in 1947 he met Claudette and within hours he was savagely, passionately in love. And on their honeymoon in Spain that winter occurred that famous freak accident in contemporary music history—the sudden collapse of a decaying and condemned building as she happened to be walking along the street, so that within moments Mme. Claudette Baudelin was crushed beneath tons of rubble, and Baudelin, who had been so full of the joy of love, was desolate.

"It was the shadow of that lost love, snatched away by sudden blind chance, that filled, one might almost say obsessed, his music from that day, and lent to his compositions a fullness and poignancy, a sense of the merciless randomness of the universe. It is to the fate of Claudette that we owe the four great Symphonies, the second Suite for Strings, the cycle of Death Songs—all the major works of Baudelin's second period which established him as the foremost French composer of the generation.

"And then last year he fell in love again. He was in New York City to conduct the Philharmonic in his Third Symphony. Elana Nassour was second violinist, and her musicianship was superb. It was her rendition of the sublimely difficult passage at the end of the *lento* movement that first stirred his heart, Baudelin told me. The night after the performances of the Symphony they slept in each other's arms.

"Suddenly he was like a boy of eighteen again, this fifty-year-old titan of world music. The universe revolved around Elana and he was soaringly happy. The sense of unutterable loss that was the hallmark of his second period vanished. He almost ceased composing, and what little he wrote was no longer worth hearing. I couldn't stand to see that happen. I loved his work too much.

"And so, four months after they were married—I allowed him that much time of happiness—I mixed an overdose of sleeping pills into the thick Turkish coffee she drank each night before bed.

"I was both careful and lucky. There has been much speculation whether her death was accident or suicide, but no suggestion of murder. And in the year since her death, out of his grief at the loss of her, Baudelin has begun to compose great work again. If she had lived, the Fifth Symphony and the tone poem *La Mort de Dieu* would never have been. That is my justification.

"But it is not enough. I have come to see that no work of art is worth a human life, not even a masterpiece by Baudelin. I have committed a great wrong which can be expiated in only one way. And so I shall go upstairs and take the revolver from my night table drawer and place the barrel in my mouth and squeeze the trigger.

"Baudelin, old friend and benefactor, do not curse my memory, I beg you."

The string suite on the stereo came to an end, and the record player shut itself off with a sharp click. He tugged the third sheet of paper out of the typewriter—it began with the words "can be expiated"—and reread the confession with infinite care.

When he was satisfied he swiveled to the oak desk and placed the final sheet of cream bond on the blotter, above the last page of a signed copy of the management contract between Paul Baudelin and H. Joshua Hawes.

And then Baudelin picked up one of the felt-tipped pens with which Hawes customarily wrote, and boldly traced the signature of H. Joshua Hawes at the end of the suicide note, deliberately permitting variations, remembering that no two signatures by the same person are ever exactly the same.

When he compared the result with Hawes's genuine signature, he gave a little gasp of delight: the forged signature, he was sure, would deceive an expert. He put the contract away in a drawer, slipped the protective lid over the typewriter, and fastened the sheets of the confession together with a paper clip. He then crossed the rooms of the spacious Connecticut farmhouse they had rented for the season.

The perfect murder, he reflected, is not so difficult after all; in fact it requires far less skill than the composition of a symphony. He sprang up the staircase two steps at a time and slipped into Hawes's room without knocking.

His manager-biographer-buffer was sprawled in a wing chair with his huge belly bulging beneath his scarlet dressing gown and his slippered feet resting on the edge of the bed. On the little teakwood table beside the chair there was a water tumbler half full of thick apricot brandy. A bright-jacketed detective novel lay open on Hawes's lap.

Baudelin sauntered casually across the room until he was within one step of the night table where he knew Hawes kept his revolver.

"What's up?" Hawes glanced up half irritated and spoke in a foggy mutter.

Touching only the end of the paperclip, not the papers themselves, Baudelin set the three sheets of the suicide note on top of the book on the other's ample lap. "You might find this document more interesting than the detective story."

As Hawes began reading, Baudelin backed toward the night table and eased the drawer open noiselessly, but kept his eyes fixed on Hawes as his fingers hunted for the weapon. First the musicologist's mouth puckered in a whistle of amusement; then as he read more and more of the confession his face seemed to turn paste-white and his thick lips trembled in sudden terror. At the moment Hawes saw the forgery of his own signature on the last page, Baudelin snatched the revolver out of the drawer and pointed it at the other. Hawes's mouth fell open in fright and disbelief.

"Wider, please." Baudelin smiled bleakly and curled his finger around the cool metal of the trigger.

And suddenly H. Joshua Hawes began to roar with laughter. Great uncontrollable waves of mirth shook his huge frame and he rocked back and forth in the wing chair as if the revolver barrel were the most outrageously funny joke in the world. He groped blindly for the tumbler of apricot brandy, lifted the glass toward Baudelin like a salute, and gulped the drink down in a single swallow.

"Oh," he mumbled, his face dripping with sweat. "What a scheme, what an absolute love of a scheme! You were right, you know. Much better than this novel."

Baudelin was laughing too, but more quietly. He returned the revolver to the night table and shut the drawer tight. "I imitated your writing style well, no? Just the right touch of the pompous and the artificially dramatic." He was delighted at the way Hawes bit down on his lower lip at his touch of criticism. "And not only your style did I capture, but your typing touch as well! You are a trained ten-finger typist, so to match your even touch on the keyboard I typed the entire confession with my one finger."

"Clever of you," Hawes admitted. "I missed that. But you did make one very bad mistake." He folded his arms in a gesture of patronizing superiority.

Baudelin lifted his graying brows in disbelief. "And what might that be?"

"The note's too damn *long*. No one would believe it was really written by someone who was about to kill himself. It rakes up too much past history. You wrote that confession as if there were a huge audience of readers out there who'd never heard of you or Claudette or Elana, so you had to tell them everything they needed to know to follow the story. That isn't the way anyone would write a suicide note."

The composer shook his head right and left. "I disagree with you most profoundly. You are a former music critic for a newspaper, so your instinct is always to write so that the great audience can follow what you are saying. Besides, my friend, your style *is* long-winded, even when you write about me."

Hawes lifted himself out of the wing chair, crossed to Baudelin, and kissed him lightly on each cheek like a French dignitary awarding a medal. "I won't argue it any further. Round Number Thirteen—this is the thirteenth round, isn't it?—goes to you. I can afford to give you one round, I think. The score is now nine to four in my favor, if I'm not mistaken?"

"Nine to four," Baudelin conceded. "But you were always a good manipulator, you know, while I am simply a guileless old naif who scribbles funny marks on music paper. Should I not have what you call a handicap?"

"You old fraud," Hawes chuckled, "you're as devious as I am any day and you know it, and just as adept at the game of plotting against me as I am at plotting against you. So no handicap. The first to take eleven rounds is the winner. I'll make my move within our usual week's time, and I warn you now that I plan to do something especially fiendish to repay you for this clever one."

"As you please." Baudelin shrugged. "Then I leave you to hatch your scheme in peace." With two fingertips he retrieved the confession he had drafted and silently left the room.

He could not restrain his excitement as he descended the stairs. It had worked! The look on Hawes's face as he read the confession had betrayed him. He had never seen such a look of terrified guilt in his life. It had been the sudden numbed panic of a person with a monstrous secret who without warning and beyond human expectation has been exposed. There was no other way of interpreting Hawes's reaction.

True, he had recovered quickly, but not quickly enough. H. Joshua Hawes had murdered Elana in the manner and for the reason Baudelin had written in the confession. His face had given him away, as Baudelin had been praying it would when he set this trap. What was it Hamlet had said? "The play's the thing wherein I'll catch the conscience of the king?"

He was not sure when he had begun to suspect—four months ago, perhaps five. He had never believed his adorable Elana could have killed herself, without explanation, without leaving a note or even a hint. And he could not accept that she had died by accident, for in that case he himself must be some kind of accursed creature, whom no woman could love without paying with her life. And so her death had to be murder, and the only person who lived with them, the only one who could have put the sleeping pills into her Turkish coffee, was Hawes.

Like an evil god Hawes had been manipulating Baudelin's life for seven years, managing his business affairs, publishing interpretations of his music, taping their conversations for use in his books—in the maze of the musical milieu Hawes was the researcher, and Baudelin the experimental rat. He had wanted Baudelin to continue the doom-haunted works of the second period, and so Elana had to die. The only difference between the typed confession and reality was that, in fact, Hawes felt no remorse at all.

Baudelin knew he could prove none of this in a court of law, that there was no way he could make that stare of blubbering terror reappear on Hawes's face for the benefit of a judge and jury. But he didn't need a judge and jury for what he intended to do.

In the study, as sunset turned the distant hills violet and orange, he reread the confession. When he had reassured himself, he swiveled to the steel typewriter table and fed a fresh sheet of cream bond into the carriage and rewrote the third page.

". . . can be expiated in only one way. And so I shall go to the liquor cabinet and pour myself a final snifter of apricot brandy, mixed with an overdose of sleeping pills. It is at least a fitting way to die.

"Baudelin, old friend and benefactor, do not curse my memory, I beg you."

He forged Hawes's signature again at the end of the

confession which now was conveniently marked with Hawes's fingerprints, and put the three sheets away in a desk drawer beneath a sheaf of sketches for a concerto. Then he took the original third sheet into the downstairs bathroom, tore the sheet into tiny bits, flushed them down the toilet, took the bottle of sleeping pills out of the medicine cabinet, brought it into the kitchen where he crushed the tablets to powder, and poured the powder into the decanter of apricot brandy. When he was finished he replaced each thing where he had found it, cleaned his work space carefully, and went back to the study to wait for the sounds of Hawes stumbling downstairs to refill his glass.

Somewhere in a distant meadow he could still hear the laughter of children playing.

Murder Will Out

by Edward Wellen

VICTIM: Here he comes, oozing crocodile tears. Could I but throw off this illness and grow pert once more, they would be real tears. Still, he will weep sincerely when he finds the vaults bare. I have spent all to buy future life. But now my heart is faint, my belly writhes, my hands clutch at the sheet as if it were the thread of life, and all my members fall to trembling. My throat is choke-full of dust. This is the taste of death.

MURDERER: *Now he dies. The sun will not sink below the horizon, I think, before he is gone and all falls to me. But I must show grief even as I rejoice in my heart. Wealth and mastery are now mine, and I will ram through great works and far outbuild him. Set your mind at rest, I keep telling myself: for the tomb will mask it. What I have done will remain forever hidden.*

DETECTIVE: Ha! Then I'm right. The state of the mucous lining and a rough chemical analysis of the skin confirm my hunch. Later I'll hike over to the lab for more conclusive tests. But I can tell you now how you met your end. Someone fed you arsenic. Unfortunately, it's a bit late for an official autopsy report in your case, you poor old bundle of rags, you poor old mummy.

An Insignificant Crime

by Maxine O'Callaghan

When the shop bell rang, I looked up from the account books and groaned. I had enough trouble managing the old man lately without that woman coming around to ruin things completely.

He watched her grimly, his mouth thinned to a tight, self-righteous line—judge, jury, and executioner. I closed the books and hurried to the end of the counter.

"Father, please," I said.

"Please, nothing. I meant what I said. If that woman steals something today, I'll turn her over to the authorities."

I kept my voice low, but his was rising in agitation. "Let's go back into the office and talk," I urged quietly. A glassed-in area lay directly behind the counter where it was possible to work and watch the aisles at the same time. He hung back stubbornly, but I coaxed him in and closed the door.

"There's no reason to discuss it," he said.

"There's every reason. Her father has a lot of influence in this town. If you think you can humiliate him without reprisal, you're dangerously mistaken. If she takes something, why can't you simply charge it to his account as you've done in the past?"

"Because it's wrong, that's why. I've compromised my principles long enough."

I began to sweat. The room was oppressively hot, but that was only partly the reason. I was shaking with inner rage. The old fool couldn't see beyond the end of his thin quivering nose. He would sacrifice the business and our future, his daughter's and mine, and feel smugly sanctimonious. And for what? An insignificant little crime that would hurt nobody.

"You mustn't judge the poor woman," I said, trying to think of a way to avoid the clash that was sure to come. "Her father says it's a sickness."

"Rubbish. She's a thief, and worse, she makes no attempt to hide it." His jaw set obstinately. There was not a drop of perspiration on that cold forehead. "I tell you I have my principles, though your generation wouldn't understand that. All you value is the dollar."

You should talk, I thought grimly. I've worked for him long enough to know how he cheats his customers. Nothing big or obvious—just a niggling penny here and there or merchandise a bit substandard. My one comfort was that he could not live forever. My wife was his only child, born late. If I hung on, the store would eventually be mine—a starting point for the ideas and plans that churned impatiently inside my head. I couldn't allow him to throw everything away because of his single-minded morality.

He kept watch like a hangman waiting on the scaffold, but I began to feel a little hope. She walked up and down the aisles fingering things and dropping them back in the bins. Perhaps the whole thing would blow over. She didn't *always* steal. It's the weather, I told myself. For weeks the heat had clamped down like the lid on a boiling pot, shredding nerves and stroking tempers. Go away, I pleaded silently; make your purchase and get out of here.

It was too late for prayers. Her plump fingers had chosen their prize for the day, bold as brass. The old man sucked in his breath sharply and prepared to charge out of the office, but I grabbed him.

"I won't let you do this," I said.

"You can't stop me." He tried to shake me off, but I hung on tenaciously. "This is my store. I know you're waiting anxiously for me to die so you can get your hands on it, but at present I am very much alive and I'll do as I please."

"Go ahead then," I said recklessly, "but listen carefully. If you do this, I'm leaving. You spend a lot of time belittling me, but you're not a stupid man. You're crafty enough to recognize the amount of work I put into this store. The truth is, you can no longer handle the business alone."

"Don't be ridiculous," he snapped, but he hesitated.

"I have another opportunity." It was a blatant lie, but I was desperate. "I'll take it tomorrow. You'll lose not only my help but your daughter and grandson as well."

He licked his lips, but I could read nothing in those hooded, fish-gray eyes. It took every ounce of my will power to fold my arms and lean casually against a desk, to pretend I could breathe the hot soggy air.

"Well," I said. "Exactly how much are your principles worth to you?"

He didn't answer, just turned his back on me and went out to the counter where the woman waited with a few pennies' worth of nails to legitimatize her visit. I thought his walk seemed slower than usual and his shoulders drooped, but I couldn't be certain. I followed him with my heart thudding painfully against my ribs, convinced that I had made a ghastly mistake and ruined my future.

He accepted payment without a word or a look at her large shopping basket where the hatchet handle was plainly visible. He even managed a stiff nod and a "Good afternoon, Miss Lizzie," while I breathed a shaky, victorious sigh and made a note to charge the stolen ax to Mr. Borden's account.

The Stray Bullet

by Gary Brandner

There were plenty of empty stools in Leo's, it being the Monday after Easter, but the kid followed Hickman all the way to the end of the bar and sat down next to him. Normally, Hickman would not have minded having company, but on this Monday evening he was tired and would have preferred to sit alone.

The kid looked to be about twenty-two or twenty-three, and he needed a shave. Hickman shifted his stool a fraction of an inch farther away and concentrated on the glassy stare of the deer's head mounted behind the bar.

"Quiet night," the kid said.

"Yeah," Hickman grunted. He motioned to the bartender who was pulling on a red vest. "One of the usual, Leo."

The bartender dropped ice cubes into a squat glass and poured whiskey over them. He set the drink in front of Hickman and turned to the kid.

"What'll it be?"

"I'll have a glass of beer," the kid said.

"How about a sandwich, Mr. Hickman?" the bartender asked while he filled a glass from the beer tap.

"No, thanks, Leo. I'm trying to lose a few pounds."

The bartender patted his own stomach. "That's what I ought to do, but I'd rather be fat and happy than thin and miserable. As long as the girls don't complain, right?"

"Sure," said Hickman.

Leo picked up the money for the drinks and went down the bar to ring it up.

"This is my first trip to Los Angeles," the kid said. "I'm from Oregon."

"Nice state," Hickman said. "Green. Rains a lot, though."

The kid leaned over and peered intently into Hickman's face. "Look, do you mind if I tell you a story? I have to tell it to somebody all the way through just one time. If you're a hunter it should interest you. It's a story about a stray bullet."

Hickman studied the kid for a few moments. He was thin, almost frail, under the too-heavy checkered jacket. He had an unruly shock of brown hair and was overdue for a shave. His eyes had a pinched, hurting look.

"Okay," Hickman said, "Let's hear it."

The kid signaled for Leo to bring each of them another drink, and began to speak in a tight voice.

"My name is Wesley Mize. Last September I was married in Portland to a girl named Judy who I knew ever since we were in grade school. She was blonde and cute with sky-blue eyes the size of half dollars.

"For our honeymoon I took a week off from my job in a sporting goods store. We planned to just drive around our own state. On the second day we were headed out Highway 58 east of Eugene when Judy spotted an old logging road leading off into the woods. She was sure there would be wild blackberries, which she loved, up that way, so I turned off the highway and drove as far as I could before the brush got too thick.

"We got out of the car and, sure enough, wild blackberries were everywhere. Judy laughed and danced around like a little girl. She got a plastic bucket out of the car and ran ahead of me to fill it up with the berries.

"She went running up on top of a little rise then, and she turned to wave for me to come on. She said, 'Hurry, Wes, come see what I found.'

"I started up to where she was waiting for me, but I never did see what she found. Just as I got to the rise where she was standing, a bullet went through her head and killed my wife of two days."

"Hey, that's terrible," Hickman said, feeling that he should say something.

"I just about went crazy," the kid went on. "I never heard the shot that killed her, but then there were three more in quick succession. I didn't see where they hit. I just started running at the sound like I was chasing the devil. My foot got caught in some roots and I fell. It broke two bones in my right leg. Somehow, I don't know how, I must have crawled back to Judy's body, because that's where they found me in shock about six hours later. If a patrolman hadn't seen where our car turned off the highway and gone up to investigate, we might both still be there."

"That was lucky, anyway," Hickman said.

"Was it?" Wesley Mize let the question hang between them like smoke. "I spent the next five months in the hospital while they tried to fit my leg back together. There wasn't a single hour of those one hundred and forty-seven days that I didn't wish it was me who died instead of Judy."

"Couldn't the police tell anything about who fired the shots?"

"Not much. They knew it was a 30-06 deer rifle. An empty whiskey bottle was found where the shots came from. They guessed the guy was shooting at an old sign-post where the logging road turned off. Just having a little target practice. He hit the post three times. His first shot was the stray that killed Judy. He never even knew he hit anybody. There was a screen of brush right there and you couldn't see to the road."

"That's really a tough break," Hickman said. "It's too bad you didn't at least get a look at the guy's car."

"Oh, but I did. I not only got a look at his car, I read the California license number, and I saw the man who did the shooting. I saw his fat drunken face as he threw the bottle out and drove away. He was weaving all over the road. Probably didn't remember a thing the next day. I was running after the car when I caught my foot and fell."

"Then why couldn't the police locate the man if you knew his license number and what he looked like?"

Wesley Mize stood up and wiped his mouth with a paper napkin. "I'll tell you the rest of the story when I get back," he said.

As the kid limped toward the Men's Room, Leo came over to Hickman and leaned on the bar.

"That guy's getting kind of loud," he said. "Is he giving you any trouble?"

"No, I think he's all right. He's all unstrung about

something that happened to his wife. I think he just wants to get the story off his chest."

"If he starts to get out of line give me the high sign. I heard him say he's from Oregon, and those people don't much like us Californians. For my money they can keep their state."

"It does rain a lot," said Hickman.

The kid came back and sat on his stool. Leo gave him a hard look and sidled away down the bar.

"The reason the police didn't catch the guy," the kid said, picking right up on his story, "is that I didn't tell them about seeing him."

"What would you do that for?" Hickman asked. "Didn't you want him punished?"

"That's exactly why I did it. I want him *punished,* not slapped on the wrist. As soft as the courts are these days, they would probably let him off with a suspended sentence. That man destroyed the most beautiful thing in my world. There is only one punishment for what he did. He's got to die.

"During those long months when I was in the hospital there was just one reason for me to live—so that I could come after the man who took my wife . . . and kill him."

"You mean you're going to try to find the guy yourself?"

"I mean I *have* found him. It was easy. I wrote to the California Department of Motor Vehicles and gave them the license number. They wrote back the name of the car's owner. It turned out he lives here in Los Angeles."

Hickman felt a sudden clutch of fear. "You have his address?"

"That's right. I went to his house today. I waited until I saw him come out to make sure he was the one, then I followed him right here to this very bar."

Hickman looked down and saw that the kid was holding a .45-caliber service automatic in his lap.

"Wait a minute, son," Hickman cried, "you're making a mistake!"

"No mistake," the kid said.

As their voices rose, Leo came hurrying up the bar. When he reached the spot across from the seated men, Wesley Mize raised the big pistol and shot him in the face. Leo was knocked back against the rows of bottles, then he pitched foward, smacking against the bar as he fell.

Hickman sat as though welded to the bar stool. Wesley Mize laid the automatic on the damp surface of the bar and pushed it toward him.

"I won't need this any more," the kid said. "The stray bullet is home now."

A Night Out with the Boys

by Elsin Ann Graffam

The lights were dim, so low I could hardly make out who was in the room with me. Annoyed, I picked my way to the center where the chairs were. The smoky air was as thick as my wife's perfume, and about as breathable.

I pulled a metal folding chair out and sat next to a man I didn't know. Squinting, I looked at every face in the room. Not one was familiar.

Adjusting my tie, the stupid, wide, garish tie Georgia had given me for Christmas, I stared at the glass ashtray in the hand of the man sitting next to me. The low-wattage lights were reflected in it, making, I thought, a rather interesting pattern. At least, it was more interesting than anything that had happened yet that evening.

I was a fool to have come, I thought, angry. When the letter came the week before, my wife had opened it.

"Look!" she'd said, handing me my opened mail. It was a small square of neatly printed white paper.

"It's from that nice man down the block. It's an invitation to a meeting of some sort. You'll have to go!"

"Go? Meeting?" I asked, taking off my overcoat and reaching for the letter.

"You are Invited," the paper read, "to the Annual Meeting of the Brierwood Men's Club, to be Held at the

Ram's Room at Earle's Restaurant, Sunday evening, January 8, at Eight o'clock."

It was signed, "Yours in Brotherhood, Glenn Reynolds."

"Oh, I don't know," I said. "I hardly know the guy. And I've never heard of that club."

"You're going!" Georgia rasped. "It's your chance to get in good with the neighbors. We've lived here two whole months and not a soul has dropped in to see us!"

"No wonder," I thought. "They've heard enough of your whining and complaining the times they've run into you at the supermarket."

"Maybe," I said, "people here are just reserved."

"Maybe people in the East just aren't as *friendly* as the people you knew back home," she said, sneering.

"Oh, Georgia, don't start that up again! We left, didn't we? I pulled up a lifetime of roots for you, didn't I?"

"Are you trying to tell me it was *my* fault?! Because if you *are*, Mr. Forty and Foolish, you've got another think coming! It was entirely your fault, and you're just lucky I didn't leave you over it!"

"All right, Georgia."

"Where would you be without Daddy's money, Mr. Fathead? Where would you be without me?"

"I'm sorry, Georgia. I'm just tired, that's all."

She gave a smug little smile and went on. "You *are* going," she nodded, making her dyed orange hair shake like an old mop. "Yes indeedly. You can wear your good dark brown suit and that new tie I gave you and . . ."

And she went on, planning my wardrobe, just as she'd planned every minute of my last fourteen years.

So the night of the eighth I was at the Annual Meeting of the Brierwood Men's Club. Totally disgusted. What crazy kind of club had a meeting annually? A service club? Fraternal organization? Once a year?

It was almost eight when the men stopped filing into the room. They were, with hardly an exception, a sad-looking lot. I mean, they looked *depressed*. A gathering of funeral directors? A club for people who had failed at suicide and were contemplating it again?

"I think this is all of us, men," Reynolds said, standing at the dais. "Yes. We can begin. Alphabetical order, as always. One minute."

A sad, tired-looking man in his fifties stood up and went to the platform.

"Harry Adams. She, she . . ."

He wiped his brow nervously and went on.

"This year has been the worst ever for me. You've seen her. She's so beautiful. I know you think I'm lucky. But I'm not, no, no. She's been after me every minute to buy her this, buy her that, so she can impress all the neighbors. I don't make enough money to be able to do this! But she threatened to leave me and take all I've got, which isn't all that much any longer, if I don't give in. So I took out a loan at the bank, told them it was for a new roof, bought her everything she wanted with the money. But it wasn't enough. She wants more. A full-length mink coat, a two-carat diamond ring. I'll have to go to another bank, get another loan for my roof. I'm running out of money, I'm running out of roofs . . ."

"One minute, Harry."

Dejected, the little man left the platform and another took his place.

"Browning. She invited her mother to live with us. The old dame moved in last April. I could hardly put up with my wife, but now I've got two of them. Whining, nagging—in stereo, yet. You can't imagine how it is, guys! I get home from work five minutes late, I've got two of them on my back. I forget my wife's birthday, my mother-in-law lets me have it. I forget my mother-in-law's birthday, my wife lets me have it."

He looked over at Reynolds, sitting on the platform.

"More?"

"Ten seconds, Joe."

"I just want to say I can't stand it at home any longer! I'm not a young man any longer! I—"

"Minute, Joe."

And it was another's turn. I sat there rigid with fascination. What a great idea! Once a year, get together to complain about the wife! Get it out of the system, let it all out! And to think I hadn't wanted to come!

Some guy named Dorman was on next. His wife had eaten herself up to two hundred and eighty pounds. And Flynn, his wife had gone to thirty doctors for her imagined ills. Herter, his wife refused to wear her false teeth around the house unless they had guests, and Klutz, his wife had wrecked his brand-new sports car three times in the year, down to Morgan, whose wife gave all of his comfortable old clothes to charity.

And then it was *my* turn. It wasn't, you understand, that I wanted to *impress* anybody—but to be able to actually say it, to tell the world what she'd done to me—heaven!

I took my place on the dais and looked at Reynolds.

"You can begin now," he said kindly.

"Freddie Nerf. Her name was Jennie and she was my secretary and she was twenty-three and I loved her more than anything else on earth and knew I always would and my wife who is cold like you wouldn't believe found out and told everybody on the west coast what I'd done and said we'd have to move thousands of miles away from 'that tramp', only Jennie wasn't a tramp and I'll never in my life see her again and I still love her so much and my wife keeps bringing the whole thing up and I try to forget because it hurts so much, but I know I'll never be able to, especially with my wife reminding me all the time."

"One minute, Fred."

"I CAN'T STAND MY WIFE!" I yelled into the microphone as I left the platform.

Never in my thirty-nine and three-quarter years had I felt so good. Almost laughing from the pure pleasure of getting it out of my system, I took my seat and half-listened to the others. Owens, whose wife told his kids he was a dummy, and Quenton, whose wife had gone back to college and thought she was smarter than he was, and Smith, whose wife slept until noon and made him do all the housework, all the way down to Zugay, whose wife made all of his clothes so he went out looking like a hold-over from the Depression. Which he certainly did.

One guy, who hadn't spoken, interested me. He was smiling. Actually sitting there with a big grin on his face. I was staring at him, wondering if I knew him, when Reynolds spoke.

"All right, men. Time to vote. George, hand out the paper and pencils, okay?"

"Vote?" I asked the man sitting next to me, whose wife hid his hairpiece when she didn't want him going out.

"Sure. Vote for the one who has the lousiest wife."

I scribbled down the name Freddie Nerf. After all, I did have the lousiest wife.

Glenn Reynolds collected the slips of paper and sorted them. In a few minutes he turned to face the men.

"For the first time, men" he said, "a new member has won. Fred Nerf. The one with the wife, you remember, who called his nice girlfriend a tramp."

I half-rose as he congratulated me, feeling somewhat foolish and yet proud. It was indeed an honor.

And then all of them, all the sad-faced, beaten-down men gathered around me and shook my hand. Some of them actually had tears in their eyes as they patted me on the back.

Later, as we all went to the lounge to have a drink before going home, I found Reynolds at the end of the bar and went over to him with my drink.

"This is some deal!" I said. "It really, *really* felt good to get it out of my system! Whose idea was this club?"

"Mine," he said. "We've met once a year for the last five years. I control the membership and I wanted you to be included this year. That wife of yours is really something, isn't she?"

"Yes," I agreed. "She sure is. How come you didn't speak? Because it's your club?"

"Oh, no. My wife passed away four years ago."

"I'm sorry," I said, feeling suddenly awkward. "That guy sitting over there, the one who's had the big smile on his face all evening, who the heck is he?"

"Gary McClellan? He's a plumber."

"Oh, *sure*. Say, didn't my wife tell me that McClellan's wife died last year in some sort of horrible accident?"

Reynolds smiled broadly and patted me on the arm. "Of *course*, old man! McClellan was *last* year's winner!"

Office Party

by Mary Bradford

Everett Willis left the main entrance of the industrial controls department at dusk after the Thanksgiving party at the office. He had hated being there, but it was the annual turkey-and-basket-of-cheer raffle and he had to oversee it. He had tried to stop the practice this year but everyone protested. Now the party was over—but the night wasn't.

It was sleeting a fine coat of ice on the vast parking lot for three hundred company cars. Everyone else had gone home. Willis stayed to the end to make sure no one had passed out behind the Xerox machine. It was always a little lonesome finding your car the only one left, he thought, and a little eerie. His car was parked in the middle of the lot.

But one thing had been a master stroke this night. He smiled to himself. And it was all wrapped up inside the small gray cardboard box he was carrying close to this side. The box contained the kickback payoffs from the shipping crew he had caught selling company goods after circumventing inventory records. The office party had been the perfect night to split the cash he knew they'd received that afternoon. Now he could meet his new car payments and the mounting credit card bills that snowballed in each month.

The sodium lights cast a strange pall over the lot as he hurried toward his car. He waved goodnight to the security guard as he passed by the old man whose head was bundled up in a scarf against the biting cold. It would be three-quarters of an hour before he got home where his wife was waiting dinner and his eldest son was waiting impatiently for the car.

His son would leave early, and after dinner his wife would

walk the two blocks to Walnut Lane to baby-sit for her sister for a few hours. His two younger children, as usual, would be glued to the TV set in the family room. Willis would put the money in the metal box in the locked cabinet above his tool bench in the basement.

He opened the door on the driver's side, placing the box carefully on the back seat. He started to slide into the seat when he noticed a large woman slumped on the passenger seat. Startled, he jumped back out.

"For God's sake, who are you? What are you doing here?

The woman pulled herself up to a sitting position. She had a wild, unkempt black hair and was wearing a green polyester pantsuit which she overflowered like molten lava. She had on a green parka jacket with a hood of ratty-like fur framing her face. She was very, very drunk. "You take me where I want to go or I'll scream. I'll scream that Everett Willis attacked me in the plant's parking lot, and the security guard'll come running."

"Who the hell are you?" he demanded, getting back into the car out of the hard-driving sleet and wind.

"Who am I? That's a good question. Whom am I?"

She turned full face toward Willis, who recoiled from the smell of cheap alcohol.

"I don't know who I am. But I know where I want to go. Mr. Boyd of marketing put me in this car. Mr. Boyd said you were a great guy and would see that I got home. That was not a nice thing to do," she broke out tearfully. "He should have taken me home himself, he should have. You take me to Mr. Boyd's house, and we'll tell him so, the two of us."

Willis swore under his breath—Stan Boyd, the office clown. He'd get even with Boyd if it was the last thing he did. My God, he thought, of all nights for this to happen. He had the box with him. He had to get it home. And now that clown, Boyd, had dumped this on him.

"Why didn't someone take you home? What happened?"

"We were having a party like yours in Building A, waiting for the raffle drawing, and some drinks were passed around. You know how it is at those parties. And they had the raffle and you know I never won anything in my whole life, not even when I was a kid, and you know what, Mr.

Willis of industrial controls? Yes, I know you. I read the employees' newsletter faithfully, *very faithfully*. You are in charge of shipping, you coach a Little League baseball team, you're on the industrial controls bowling team, and you're a Sunday school teacher. You have a wife and three children—one, two, three—and you have been with the company for ten years—one, two, three, four . . ."

Willis exploded. "Okay, you know all about me. What about you? I don't remember seeing you around, Miss, or is it Mrs.? What's your name and why did that clown, Boyd, bring you here?"

"I was telling you. I had never won anything in my whole life and you know what—I had to win that damn turkey! Now what the hell do I want with a twenty-pound turkey. I live alone. I don't need a twenty-pound turkey. I need . . ."

She tossed her head back and laughed. "You know I left that turkey on top of the file case and after this three-day holiday it will be a little ripe, don't you think so, Mr. Willis of industrial controls? Say, let's go get him. Let's go get Mr. Boyd of marketing. Now, let's go now. If you don't, I'll scream. You want to hear me? I can scream good and loud. I've had lots of practice."

Willis sat back in the seat and rubbed his face in his hands. He felt hot and his throat was dry. The sleet was coming down heavier, and the windshield was icing up. He started the car to defrost the windshield.

"No cabs," she said. "Don't go back and call me a cab. Take me to Boyd or I scream."

"I don't know where the s.o.b. lives! And I'm expected home by six o'clock!"

"I know where he lives. It's in Lakewood at the corner of Mulberry and Vine."

It was hot and oppressive in the car. The alcoholic fumes and the stale aroma of cheap perfume were overwhelming. God, what can I do, he wondered. I could take her up to the night watchman, but I don't want this to get around. No, it's up to me to take care of it. I'm the senior official. It's my responsibility. If I take her to Boyd's, it will embarrass his family. His wife and mine are good friends.

"Look, I'll take you to Boyd's. But you stay in the car. I'll do the talking. Is that understood?"

"Yeah, let's go to Boyd's." She had a self-satisfied smile on her face, and she sunk lower in the seat. Willis opened the window on the driver's side. The cold, biting air felt good against his hot, dry skin and the dryness of his throat.

"Remember, you stay in the car," he ordered.

She looked at him through half-closed eyes.

"You know, Mr. Willis of industrial controls, I'm a woman who was never meant to be a career woman. I liked being a dumb housewife. Yeah, you're looking at a liberated woman, Mr. Willis. I've got a lot to thank women's lib for. My husband liberated me. He didn't want to stand in the way of my development.

"That Boyd is a so-and-so. He had no right to put me in your car. I thought he was taking me home. I guess I got a wee bit drunk—or stoned—and I was slumped against the file case, and when he was closing up the place he found me. He was really swearing. He picked me up and brought me outside, and I thought he was going to take me home. That's what I thought, Mr. Willis. That he would take me home. But, instead, he put me in your car and drove off in his own. And that was not a nice thing to do, was it?"

Willis drove the streets of Lakewood through the northwest residential section. He came to the corner of Mulberry and Vine. It was an area of large, pleasant homes. Boyd's house was a two-story brick with green shutters and a two-garage. It was handsome and impressive.

Willis got out of the car. The sleet was coming down hard now, and he moved slowly across the slick flagstone walkway. The woman remained inside.

Boyd's wife came to the door and invited him in. "No," Willis said evenly, "if Stan could just come to the door, please. I have something to discuss with him."

Boyd wasn't home. Willis swore under his breath. What am I going to do now, he thought grimly as he returned to the car.

"Now what?" he said to the woman. "He's not home. Now, look, whoever you are. This is not my fault. I have nothing to do with this. I should be home right now, not driving around with a . . . I've got to take you home or someplace. Do you live in an apartment, a house? Just tell me. Do you have any friends you could go to?"

She sank farther down in the seat. "I'm gettin' cold. Let's stop at Marty's Coffee Shop and get some hot black coffee."

The coffee shop was empty except for two men at the counter sitting on stools. A young waitress slowly wiped off the table tops of the booths. Willis guided the woman into a booth where she wedged herself into the corner. She seemed to be a little more manageable. The drunkenness was wearing off a bit, he hoped fervently.

The waitress brought them mugs of hot black coffee. The woman sipped the coffee slowly, much to Willis' relief.

"Look, I've got to call home. I'll be right back," he said. The phone booth was at the front of the coffee shop. He saw the woman get up and go to the ladies' room at the back of the shop. He put the box of cash beside the telephone.

His wife's voice was frantic. "Where are you? What's happened?" She listened attentively and patiently, as he knew she would. He explained slowly and carefully all that had happened. She was understanding but apprehensive.

The woman was sitting in the booth when he came back from the phone. She had straightened up considerably. She seemed much younger. Her hair was combed, her face freshly made up, and the dark green print scarf at her neck was tied in a fashionable bow.

She lit a cigarette and looked evenly at Willis.

"I do a pretty convincing drunk, don't I? I've had enough practice. I can also be a salesclerk, a garden club president, a mother-in-law waiting for her kids to show up, and a new clerk in the accounting division of a large company. I'm one of twelve women in this state licensed to be a private investigator. I'm fifty-five years old, a grandmother, and being an old lady is no stumbling block in this work."

Willis' face had gone ashen white.

That box you have with you, Willis. Mr. Boyd and another company man are coming in the front door now. And if it's cash payments for all those company machines and supplies you and the shipping crew have been funneling off on the side, you'll have to explain it to them."

Her face was calm and serene—and smiling. Now she looked like what she really was—somebody's sweet old grandmother.

Comes the Dawn

by Michael Kurland

The sun was just sending its slanting rays over the mountains to the East, etching the pattern of the adobe rooftops into the walls of the buildings across the street, when the first daylight patrol of the *Guardias Municipales* found the twisted body of what had been a man lying in the dust. At first they thought it was just another looter. . . .

Civil insurrection, even in a country where it is almost the normal pattern of life, is always an ugly thing. Whether it is right or wrong, good or evil, necessary or irrelevant, it is the handmaiden of chaos. Looting, raping, fire, and death are always within its domain. Its borders spread, and are not sharp or distinct. Unconnected events are swept before it as flotsam before the ocean tide.

Manuel Hispoza Forgas had a brother. This brother's name was Philippe. Manuel did not like Philippe; a feeling which was reciprocated. These brothers lived in widely separate parts of the city and saw each other but seldom. Philippe's dislike for his brother remained fairly constant through the passing years, he preferred to just not ever think about Manuel. Manuel's feeling festered and grew into a supreme, blinding hatred; he could not help but think about Philippe constantly.

Philippe and Manuel shared jointly in their father's estate. Philippe prospered with his portion, establishing a small furniture shop which grew into a major store over the years. Manuel tended to try more speculative ventures: mostly at the racetrack and cockfight. As Philippe's fortunes rose, Manuel's fell; and Manuel's dislike of his brother increased.

It is incidental, perhaps, that Philippe married the very girl that Manuel, on afterthought, decided he would have liked to marry. It is predicatable that, of all the houses in the city, Manuel was most fond of the one in which Philippe happened to live.

. Manuel's hatred of his brother drove him to thoughts of murder. Shooting, strangulation, poison, defenestration; murder by axe, knife, car; all these fancies and more took up a large part of his imagination. He planned accidental deaths, locked room murders, and murders of passion. He read detective stories, true crime books, and medical journals. He became cognizant of every famous killer from Cain to Torquemada, from Richard III to Lizzie Borden. That he restrained from committing that most horrible and fascinating of all crimes can be attributed only to one fact—Manuel's extreme cowardice. These famous murderers, Manuel would reflect when reading about Mrs. Simms or Doctor Crippen, became famous not because they committed murder, but because they got caught. Manuel didn't have a very high regard for the local police, but if there were the slightest chance—however small—of hanging for his crime, Manuel would keep it a secret dream.

The wonderful idea came to Manuel on the second day of the insurrection. On the evening of the third day he went to find Philippe to tell him about it. Philippe, who as usual was working late in his store after the clerks had gone home, let Manuel in when he knocked.

"You want something?" Philippe asked.

"Don't be unfriendly," Manuel replied. "I've come here this evening out of concern for you. The riots in this part of the city are horrible: looting, burning, killing."

"I'm touched that you have such concern for me," Philippe commented, and went back to his desk. "But you could have seen me at the house, I have to be leaving soon."

"Ah, yes. The curfew starts shortly, doesn't it?" Manuel asked.

"It does. And I don't want to have to spend the night here."

"If the riots start again tonight, aren't you afraid the store will be looted, or perhaps burned?"

"I should think that would please you," Philippe commented. "I think the *Guardias Municipales* have the situation well under control. Besides, I carry heavy insurance."

"Ah!" Manuel shrugged. "Insurance, of course." He sat down on the desk Philippe was working at, and leaned over Philippe. "Before you leave," he said, "I want to tell you of the brilliant idea I had yesterday. I've been thinking about it for two days, and it seems perfect. Perhaps you can find a flaw in it?"

Philippe threw down his pencil. "You're sitting right on the papers I've been trying to work on. I don't give a fig for your ideas—get up and get out of here!"

"Ah, but this idea concerns you," Manuel said. He took a large, heavy revolver from under his shirt, and pointed it at his brother.

Philippe jumped up, upsetting his chair. "What's this?" he demanded shrilly.

"A revolver," Manuel told him. "It's quite old, but I think it will work. I'm going to kill you with it."

Philippe straightened the chair, and sat down again: slowly, as though he were sitting on a case of eggs. "Kill me? You wish to kill me?"

"I've wished nothing else for many years."

"They'll hang you," Philippe said.

"I think not," Manuel answered. "And I've been thinking about it quite a lot. Let me explain."

"You're insane," Philippe said.

Manuel went on as if he hadn't heard. "The trouble, of course, is the police," he explained. "They find a body, and they start searching for a murderer. They check for clues; they try to find witnesses; they try to establish a motive. They slowly close their net until they find their killer. It is almost inevitable."

"Yes, yes. Inevitable. If you kill me, they will find you and hang you." Philippe pounced on the thought. "You don't want to be hanged. Now leave here, and we'll forget all about it. I promise you, I shall not say a—"

"The trick," Manuel went on, as if his brother had said nothing, "is to stop this process before it starts. And I've found a way. It came to me while I was listening to the radio. It's a clever idea, but very simple. What bodies do they find that do not cause them to search for a murderer?"

Philippe said nothing.

"I will tell you. Now, in this part of the city, during the riots, there is much looting going on at night. The *Guardias* shoot anyone they find looting. Such bodies are buried without question. If one of the bodies happens to be the owner of a store instead of a looter, a regrettable mistake has been made, and that is the end of it. You see how simple it is?"

Manuel took the revolver in both hands and pointed it at his brother's head. "Bang," he said.

"You're crazy," Philippe said, starting to shake uncontrollably.

"You see something wrong with the plan?" Manuel asked.

"They'll hang you."

"How are they going to catch me?"

Philippe did not answer.

"Turn around," Manuel said.

"What?"

"Turn around. I'm going to tie you up. When I hear some shooting, so I know the *Guardias* are out, I'm going to drag you outside. Then, bang! The *Guardias* never come up the street to see the looters they've shot until morning, for fear of ambush, so you'll lie there until daylight. Of course, I'll untie you before I leave. Regrettable accident. I shall cry when I hear the news."

Manuel tied and gagged his brother with rags that wouldn't leave marks, and continued sitting on the desk staring at Philippe. Philippe tried to meet his brother's stare with a defiant look. "Bang," Manuel said softly, and Philippe looked away.

Manuel took a thick, black cigar out of a box on the desk, and lit it with a wooden match from his pocket. "Would you also like a cigar?" he asked his brother politely. Philippe shook his head.

Time passed. Manuel lit another cigar from the stub of the first one, and then a third from the stub of the second. The street outside was dark and silent. Suddenly there was the sound of breaking glass, and then of running feet. A loud cracking sound was heard, and the feet stopped running.

"It's almost time," Manuel said.

From a few blocks away there were new noises, and then more gunshots. Soon the siren of a fire-engine filled the night with its wail.

"Time," Manuel announced. He dragged his brother to the door of the shop, and then outside to the slightly set-in doorway, and propped him up against the wall.

"Good-bye, Philippe."

Manuel took three steps away from the doorway, turned and raised his pistol as though he were engaged in a duel. He took a last, deep drag on the cigar, and . . .

At first they thought it was just another looter. "There he is," one of the *Guardias* said to his partner, "the one I shot at last night. I told you I saw a burning cigarette."

"Cigar," the second one said, looking down.

"Look over here," the first one called, "there's someone tied up in this doorway."

Acting Job

by Richard Deming

The man was tall and pale, with a wooden expression and hooded eyes. He would have been perfect in the movie role of Jack-the-Ripper. Myrna Calvert hesitated before letting him in, then seemed to decide it was silly to let his appearance bother her.

"Come in, Mr. Moore," she said coolly, stepping aside to let him go past her into the apartment and closing the door behind him.

He glanced around the actress' front room, approving its tasteful furnishings. When she invited him to sit, he gave his head a nearly imperceptible shake.

"I won't be here that long," he said, barely moving his lips.

"I'll just say what I have to say and leave. But first, I didn't quite tell you the truth over the phone."

The woman's green eyes narrowed. "You don't really have any life-or-death information for me?"

"Oh, that part was the truth. Only my name isn't Moore. I'm not going to tell you my real name."

Myrna's lovely features were marred by a frown. She studied him suspiciously.

He said, "Before I explain just what this is all about, I want you to know why I'm telling you. I've seen every play you've ever been in, Miss Calvert. I think you're the finest actress and the loveliest woman who ever walked on a stage."

Myrna's back stiffened. "If this is just some trick to get an autograph—"

"It isn't," he interrupted. "I just don't want you to be scared of me. You would be if I told you why I'm here before letting you know how I feel about you. I want you to know I wouldn't harm you for anything."

The actress looked surprised. "Why should you harm me?"

"It's my business," he said dryly. "I belong to an organization which disposes of people for a handsome fee."

Myrna's eyes gradually widened until they were enormous. In an incredulous tone she said, "You mean you've been hired to kill me?"

"My organization has. I've been assigned the job. I don't intend to do it."

After a period of shocked silence, she asked faintly, "Who wants me dead?"

The man raised his eyebrows. "I figured you'd know that. I was just given the job, not the reason."

Myrna paced to a sideboard, took a cigarette from a box and lit it. "Why have you risked telling me this, Mr. whatever-your-name-is? Won't your organization be angry with you?"

"I don't plan on them finding it out."

"Suppose I called the police and asked for protection? Wouldn't they know then?"

He shrugged. "You could probably get me killed, if you're that ungrateful. Are you?"

She studied him with an undecided expression on her face. "You're taking this risk just because you're a fan of mine?"

"A little more than that, Miss Calvert."

"Oh? What?"

"I've been in love with you for five years," he said quietly. "Don't let it upset you. It's from a distance and I never expected to meet you. I don't plan to bother you. When I walk out of here you'll never see me again. I just don't want you dead."

After contemplating him for a time, she said, "I'm flattered. And very lucky too, I suspect. You look like an efficient killer."

"I am," he said dryly.

She took a quick, nervous puff on her cigarette and stubbed it out. "You don't know any details of this plot?"

"There was a condition attached," he said. "I'm supposed to tail you. If you caught a plane for Europe tonight, I was supposed to forget it. If you didn't, I was supposed to move in and do the job."

Her nostrils flared. "Max Fenner!" she said.

"The theatrical producer?" he inquired.

She gave a jerky nod. "I knew he hated me, but I didn't think he'd go this far. He must be mad."

"What's his beef?"

"He's over a barrel," she said viciously. "I want the lead in his new play. He's already signed Lynn Jordan, and he knows she'll sue his pants off if he reneges on the contract. But I'm in a position to cause him even more trouble if he doesn't play ball."

He said, "I thought I read you were supposed to make some picture in France."

Myrna made an impatient gesture. "That's peanuts compared to the lead in *Make Believe*. Max knows I have no intention of catching that plane. I told him yesterday if he didn't bring around a contract by this evening, I'd talk to his wife."

He examined her curiously. "You're blackmailing him into giving you the part?"

"This is a cutthroat business, mister. You get to the top any way you can. Lynn Jordan signed her contract on Max's casting couch. I'm in a position to wreck his marriage if he doesn't break the contract and sign me. There isn't an actress on Broadway who wouldn't use that position in the same way I am. It isn't amoral, because there aren't any morals in the theatrical business."

He shrugged. "It's nothing to me. You ought to know something, though."

"What?"

"You're not off the hook just because I'm turning down the job. The organization will assign somebody else. And maybe he won't be a secret admirer."

Myrna paled a little. "They won't just forget it when you back out?"

He shook his head. "Not a chance."

"And if I ask for police protection, they might kill you?"

"Uh-huh. It wouldn't save you anyway. You'd get by tonight, maybe, but the cops can't guard you forever. They'd get to you eventually. I doubt that the cops would believe you anyway. They'd think it was a publicity stunt. And I'm not about to back up your story. Tipping you off is as far as I can afford to go."

Nervously she lit another cigarette, immediately punched it out again. "What do you think I ought to do?"

"You could save everybody trouble by catching that plane. I wouldn't even have to turn down the job if you did that. I could just report that you caught it."

"And miss the best part I ever had a chance at?"

He shrugged again. "My outfit is pretty efficient. You won't star in anything if you're in the morgue."

Myrna paced back and forth. "Suppose I hired you as a bodyguard?"

He gave her a bleak smile. "I might as well commit suicide. They'd just get both of us."

She stopped pacing, lifted another cigarette from the box, then dropped it back again without lighting it. "You don't think I have a chance?"

He gave his head a slow shake.

Biting her lip, she considered. "But if I catch that plane, nothing at all will happen?"

"That's right," he said tonelessly. "You make your picture in France without a care in the world."

"All right," she decided. "Tell your people I'm on my way to France."

His wooden expression momentarily relaxed into the barest suggestion of a relieved smile. "Thanks, Miss Calvert. That will keep both of us out of bad trouble."

When the tall, pale man entered Max Fenner's office, the fat, bald-headed producer eyed him worriedly.

"How'd it go, John?" he asked.

"Like shooting fish in a barrel," the pale man said, sinking into a chair. "She's catching the plane."

"She didn't suspect you were a phony?"

The pale man looked pained. "I told you I do the best gangster act in the business."

"Yeah, but are you sure she didn't recognize you?"

"Where would she see me? I've been ten years with the Cleveland Players. She doesn't even catch off-Broadway shows, let alone out-of-towners. I tell you she swallowed it hook, line, and sinker."

Max Fenner breathed a sigh of relief. "That's a load off my mind. If she'd ever played those tape recordings for my wife—" He paused to shudder. "John, if you ever carry on an affair with an ambitious actress, make sure her apartment isn't wired for sound."

"How could anybody blackmail me?" the character actor inquired. "I can't hand out parts in Broadway plays."

"I guess you wouldn't have the same problem," the producer agreed. "You're going to follow up by being at the airport to make sure she doesn't change her mind, aren't you?"

"Sure. You can phone me at my rooming house about nine P.M. I'll be back from the airport by then."

Max Fenner nodded. "I won't forget this, John. The minute you tell me she's on that plane, you've got a part in *Make Believe*."

When the character actor came to the phone, Fenner asked, "Did she make it?"

"Yeah," Blake said. "She's gone. I told you there was nothing to worry about."

"Good job," Fenner said with relief. "Drop by tomorrow and we'll draw up your contract."

"What sort of message is it?" Fenner asked dubiously.

"I told you it has to be delivered personally," the man said in a patient tone. "May I come up?"

"All right," Fenner agreed. "You know the apartment?"

"Uh-huh. See you in five minutes, Mr. Fenner."

When the doorbell rang five minutes later, Fenner found a plump, middle-aged man standing in the hall. The man had a round, pleasant face and a deferential manner.

"Mr. Fenner?" he inquired.

"Yes. You're Howard Smith?"

The man nodded. Letting him in, Fenner closed the door behind him. Howard Smith glanced around the front room.

"You're alone?" he asked.

"Yes. What is this message?"

The plump man smiled. "Miss Calvert resented what you did to her today, Mr. Fenner. She was really quite frightened."

Fenner said coldly, "I don't know what you're talking about."

"Hiring a professional killer to work on her, Mr. Fenner. She wasn't sure whether the man actually was sincere when he said he couldn't kill her because he admired her so, or was merely subtly warning her that he would kill her if she didn't catch that plane. But she was too frightened to risk not catching it. I suppose you know she's on her way to France."

"You're saying nothing which makes sense to me, Mr. Smith," Fenner said in the same cold voice. "I haven't hired any professional killer."

"Of course you did, Mr. Fenner. But I won't press the point. What Miss Calvert wanted me to tell you was that she has contacts too. You've heard of Vince Pigoletti, I suppose?"

"The racketeer?"

Howard Smith nodded. "He's a great admirer of Miss Calvert. He is one of the numerous men with whom she has had—ah—romantic alliances, I understand. Mr. Pigoletti was kind enough to put her in touch with the organization I represent."

Fenner frowned. "What organization is that?"

"We don't advertise its name, Mr. Fenner. But it's a competitor of the one you engaged. Miss Calvert resented your action so much that she decided to retaliate in kind. Ordinarily we don't explain things like this, but she stipulated that she wanted you to understand exactly what was happening."

Fenner's face gradually paled. "I don't think I follow you," he said faintly.

"I think you do," the plump man said.

He drew a silenced revolver from beneath his coat. Staring at him in fascination, Max Fenner realized that this was no character actor.

Myrna Calvert had hired the real thing.

The Last Smile

by Henry Slesar

The arrogance went first. The clanging of the death-cell door drove it out of Finlay the first day. Then he turned sullen, uncooperative, his young face taking on the protective coloration of the cement block that lined his prison. He wouldn't eat, talk, or see the chaplain. He snarled at his own lawyer, muttered at the guards, and kept his own company. A week before the scheduled execution, he began to cry in his sleep. He was twenty-one years old, and with the aid of an accomplice, had mercilessly beaten and slain an aged storekeeper.

On the morning of the fifth day, he woke out of a nightmare in which he had been sentenced to die. Finding the dream sustained by reality, he began to scream and hurl himself against the steel bars. Two guards came into his cell and threatened him with mechanical restraints, but they failed to quiet him down. An hour later, the prison chaplain, a silver-haired, stocky man with the pained face of a colicky infant, looked in on him and said the same old things. This time, however, there was an air of pleading that made Finlay listen harder.

"Please," the chaplain whispered. "Be a good fellow and let me come in. It's important, really."

"What's important?" he said bitterly. "I don't want you praying over me."

"Please," the chaplain said in a curious, begging tone. The boy in the cell wondered at it, and wearily gave his permission. Once the chaplain had been admitted, however, he regretted the decision. The silver-haired man took a small black book from his pocket.

"No!" Finlay yelled. "None of that! I don't want no Bible reading!"

"Just look at it," the chaplain said, his face reddening. "Here, take a look."

Finlay took the small thick volume from the plump fingers. Outside the cell, a guard with a comfortable paunch stood profiled against the hall light. Finlay looked at the open page, marked *Revelation,* and then at the tiny slip of white paper that had been stuck into the binding of the book. The handwritten message read:

Trust me.

Finlay blinked at it rapidly, and then looked at the cherubic face of the man beside him. The round chin fitted the turnabout collar like an egg in an eggcup, and the expression on the baby features was impassive.

"Now can we talk?" the chaplain said cheerfully. "There's so little time, my son."

"Yes," Finlay said vaguely. "Listen, what's the—"

"Shush!" A chubby finger crossed the chaplain's lips. "Let us not speak any longer, son. Let us pray." He placed his palms together, and closed his eyes. Bewildered, Finlay mimicked him, and the chaplain droned on in a convincing monotone about salvation and redemption. When he was through, he beamed at the prisoner and took his leave.

Finlay didn't see the chaplain again until late that evening. This time, there wasn't any hesitation about admitting the chubby little man to his cell. As soon as he was inside, Finlay whispered hoarsely at him:

"Listen, I gotta know. Was it Willie sent you? Willie Parks?"

"Shush," the chaplain said nervously, looking at the strolling guard. "Let us not speak of earthly matters . . ."

"It *is* Willie," Finlay breathed. "I knew Willie wouldn't let me down." As the chaplain opened his little black book, he grinned and leaned back on the cot. "Go on, pal, I'm listening."

"The Bible tells us to have courage, my son," the chaplain said meaningfully. "The Bible tells us to keep faith in ourselves, our friends, and our Lord. Do you understand?"

"I understand," Finlay said.

That night, he slept well for the first time since his imprisonment. In the morning, he asked for the chaplain again, and the guard raised an eyebrow at the sudden conversion. When the little man arrived, Finlay smiled broadly at him and said: "What's the Bible say this morning, chaplain?"

"It speaks of hope," the chaplain said gravely. "Shall we read it together?"

"Sure, sure, whatever you say."

The chaplain read a lengthy passage, and Finlay began to stir restlessly. Then, just as he was about to explode with impatience, the chaplain handed the small book over, and Finlay saw the written message in the binding:

Everything's set.

The chaplain smiled at the prisoner, patted his shoulder, and called the guard.

On the beginning of what was officially his last day on earth, Finlay was visited by his attorney, a small man with a perennially moist upper lip. He had nothing to offer in the way of hope for commutation of the sentence, and Finlay gathered that his visit was merely to satisfy the contract. He seemed surprised by the condemned man's congeniality, a sharp contrast to the hostility he had shown before. In the afternoon, the prison warden came by and asked Finlay again if he cared to reveal the name of his accomplice in the murder of the storekeeper, but Finlay merely smiled and wanted to know if he could see the chaplain. The warden pursed his lips and sighed. At six that evening, the chaplain returned.

"How's it gonna work?" Finlay whispered to him. "Do I crash outa here, or—"

"Shush," the little man warned. "We must trust a Higher Power."

Finlay nodded, and then they read the Bible together.

At ten-thirty that night, two guards entered Finlay's cell and performed the ugly duties of shaving his head and slitting the cuffs of his trousers. The ceremony made him nervous, and he began to doubt that his escape was ordained. He started to rave and demanded to see the chaplain; the little man appeared hurriedly and talked to him in quiet, firm tones about faith and courage. As he spoke, he placed a folded slip of paper into the boy's hands; Finlay swiftly hid it under the blanket of his cot. When he was alone once more, he opened the note and read it. It said:

Last-minute escape

Finlay spent the rest of the time tearing the note into the tiniest possible shreds and spreading them around the floor of the cell.

At five minutes to eleven, they came for him. The two guards flanked him, and the warden took up the rear. The chaplain was permitted to walk beside him all the way to the green metal door at the end of the corridor. Just before they entered the room, with its silent audience of reporters and observers, the chaplain bent toward him and whispered:

"You'll be meeting Willie soon."

Finlay winked and allowed the guards to lead him to the chair. As they strapped him in, his features were calm. Before the hood was dropped over his face, he smiled.

After the execution, the warden asked to see the chaplain in his office.

"I suppose you heard about Finlay's accomplice, Willie Parks. He was shot and killed this afternoon."

"Yes, I did. Rest his poor soul."

"Strange, how Finlay took it all so calmly. He was a wild man before you started working on him. What did you do to that boy, chaplain?"

The chaplain put his fingertips together, his expression benign.

"I gave him hope," he said.

Grief Counselor

by Julie Smith

I started to give Sidney Castille my usual rappity-rap. "This is Jack Beatts," I said, "with the Grief Protection Unit of the county coroner's office . . ."

That was as far as I got before he hung up.

Sidney's wife, Dawn, had died two days before in a freak accident. He'd found her with a broken neck and her copy of *Vince Mattrone's 30-day Yoga Actualizing Plan* lying on the floor beside her. It was open to the section on headstands.

I'd called him because it was my job. After the death certificates are signed, they're sent to me or one of the other grief counsellors so we can get in touch with the victim's families.

As soon as Sidney hung up, I knew he was out of touch with his feelings. He was in the first phase of the grief cycle—what we psychologists call the stage of "disbelief and denial." He was refusing to deal with death.

That's normal and that's okay, but I wanted Sidney to know he had alternatives. I had things I could share with him. So I decided to pay him a visit.

I meditated a few minutes to get myself centered and then I drove my Volkswagen over to Sidney's house on Bay Laurel Lane. It was a typical northern California redwood house set back from the road in a grove of eucalyptus. Smoke was coming out of the chimney.

As I got closer, I could see the living room through sliding glass doors that opened onto a deck. Several cats prowled in the room like tigers in a forest. Dozens of plants hung from the ceiling and took up most of the floor space as well. There was nothing to sit on but oversized cushions.

On the far wall of the room was a fireplace with a pile of

books in front of it. A man was squatting there, burning the books, feeding them one by one into the fireplace.

"Sidney?" I said. "I'm Jack Beatts from . . ."

"Oh, yes, the man from the coroner's office."

He let me in and waved me to a cushion, but he didn't seem pleased about it. In fact, he went right back to feeding the fire.

"Sidney," I said, "I'm going to be up front with you. When you hung up, I sensed I'd better get over here right away."

"Yeah, that's what I thought. I guess I panicked when you said 'coroner's office.' "

"A lot of people are uptight about that. But I'm going to ask you to forget about the bureaucracy and just be open with me."

"I guess we may as well get it over with." He put a copy of *Zen Flesh, Zen Bones* in the fireplace and turned around to face me. A tear rolled down each cheek.

"That's it, Sidney," I said. "Flow with it. Experience your feelings."

"You talk like Dawn."

"I know how it is, Sidney. Everything reminds you of her, doesn't it? But that's okay at this stage. I don't want you to be negative about it."

"*Negative!*" he snorted. "What am I supposed to . . ."

"I'll bet those are Dawn's books you're burning." He nodded. "And it looks like you're about to take the cats to the pound. You're getting rid of everything that reminds you of Dawn, aren't you?"

Tears came into his eyes again. "I couldn't take it any more, Mr. Beatts. I never should have married her in the first place."

"I know where you're coming from, Sidney. You felt inadequate because you were a lot older than Dawn, right?"

"She was twenty-two," he said, "and looking for a Daddy. A rich daddy. And I was just lonely, I guess. I picked her up hitchhiking on my way out here from Ohio after my first wife died." He winced. "But *she* died of natural causes."

"Death *is* natural, Sidney. I mean life is a circle, you know? I want you to choose to recognize that. And if burning books is what's happening for you, I don't want you to feel guilty behind it. Just acknowledge that it's okay."

"Look, are you going to take me in or what?"

"Take you in? Oh, you mean to the Grief Center."

"Is *that* what they call it in California?"

"For sure. We can rap anywhere you like if the vibes are wrong here."

"What is a vibe, Mr. Beatts? If I heard Dawn use that word once I . . ."

"Now stay loose, Sidney. I hear what you're saying and I sense you're uptight behind it. You couldn't relate to Dawn's lifestyle, right?"

He began picking up cats and taking them to the carriers on the deck. I didn't want to blow the energy we had going, so I followed along beside him.

"She was all caught up in what they call the human potential movement," he said. "Transactional analysis, transcendental meditation, self-actualization, bioenergetics, biofeedback . . ."

"She must have been a heavy lady."

"She talked funny. Like you. And she cooked things like wheat germ soufflé. And she wanted the house to be 'natural.' You couldn't go to sleep without a cat curled around your neck, or a spider plant tickling your nose. It got so every time I saw her do that crazy yogurt . . ."

"Yoga."

He closed the last carrier and we went back into the house.

"I used to call it yogurt to annoy her," he said, squatting by the books again. "Anyway, when she started to stand on her head, she'd do it first with her feet against the wall and then she'd let go of the wall and stick her legs up in the air. Well, every time I saw her with her feet like that, getting little toeprints all over the paint, I'd think how easy it would be just to grab her and . . ." He stopped.

"And what?"

"And snap her neck."

I nearly clapped him on the back I was so relieved. At last he'd gotten his energy flowing in a positive way! "I have to acknowledge you, Sidney," I said. "It's really a far out thing to see someone being so open about his fantasies."

Sidney tried to speak, but he couldn't. He took out a handkerchief and blew his nose. Sometimes you have to hurt people to help them so I took a chance.

"You killed her, didn't you, Sidney?" I said.

He kept his eyes down as he put the handkerchief back in his pocket. "You knew all along," he said finally.

"For sure," I said supportively. "Self-recrimination is very common in the first stage of the grief cycle, and I want you to know that it's okay."

"Okay?" he said. "I don't understand."

"A lot of people get on that kind of trip when something like this happens. You and Dawn weren't getting along and you feel guilty about it now, right? You think she died because of something in your karma."

The way Sidney looked at me I could tell he was surprised. He didn't really expect anyone else to understand. He started to speak, but I stopped him.

"That's okay," I said. "You know? Because it's only the first part of the cycle. You know what's next? Personality reorganization! Sidney, you've got a really positive thing to look forward to."

Sidney sat down on one of the cushions and started to laugh. It doesn't happen often that somebody really flashes on the whole cycle like that, and it was a far out thing to see.

"Mr. Beatts," he said. "I don't remotely understand where you're coming from . . ."

"Don't try, man."

"But I think I can flow with it."

The Best Place

by A. F. Oreshnik

Dr. Jason Whitney saw the two federal agents enter the crowded restaurant. Their rumpled suits and stubble-covered cheeks betrayed the fact that they had been too busy to think of appearances for some time. They moved wearily toward him along the line of booths against the wall, looking for an empty one. When they reached the booth where the young doctor was sitting alone, he spoke to the agent he recognized, a deceptively soft-looking man in his forties.

"Hello, Tom. Have a seat." He indicated the place opposite him with a sweep of his hand. "There probably aren't any empty booths at this hour. A lot of people stop here for breakfast on their way to work."

Tom Campbell slid heavily into the booth and was followed by his look-alike companion. "I'd like you to meet my partner, Joe Moffet, Dr. . . . Dr. . . . ." Campbell snapped his fingers, trying to dislodge the name from his memory.

"Whitney. Jason Whitney," the doctor offered with a smile, not the least offended at not being remembered.

"Yeah, that's right," Campbell acknowledged with a nod as Joe Moffet and the young doctor clasped hands briefly.

"You men look like you've had a hard night," the doctor said.

"You can say that again," Campbell answered. "We haven't been out of our clothes in two days. Just brought a man back from Spain."

"Extradition?"

Campbell gave a wry smile. "You could call it that. Our man was staying in Andorra, that little postage-stamp country on the border between Spain and France. They'd have let him stay there until his money ran out, which would've taken a couple of thousand years or so. We have no treaty with them."

"So what happened?"

"The usual. We pretended we'd lost interest in him and waited for him to get careless. When he made the mistake of taking a walk too close to the Spanish border, we were ready. Next thing he knew, Joe and I each had one of his arms and were marching him past the Spanish custom-house. We tossed him into a car and rushed him to a plane we had waiting at one of our bases. The Spanish authorities pretended they didn't see a thing."

"Seems like a lot of trouble and expense over just one man," Dr. Whitney said.

"It was Henry Hammond." Campbell had a touch of pride in his tone.

A waitress came to take their breakfast orders. As soon as she was gone, the doctor repeated the name. "Henry Hammond . . . It *does* sound a bit familiar. Should I know the name?"

"He's the big-shot financier who jumped bail and skipped the country a couple of years ago. He'd built himself an empire, using phony balance sheets and illegal manipulations. He got away with just about every nickel from his companies' treasuries."

"Oh, yes, now I remember. It made quite a splash in the papers at the time. What did you do with him?"

"Dropped him off at your place ten minutes ago," Campbell said.

The second agent, Joe Moffet, had been sitting quietly, but now he twisted his face into a puzzled expression and said, "Huh?"

Campbell turned to him. "The doctor is in charge of the infirmary at the Federal House of Detention on West Street," he explained. "He'll probably be giving our friend a physical examination today."

"I check all new prisoners," Dr. Whitney agreed.

The waitress returned with their orders. They didn't say much until they had settled back to enjoy their coffee. Then the conversation returned to Henry Hammond.

"Do you think he'll return the money he stole?" the doctor asked.

"That's something you'll have to ask Hammond. We couldn't get a word out of him all the way across the Atlantic. He probably has it safely stashed away in a couple of dozen Swiss banks. One thing's sure—no one will ever see it again unless he wants them to."

"I wonder what makes a man decide to be a criminal?" the doctor mused.

Campbell shrugged. "Who knows? People don't always do the things you'd expect, or fit into patterns the way you think they should. Take yourself, for instance. What's a bright young guy like you doing in the Public Health Service? There's no military draft anymore, so you didn't choose it as an alternative service the way doctors and dentists have in the past. I'll bet you could have had your pick of the private hospitals."

"Yes, I probably could have, but I'm happy where I am. I think it's the best place for me. If I didn't, I'd go somewhere else or do something else. That's the way you feel about your job, isn't it, Tom? That active police work is the best occupation for you?"

"You certainly have Tom figured out," Joe Moffet said. "And you put it into words better than he does, too. He's turned down two promotions in the last year. He could have a comfortable desk job in D.C., but he prefers to transport fugitives. Everyone thinks he's crazy, but he says he's happy where he is."

They exchanged small talk for a few more minutes, then left the restaurant together. They paused to say good-bye on the sidewalk outside, and Tom Campbell's face clouded with confusion and embarrassment. "I'm terribly sorry, Doctor, but I—uh—I've forgotten your name again."

Jason Whitney smiled. "That's all right. You'd be surprised how many people have trouble remembering me. The next time you're at the House of Detention stop by my office to say hello. I always have a pot of coffee on the hot plate." He turned to the other agent. "That goes for you, too, Mr. Moffet. Stop in any time. It's been nice meeting you."

Jason Whitney waited until ten that morning before

having Henry Hammond called to the infirmary. He chose that time because the morning sick call had been taken care of by then, and his assistants were enjoying a coffee break.

"Good morning, Mr. Hammond. I'm Dr. Whitney, the Chief Medical Officer here. I'm in charge of the health and physical well-being of you and the other prisoners. It's my job to examine each new arrival and determine whether or not he'll require treatment of any kind."

Hammond nodded his understanding. He had dark circles under his eyes and stood nervously in the doorway of the infirmary. He clenched and unclenched his right fist in an uneven rhythm, and his eyes swept back and forth, taking in all the cabinets and equipment. It was obvious his sudden arrest and transportation to the United States had been a severe shock.

"Step this way, please," Whitney said, leading the way to a side room.

Here there were bare white walls and the only furniture was an examination table for the patient. There was nothing that might prove distracting.

"Lie down, please. I'm going to take your blood pressure. I'm sure you've had it done before."

The doctor wrapped the instrument around Hammond's arm, and squeezed the bulb to pump air into it.

"Be as quiet as you can. I want the lowest reading possible. Relax as much as you can and try not to think of anything in particular."

Whitney busied himself with the instrument.

"Your reading is a bit high, Mr. Hammond. I think you're a little too tense. I you don't mind, I'll show you how to relax. Just close your eyes. That's right, close your eyes and relax the eyelids. I think you can get the feeling of complete relaxation if you'll follow my suggestions. Relax your eyelids completely. Now turn your attention to your arms. Let them become completely limp. Think of them as a pair of limp rags and when I lift them let them fall back to the table just as a couple of limp rags would. That's very good. Now we'll do the same with your legs. See, you're much more relaxed and at ease now.

"I'll just take your blood pressure again and see how well you've done. Oh, that's very good. That's very, very good.

You're far more relaxed than before. Let's try it again, Mr. Hammond, and this time keep your eyes closed all the while. That will aid the relaxation process.

"Okay, now, relax your eyes. Now your arms. Let them become as limp as rags. Now your legs. Relax them. Just relax your whole body. Let your whole body go limp. Let your whole body become heavy. Get completely comfortable. Now, if you are truly relaxed, you will find that your eyelids won't open. Relax your eyelids and body completely. When you feel you're completely relaxed you may try to open your eyes. If you are completely relaxed, they won't open. If you cannot open your eyes, you will be completely relaxed. That's fine. Now try to open your eyes. See—you cannot open them. You are completely, deeply relaxed and you cannot open your eyes. Your arms and legs are heavy and limp and you cannot lift or move them."

As quickly and easily as that, without once using the words sleep or hypnosis, Dr. Jason Whitney placed Henry Hammond into a deep trance.

In the next half hour he deepened the trance still further, then extracted from Hammond the code numbers and balances of ten secret bank accounts. Immediately before allowing the man to wake up, he directed Hammond to forget forever that the secret accounts had ever existed. "And you will never be able to remember my name," he told him.

That reminded Whitney of Agent Tom Campbell. When he had hypnotized Campbell a year before and instructed the man to keep him informed about criminals with hidden money, he had neglected to order him always to come to the restaurant alone. He would have to rectify that oversight at the first opportunity.

As Hammond left the infirmary to return to his cell, Dr. Whitney watched him walk away and felt a wave of satisfaction. This *was* the best place for him. He didn't have to work the long hours a hospital might have demanded, and he was collecting far, far more money in a single year than his professional hypnotist parents had earned in their lifetimes.

Dead End

by Alvin S. Fick

What a surprise it was to see Sweets yesterday—and not altogether a pleasant one.

By the time I got my chair turned around in the kitchen after I heard him knock and rolled through the arch into the living room, he had walked in.

It was just like Sweets to do that, just walk in. He stood there in the center of the room looking around, his pudgy face divided by a wide toothless grin that made his head look like a Bender melon split by a cleaver. Not a bad idea, that.

I had come back from a ride down to the Heron Valley overlook just before his car pulled up in front. "You've put on weight, Sweets," I said. I looked at the bulge above and below his narrow belt. He eased into a rocker facing the couch. Aside from my bed and a dresser, that's about all the furniture left in my house. When you live in a wheelchair, that's the first move you make—you get rid of all the road hazards.

"It's been near four years, old buddy," Sweets said. He shifted his weight in the rocker. It creaked in protest. I noticed that the pressure within had tested every fiber in his soiled chino pants. The stitching down the front had surrendered in the struggle and the zipper was exposed, a silver snake that caught the light from the west window. It was like Sweets to go around that way. My distaste for him spilled over into my voice.

"Don't 'old buddy' me, Sweets. What do you want? What are you after now, after all this time? I have nothing left."

"That ain't no way to talk to an old friend. Ain't I the one who told the boys they should build the ramps for you?

Ain't I the one who said you need a low counter in the kitchen for cooking and eating? Ain't I the one who hung those bars on chains in the bathroom so you could get in and out of the tub—take care of yourself?"

I couldn't help but mimic him. "Yeah, and ain't you the one that got careless setting off that dynamite charge in the quarry that put me in this chair for life?"

Sweets wriggled his button nose as if he smelled something bad. It twitched side to side, a pink crabapple adrift on a sea of bread dough.

"That was a accident. That was five years ago. You shouldn't oughta hold a grudge like that. Lord knows I wouldn't hurt a flea."

Wouldn't hurt a flea. When he was eleven, after having been punished by his father for beating his dog, Sweets had let a mean bull out of its stall into the barnyard. There it gored and killed the old man, who was patching a watering trough. Everybody thought the bull had broken the tie rope, but a few days later in school I heard him bragging how he had cut the rope and rubbed dirt on the frayed ends.

Wouldn't hurt a flea. I remembered how Sweets used to catch flies when we were kids in the one-room country school we both attended. He'd pull off their wings, then tie a thin thread to one leg.

"See my pet," he'd say. He would draw a blob of ink from the inkwell with his pen and wet the fly with it. Then he'd walk the fly across the paper on his desk, or on the nice white collar on the dress of the girl in front of him.

"Chinese writing," he used to say, and his laugh shook fat even then.

Why the girls took to him so, I never understood. But if I did not understand then, his success with women when he grew older was even more of a mystery to me. He'd had three wives—my Norah among them. His first, Charlene, fell from a boat and drowned when the two of them were fishing in Heron River. Ellie hung herself from a rafter tie in the attic of their house. I stopped taking the *Heron Falls Gazette* when I read Norah's obituary six months after she left me for Sweets. The story said she fell down the cellar stairs with a load of laundry in her arms and hit her head on a protruding rock in the fieldstone foundation.

Sweets. What a name. Did I tell you how he got it? His last name is Sharger, but the kids in school found it hard to say and seeing it was so close to the kitchen staple and how the girls loved him, they hung Sweets on him.

My life has always been tied to his in some way. My dislike for him, begun in boyhood, hardened into something deeper long before he hit the switch that sent a piece of rock into my spine, long before he took away my Norah. I never held anything against her for leaving half a man. The bitter part was her going to Sweets.

"You still in the quarry?" I said, desperate for any topic to get my mind off Norah.

"Yep." Sweets brightened. "Been foreman ever since Jeff Bellins died."

"Jeff's dead? He was younger than either of us."

"One of those things. An accident. You know better than most that stone quarries is dangerous places." He stared at my wasted legs.

"How did it happen?"

Sweets' voice turned slick and oily. "He was careless. I seen it all happen. He was standing by the big flat belt that drives the crusher. He must of leaned over to look at something and the belt caught his clothes—pulled him kerspang right into the pulley. Tore him up fierce. I was only a step away but I couldn't do anything for him. Poor guy. He yelled just once."

"How long ago was this? How did Debbie take it?" I remembered Jeff's slender little auburn-haired wife. She was nearly as pretty as Norah and ten years younger.

"Yes, Debbie. I felt terrible sorry for Debbie. Guess I understood better than most how lonely she was. Let's see, that was a couple of months after Norah passed on, and we both—me and Debbie—took to leanin' on each other. We had happy times together so we up and got married."

"Is she out in the car? Is she with you? I'd love to see her."

The corners of Sweets' mouth turned down and for a moment I thought I detected a hint of moisture in his eyes.

"I wish I could. Sure wish I could. But she took sick less than a month back. Got off her feed and just kind of pined away." Sweets seemed genuinely moved. "I buried her two weeks ago."

"I'm sorry to hear that, Sweets."

"Well, we got to go on living." His mood changed. "I just came over to see how you're getting on. It don't pay to lose touch with old friends. That's the way I've always felt about your family. A day or two ago I got to thinking on it, the way I haven't seen you in years. Then I got to wondering about your brother, Harry. He moved to California, didn't he?"

I nodded.

"And Hester, your younger sister, where is she now? I suppose she's off and married with a slew of kids."

"No, Hester isn't married. She's up in Augusta. She has a job with the state." The moment the words were out I wished my tongue had been paralyzed too.

"Say! I bet she's on Debbie's Christmas-card address list I threw out when I was cleaning her dresser this morning." He brushed away an imaginary tear. "I haven't burned that trash yet. When I get home I'll dig that list out and sit right down and write Hester a letter. Maybe I'll phone her. That would be nice."

My insides felt knotted and cold. I hoped he hadn't noticed the way I'd gripped the arms of the wheelchair.

He rambled on. "I ought to drop in on her someday just for old times' sake. She was just a pretty little snippet when we was getting out of school, but I bet she's a real lady now."

The fear in my belly was a coiled cold serpent. "Sweets, why don't you wait a day or two?" My mind raced in search for something to delay him. "I have some pictures of Hester taken when she and some of her girl friends were on a swimming party last summer." I struggled to keep my voice calm. "She's a real beauty."

Sweets heaved his bulk out of the chair. "Are they in your bedroom? I'll go and get them. What drawer are they in?"

I rolled my chair across his path.

"That's not necessary. I have them in a box somewhere in the closet. Tell you what. You come by tomorrow and I'll have them out to show you. We can call Sis on the phone from here. It will pave the way for your visit if I tell her you're coming to see her."

"Good!" Sweets rubbed his hands together. "I'll bet little Hester is a livin' doll." He gave me a good view of pink gums and a tip of tongue wetting his lips.

"And, Sweets, as long as you're coming over tomorrow, could you bring a load of wood in your pickup for my

Franklin stove? Do you still have the old pickup? It's getting toward fall and I could use some firewood." I added, "I just got my disability check. I'd pay you well for some wood."

He stood by the door with his hand on the knob. "Well, I don't know. The brakes ain't so good on the pickup."

Sweets paused while the cold coil in my belly turned slowly.

"I guess if I'm your friend I can haul a load of wood for you. After all, we're almost family." The quality of reeking old motor oil was back in his voice.

"Good, then. I'll see you tomorrow," I said to his back as he walked out the door.

As soon as he was gone, I rolled down the front ramp to the sidewalk and on out to the narrow blacktop road. I live around a bend on this dead-end highway, the last house on the road the town extended a quarter of a mile some years ago to a small picnic area. It's beside a scenic view that looks out over Heron Valley and the mountains beyond. I'm about the only person who goes there any more. Every day, weather permitting, I wheel down to the overlook, poking here and there among the grass and weeds with the stout walking stick I always carry across my lap. It's like an extension of my arms.

The seclusion and beauty of the place have been my joy, and the exercise has given me tremendous arm and shoulder development that makes getting around in the house easy. Even swinging on the bars in the bathroom seems like play to me.

The town paved a turn-around area at the end of the road and erected posts and crossbars around it. The dropoff at the ledge is perhaps six hundred feet. It's so abrupt no trees grow on its face to obscure the view. Grass and weeds grow in the cracks in the amesite. The wood posts are rotten at the base. They cracked ominously when I set the brakes on my wheelchair and pushed against them.

When I got back to the house I had a sandwich. A little later I drank a glass of scotch over ice before I went to bed. I slept well.

This morning I brought the bottle and a couple of glasses into the living room. I think Sweets and I should have a few drinks to celebrate our renewed friendship. Today I feel calm and at peace with my narrow world as I wait for

Sweets. Surely he'll be so happy at the prospect of seeing Hester that he won't mind giving me a ride in his truck down to the scenic overlook where we can admire the view across Heron Valley.

While I wait, I've been jamming my stick against the baseboard by the front door. I'm certain it's just the right length to reach a pickup gas pedal.

Pure Rotten

by John Lutz

May 25, 7:00 A.M. Telephone call to Clark Forthcue, Forthcue mansion, Long Island:

"Mr. Forthcue, don't talk, listen. Telephone calls can be traced easy, letters can't be. This will be the only telephone call and it will be short. We have your stepdaughter Imogene, who will be referred to in typed correspondence as Pure Rotten, a name that fits a ten-year-old spoiled rich brat like this one. For more information check the old rusty mailbox in front of the deserted Garver farm at the end of Wood Road near your property. Check it tonight. Check it every night. Tell the police or anyone else besides your wife about this and the kid dies. We'll know. We mean business."

Click.

Buzz.

Snatchers, Inc.
May 25

Dear Mr. Forthcue:

Re our previous discussion on Pure Rotten: It will cost you exactly one million dollars for the return of the merchandise unharmed. We have researched and we know this is well within your capabilities. End the agony you and your wife are going through. Give us your answer by letter. We will check the Garver mailbox sometime after ten tomorrow evening. Your letter had better be there.

Sincerely,
A. Snatcher

Snatchers, Inc.
May 26

Mr. Snatcher:
Do not harm Pure Rotten. I have not contacted the authorities and do not intend to do so. Mrs. Forthcue and I will follow your instructions faithfully. But your researchers have made an error. I do not know if one million dollars is within my capabilities and it will take me some time to find out. Be assured that you have my complete cooperation in this matter. Of course if some harm should come to Pure Rotten, this cooperation would abruptly cease.

Anxiously,
Clark Forthcue

Dear Mr. Forthcue:
Come off it. We know you can come up with the million. But in the interest of that cooperation you mentioned we are willing to come down to 750,000 dollars for the return of Pure Rotten. It will be a pleasure to get this item off our hands, *one way or the other.*

Determinedly,
A. Snatcher

Snatchers, Inc.
May 27

Dear Mr. Snatcher:
I write this letter in the quietude of my veranda, where for the first time in years it is tranquil enough for me to think clearly, so I trust I am dealing with this matter correctly. By lowering your original figure by twenty-five percent you have shown yourselves to be reasonable men, with whom an equally reasonable man might negotiate. Three quarters of a million is, as I am sure you are aware, a substantial sum of money. Even one in my position does not

raise that much on short notice without also raising a few eyebrows and some suspicion. Might you consider a lower sum?

Reasonably,
Clark Forthcue

Dear Mr. Forthcue:

Pure Rotten is a perishable item and a great inconvenience to store. In fact, live explosives might be a more manageable commodity for our company to handle. In light of this we accede to your request for a lower figure by dropping our fee to 500,000 dollars delivered immediately. This is our final figure. It would be easier, in fact a pleasure, for us to dispose of this commodity and do business elsewhere.

Still determinedly,
A. Snatcher

Snatchers, Inc.
May 29

Dear Mr. Snatcher:

This latest lowering of your company's demands is further proof that I am dealing with intelligent and realistic individuals.

Of course my wife has been grieving greatly over the loss, however temporary, of Pure Rotten, though with the aid of new furs and jewelry she has recovered from similar griefs. When one marries a woman, as in acquiring a company, one must accept the liabilities along with the assets. With my rapidly improving nervous condition, and as my own initial grief and anxiety subside somewhat, I find myself at odds with my wife and of the opinion that your 500,000 dollar figure is outrageously high. Think more in terms of tens of thousands.

Regards,
Clark Forthcue

Forthcue:

Ninety thousand is *it! Final!* By midnight tomorrow in the Garver mailbox, or Pure Rotten will be disposed of.

You are keeping us in an uncomfortable position and we don't like it. We are not killers, but we can be.

A. Snatcher

Snatchers, Inc.
May 30

Dear Mr. Snatcher:

Free after many years of the agonizing pain of my ulcer, I can think quite objectively on this matter. Though my wife demands that I pay some ransom, ninety thousand dollars is out of the question. I suggest you dispose of the commodity under discussion as you earlier intimated you might. After proof of this action, twenty thousand dollars will accompany my next letter in the Garver mailbox. Since I have been honest with you and have not contacted the authorities, no one, including my wife, need know the final arrangements of our transaction.

Cordially,
Clark Forthcue

Forthcue:

Are you crazy? This is a human life. We are not killers. But you are right about one thing—no amount of money is worth more than your health. Suppose we return Pure Rotten unharmed tomorrow night? Five thousand dollars for our trouble and silence will be plenty.

A. Snatcher

Snatchers, Inc.
May 31

Dear Mr. Snatcher:

After due reflection I must unequivocally reject your last suggestion and repeat my own suggestion that you dispose of the matter at hand in your own fashion. I see no need for further correspondence in this matter.

Clark Forthcue

Snatchers, Inc.
June 1

Clark Forthcue:
There has been a take over of the bord of Snatchers, Inc. and my too vise presidents who haven't got a choice agree with me, the new president. I have all the carbon copys of Snatchers, Inc. letters to you and all your letters back to us. The law is very seveer with kidnappers and even more seveer with people who want to kill kids.

But the law is not so seveer with kids, in fact will forgive them for almost anything if it is there first ofense. If you don't want these letters given to the police you will leave 500,000 dollars tomorrow night in Garvers old mailbox. I meen it. Small bils is what we want but some fiftys and hundreds will be o.k.

Sinseerly,
Pure Rotten

Grounds for Divorce

by James Holding

The power failure lasted less than five minutes—but it came at an awkward time.

John Marcy, soup spoon in hand, was seated at the dining table ready to start his dinner. He was hungry.

Angela, his wife, who had just carried the filled soup plates in from the kitchen and taken her own seat across the table, was reaching out a hand toward the cracker dish when the house lights flickered once, then winked out.

"Oh, dear!" Angela said, startled. "Now what? Look out the front window in the living room, John, and see if the neighbors' lights are out, too. Maybe it's just ours."

John put down his soup spoon obediently, groped his way into the living room, and looked out the front window. "Even the street lights are out," he reported over his shoulder. "It's a general power failure, I guess."

He could hear Angela moving in the darkness of the dining room behind him. "I've got candles," she said in a moment, "if you'll get the matches from the coffee table in there."

John cautiously located the coffee table in the blackness and explored its surface for the book of matches always kept near the ashtray. As his hand closed on it, a match flared in the dining room, and a second later two candles set in silver candlesticks on the table were dissipating the darkness.

"Never mind, John," Angela called, "I found a match in the buffet drawer. Come on and eat your soup now. It'll get cold."

Before John got back to his chair at the table, the electric lights came on again.

"Ah," said Angela with relief. "That's better." She didn't blow out the candles.

John picked up his soup spoon and then, with a distraught air, put it down again. He looked across the table at Angela whose gentle blue eyes were regarding him anxiously. "Is the soup cold, dear?" she asked. She took a sip of her own. "Mine isn't."

He shook his head. How lovely she is, he thought, and what a heel I've been to go running after those other women. His conscience was suddenly tender. An unaccustomed pang of shame caused him to lower his eyes.

"No," he said, "I don't suppose it's cold, darling, but I'm not very hungry tonight."

"It's yellow pea soup, John. You love it."

"I know." He raised his head. "And I love you, too, Angela. You know that, don't you?"

Her eyes filled with tears. "Let's not go into that again," she said, trembling.

John said, "I'm an All-American heel, Angela, I admit it. A woman-crazy, middle-aged wolf who ought to know better. And I'm genuinely sorry for it."

Angela brushed aside her tears with the back of a flexed

wrist, a somehow pathetic gesture. She stood up. "Now you've spoiled *my* appetite," she said. She picked up the two soup plates and carried them out to the kitchen.

"So I want to divorce her," John Marcy told his lawyer quietly the next day.

Bartley, the lawyer, aimed a faintly disapproving glance at his client and friend. "Divorce her?" he echoed. *"You want to divorce her?"*

"Yes."

"Don't make me laugh, John. It's common gossip in town that *she* ought to divorce *you*. And I know the score, John, so don't try to kid me. I haven't forgotten those breach-of-promise suits and the paternity action I had to settle for you, John."

"I'm not forgetting them either. I just want to divorce Angela, that's all. And I need your advice on how to go about it. That's simple, isn't it?"

"Not all that simple, no. Why?"

"Why what?"

"Why do you want to divorce her all of a sudden after letting things drift along like this for years?"

"Because she won't divorce me, that's why. And I want to be free of her."

"Yes, but why won't she divorce you? Some foolish idea that this way she can punish you for your past peccadillos?"

"No. You'll think I'm even more insufferable than you do now if I tell you the true reason."

"Try me and see."

John hesitated. Then he said, "Well, it's my considered opinion, knowing Angela as I do, that she won't divorce me because she still loves me."

"That's no reason," Bartley said.

"It is if she doesn't want another woman to get her hooks into me permanently," John said. "She knows how vulnerable and—uh—undiscriminating I am." He paused. "You realize it isn't easy for me to talk like this, Bart."

"Go on," Bartley said, and with the privileged candor of long friendship he added, "Everybody knows you're a heel, John. No need to be embarrassed in front of me."

Marcy flushed and plowed on doggedly. "Angela has

decided that if she can't enjoy my full-time love and loyalty, no other woman will get a chance at it, either."

"Is that what Angela says?"

"Not in so many words, no. But I'm positive it's how she feels."

"How can you be positive about a thing like that?"

"From her actions, Bart. From her attitude lately."

"And you want to charge mental cruelty, is that it?"

"No, you don't understand at all." Marcy sighed.

"I'll say I don't. But I might remind you, John, that even in these enlightened times you need stronger grounds for divorce than a simple statement that your wife loves you and you're sure of it."

John said, "Don't clown with me, I'm serious. I tell you I want to divorce Angela."

"I'm not clowning. But you've got to have grounds. Angela's got plenty—but you haven't. Understand?" Bartley didn't wait for an answer. He went on, "Exactly when did you decide you had to divorce Angela? Maybe that'll help."

Resignedly John said, "Last night. At the dinner table."

"What happened?"

"We had a power failure in our neighborhood. The lights went out."

"Well, well." Bartley lit a cigarette and examined his client's glum face with interest. "That certainly explains a lot."

"It did to me," John said, "even if you think it's some sort of joke."

Exasperated, the lawyer leaned back in his swivel chair. "Nothing about divorce is some sort of joke, as you call it," he snapped. "So be serious about this, John! Tell me about the lights going out, if you think it's important."

"It's important, all right. The lights were out for only a couple of minutes, but during that brief period of total darkness I suddenly found out Angela's true feelings for me, Bart." John was dragging out the words reluctantly. "I'm being honest with you."

"Good," Bartley said. "So in the dark you had this great revelation of Angela's true feelings. What did she do—try to seduce you, or what?"

Marcy shook his head. "I'm sorry to make you pry it out of me like this, Bart," he apologized. "But I was pretty surprised at the time, and I'm not over my confusion yet."

"Obviously. But let's have it. You're stalling."

"I suppose I am," Marcy admitted. He took a deep breath. "Well, you've got to get the picture. Angela had just brought in our soup. We were ready to begin eating. And it was at that instant, with our soup plates on the table before us, that the lights went out."

"All right. What then?"

"Then," Marcy said, "then I saw that Angela was trying to kill me."

"Kill you!" Bartley dropped his cigarette on the rug and swore as he stamped it out.

"That's what I said. Kill me. Poison me. She had poisoned my soup."

Bartley stared at him, shaking his head. "But in the dark—" he began.

"If the lights hadn't gone out, I'd be dead. I'd have eaten that damned soup and gone where no waitress or chorus girl could ever give me the come-on again." For the first time Marcy smiled. "My soup was loaded with yellow phosphorus."

"How did you know?"

"High school chemistry. When the lights went out, my soup glowed in the dark like a plate of incandescent paint." After a dazed moment Bartley managed to whisper, "Attempted murder."

"Is that grounds for divorce?"

"Should be enough for a starter," Bartley said, swallowing.

"Angela, poor darling, tried to distract my attention from the soup," John went on. "She got candles lit as soon as she could, to hide the soup's phosphorescence." He paused. Then he said, "Understand, Bart, I'm telling this to nobody but you. If you go to Angela and tell her you know all about her attempt to murder me last night, I think that out of shame she'll consent to divorce me for the old-fashioned reasons. But I don't want the police to hear a word about this."

"Why not?" asked the lawyer. "After all, attempted murder—".

109

"Because Angela still loves me, as I told you—enough to want to kill me, if that's the only way she can keep me straight. And in my own stupid way I still love her—now more than ever, perhaps. I don't want the police hounding her."

Bartley hunched his shoulders in pure bafflement. He said, "If you and Angela still love each other so much, why not stay together? Why not go on through life hand in hand, as the poet says? Why a divorce?"

John Marcy stood up. He gave the lawyer a crooked grin. "Everybody knows I'm a heel," he said. "But that's a little different from being a fool. There might not be a power failure the next time."

Inside Out

by Barry N. Malzberg

I've got to start stacking the corpses in the bedroom now.

The living room, alas, is all filled. It was bound to happen sooner or later. Still, it's a shock to realize that the day of inevitability has come. There is simply no room any more. Floor to ceiling in four rows the bodies are stacked except for the little space in the corner I've left for my chair and footrest. Even the television set is gone. It was hard to sacrifice the television set but business is business. I put it at the foot of my bed, dreading the time when I'd have to start putting the bodies where I slept. But I must face up to reality and the living room is finished. *Fini. Kaput.* Used up. Cheerlessly I accept my fate. If I am to go on murdering I will have to bring the bodies, as the abbess said to the bishop, into the boudoir. And I am, of course, going to go on murdering.

When I do away with Brown the superintendent tonight, therefore, his corpse will go in the far corner beside the dresser. Virgin territory to be exploited—not that there is any sexual undertone to this matter. None whatsoever. It is what it is. It is not a metaphor. It is not a symbol. It is the pure sad business of murder.

Brown rolls the emptied garbage cans across the lobby, filling my rooms with a sound from hell. He also refuses to clean the steps more than once a week. Time and again I have asked him to desist from the one and do the other, but the man is obdurate. He pretends not to know English. He pretends he doesn't hear me. He pretends he has other duties. This morning I saw four disgusting orange peels on the third-floor landing, already turning brown. There is no way that a man of my disposition can deal with this any more, but I'm not able to move out. For one thing, what would I do with my bodies? It would be such a job to transport them all.

Therefore Brown, or what is left of him, will repose in the bedroom tonight. *Au boudoir.*

The murders are fictive, of course. I am not actually a mass murderer. These are imaginary murders, imagined corpses that have slowly filled these quarters since I began my difficult adjustment about a year ago. Abusive peddlers, disgusting street persons, noxious fellow employees in the Division. In my mind I act out intricate murders, in my body I pantomime the matter of conveying the corpses here, in my heart all of the dead stay here with me, mild in their state. It is a fantasy that enables me to go on with this disgusting urban existence; if I could not banish those who offend me I would be unable to go on. It is of course a perilous coupling, this fantasy, since I might plunge over the fine line someday and actually believe I've done away with these people, but it is the only way I can continue in circumstantial balance.

Giving the fantasy credence, however, demands discipline and a good deal of scut work. It is with regret that I have given up all of my living room except for the chair and footrest, but also out of simple respect for will. If I were not to make reasonable sacrifices in order to propitiate this accord it would be meaningless. One cannot play the violin well without years of painful work with wrists and hands acquiring technique. One cannot be a proper employee of the Division without studying its dismal and boring procedures. One cannot be an imaginary mass murderer without taking responsibility for the imaginary bodies.

The derelict who wipes my windshield with a dirty rag at the bridge exit is still there, of course, although I murdered him six months ago. This morning he cursed me when I gave him only fifteen cents through the cautiously opened window. His rag hardly infiltrated my vision, his cursing fell upon a benign and smiling countenance. How could I tell him, after all, "You no longer exist. Since I did away with you half a year ago your real activities in the real world have made no impression upon me. Your rag is a blur, your curses a song. I drove a sharp knife between your sixth and seventh ribs in this very street before witnesses, threw your body into the trunk, and conveyed it bloodless to my apartment where it now reposes. The essential you lies sandwiched in my apartment between the waitress from the Forum Diner who spilt a glass of ice water in my lap and the medical social worker from the Division who said I had no grasp at all of schizophrenia. I possess you, do you understand that?"

No, I don't think he would understand that. This miserable creature, along with the waitress, the medical social worker, and many others, cannot appreciate the metaphysics of the situation.

I did away with Brown in his apartment two hours ago. "Mr. Brown," I said when he opened the door, "I can't take this any more. You're totally irresponsible. It's not only the orange peels, the hide-and-seek when the toilet will not flush, and the terrible smells of disinfectant when you occasionally wash the lobby. That would be enough, but it's your insolence that degrades my spirit. You do not accept the fact that I am a human being who has a right to simple services. By ignoring my needs you ignore humanity." I shot him in the left temple with the delicate .22 I use for extreme cases. The radio was playing Haydn's Symphony 101 in D Major loudly as I dragged him out of there, closing the door firmly behind. I would not have suspected that he had a taste for classical music, but this doesn't mitigate his situation. He now lies at the foot of my bed. Now and then he seems to sigh in the perfectitude of his perfect peace.

The medical social worker commented today during a conference upon my abstracted attitude and twice she tapped me on the hand to bring me back to attention. I know she feels I'm exceedingly neurotic and not a diligent caseworker, but how could I possibly explain to her that the reason my attention lapses during these conferences is that she was smothered several weeks ago and has not drawn a breath, even in my apartment, since?

Brown's corpse is curiously odorous. This is a new phenomenon. I am a committed housekeeper and can't abide smells of any kind in my apartment (other than pipe and coffee, of course), and my corpses are aseptic. Brown's, however, is not. It is progressively foul and disturbed my sleep last night. Heavy sprays of household antiseptics don't seem to work. The apartment was even worse when I came home tonight.

I knew it was a mistake opening up the bedroom for disposal, but what choice did I have? There is simply no room left outside of here and I refuse to have corpses in the bathroom. There are, after all, limits. I'll just have to do the best I can. After a while either I'll get used to it or the smell will go away.

I should get rid of Brown's body—the smell is impossible now—but I am reluctant to do so. It would set a dangerous precedent, it would break a pattern. If I were to dispose of his body he would not then be symbolically dead, and if I did it with him might I not then be tempted to do it with one of the others? Or with succeeding victims? My project would become totally self-defeating—I would have accomplished nothing.

It has of course occurred to me to call the real Brown to help me dispose of the body of the imaginary Brown, but I won't do that either. It would be a nice irony but one he would not understand. I will either have to do the job myself or hold on.

Besides, I have not seen the foul man here in days. . .

It's all too much. I couldn't deal with it any more and accordingly dragged Brown's body to the landing for pickup tomorrow morning. That should solve the problem, although I'm concerned at the rupture of my pattern and also by the curious weight of his body as I lumbered with it, fireman-carry fashion, to the stairwell. He's the most un-usually corporeal of all my victims. Even in imaginary death he seems capable, typically, of giving me real difficulties.

Two policemen at the door in full uniform, with grim expressions, demand entrance to the apartment. Behind them I can see a circle of some tenants from the building.

I seem to be in some kind of difficulty.

At my very first opportunity during this interview I intend to distract the police and kill them—put an end to this harassment—but I have a feeling that won't work.

I should never have abandoned the living room as a disposal unit. That was my only mistake. I should have begun disposing of old corpses as they were replaced by the new. It would have been sufficient.

But it's too late now, the police say.

The Bell

by Isak Romun

I'm standing here on the stairwell, waiting. He comes by here every evening, usually the last one out of the office. He takes this stairwell because it lets him out into that part of the parking lot where his car stands alone.

Not tonight, though. He'll never make it to the lot. The steps are sharp, angular. And hard, made of unyielding metal. When he comes down, I'll be waiting, a hello on my lips, an arm raised in greeting. A strong arm, an arm that will send him bouncing and bruising down the stairs. If that doesn't kill him, I'll simply finish the job by smashing his head against the angle of a step. An accident. That's what it will look like. Something that could happen to anyone hurrying down these stairs.

It started early this morning with the forlorn shape of Yuddic—an old Gaelic name, he told me one time—with Yuddic McGill slouching against my desk. Mac isn't a pushy sort, and it took me a few moments to become aware of his presence and a few more to note the worried look on his face.

"Talmage, I've got bad news."

"Bad news?" I remarked unconcernedly. Mac was always blowing things out of proportion, so I rather pointedly kept on with my job of sorting and posting vouchers.

"Yes. Stromberg just fired me."

Now, this gave me a turn, caused me to look up, perhaps feel a twinge of fear—you know, don't ask for whom the bell tolls, it tolls for thee, and that sort of thing. Always believed in it. Well, I thought, who diminishes old Yuddic diminishes me. If Stromberg could get away with this arbitrary action, then the old domino theory might come into play and who knew who'd topple next?

Besides, the figure Mac cut was one to invite compassion. He was a diminutive, retiring, almost ridiculous man. Atop his sloping shoulders resided a head on which was impressed a face of such undistinguished features as to foster the belief that the die of character had been applied too lightly, or had been nudged at the precise moment of contact. Around this was arranged a head of listless, squirrel-gray hair allowed, mod fashion, to grow to his jawline, intimating a spirit to which the remaining cut of his Establishment jib lent the lie.

Mac's news, matched with the sympathy that the image of Mac himself always evoked, goaded me. I jumped from my seat and said to him earnestly, "He can't do that to you, Mac! You're one of the key men in this outfit. Have you gotten the formal notice?"

"I'll get written notice later today. The old pink slip. He called me into his office for a little oral preview so I wouldn't faint dead away later on."

"Well, that's good. It's not official until you receive the slip. You can't let him get away with it, Mac. You've got to do something."

"What's to do?" He shrugged and stood there, a pitiable, defeated sight.

"March right back in there and let him know what'll happen if he lets you go. Give him a picture of the impact that the loss of your expertise will have on this organization."

"Oh, Tal, I can't do that. I can't blow my own horn," he said despairingly. "He wouldn't believe me as much as he would someone else."

"By God, then I'll do it!" I exclaimed, not unaware of the admiring attention I was receiving from the other workers sitting nearby. "I'll go in and lay it out for Stromberg. Don't worry, Mac, you'll still have your job at the end of the day."

Then to the silent huzzas of the people in the outer office I marched down the long aisle formed by two rows of identical desks to the ominous green door behind which sat the equally ominous Stromberg. I tell you it took nerve and I won't say I didn't look back. I did once and was confirmed in my resolve when I saw the glimmer of hope spreading across the face of my little buddy, Yuddic McGill.

I pushed myself forward, ignoring the protest of Miss Frisby, Stromberg's secretary, and threw open the door. Stromberg looked up from a pink form in front of him and smiled inquiringly as if he had been expecting me (the man has spies everywhere). I recognized the form and noticed it was still blank. Talk about timing!

I moved into the office, slammed the door, and before Stromberg could say one word, was all over him.

"Mr. Stromberg, if you fill in that pink slip you're getting rid of one of the best men we have. McGill's a man of unquestioned ability. Firing him will be like slicing off your right arm. Accounts Receivable will pile up a week's backlog in two or three days. He's the real strength in this department."

And I went on with much more of the same puffery, but that gives you the idea. All the time Stromberg just sat there silently and smilingly taking it in. When I paused to catch my breath, he said crisply, "Thanks. Appreciate it." Then he picked up the phone and pressed an intercom button.

Miss Frisby came on and Stromberg barked, "Ring McGill's desk!" A pause during which he smiled some more at me. "That you, Mac? Forget what I told you earlier. Right, you're not fired. Good God, man, stop blubbering and get back to work!"

He slammed down the instrument and looked at me. I'm sure my face showed real gratitude as I said, "You won't regret it, sir. McGill will give you a fair shake. Nine for every eight you pay him, I'm sure."

"Took a lot of courage coming in here," Stromberg said briefly and then went back to the pink form in front of him and began filling in the spaces.

What's this? I thought. Was it all some sort of unfeeling joke played on poor Mac?

I was wrong. Stromberg handed me a copy of the completed form. *My* name was on it. There I had it, my two weeks' notice. *I was fired!* I could hardly keep myself from strangling the man right there at his desk.

"It was either McGill or you," Stromberg explained. "It was McGill until you barged in here and did a good selling job on him."

"Oh, sir," I whined, all the starch gone from my voice, "won't you please reconsider?"

"Sure, if you can get McGill to quit," Stromberg said and cackled cruelly.

In the outer office I joined the others in congratulating Mac on his deliverance and in accepting accolades for my part in it. I didn't tell anyone that I'd gotten the ax, particularly not Mac. I couldn't spoil his good news with my bad; nor could I make the ridiculous request that he decline Stromberg's benevolence so that I'd be kept on.

Instead, I put on a good face and only let it slip when my eye chanced on the green door at the end of the aisle. Then and there I devised a course of action that, while precipitate, would be extremely satisfying.

That's why I am waiting now on this stairwell. My character is repulsed at what I have resolved to do, but a spirit of survival possesses me. I've finally learned that, these days, the bell tolls only for the guy going to his own funeral. A bystander's got to close his ears to the ding-dong.

He's up there in the office, concluding the conscientious extra hour he always puts in. Stromberg left some time ago. Only Mac and I are in the building.

Sorry, little buddy.

The Box

by Isak Romun

Working for Stromberg was like being locked in a box. No matter how you tried, you couldn't get out. That's how I felt—as if I were in a box, and only Stromberg had the key.

But one day I found another key, one that would unlock the lid of the box just as effectively as Stromberg's key. Which he would never use. So I would use my own.

My key was death.

Once I had made the decision, I found it quite easy to live with. With something like gusto I attacked the matter of a plan—how I would kill Stromberg. It should not be something complex or difficult. Simple plans are usually the safest. But I had no experience.

Oh, certainly, I had read mystery stories, had even in my mind concocted ways and means of putting to rest the fictional victims I met on the printed page. And with more panache than many of their creators! But there's a difference between a cold, paper thing and a warm, pulsing human organism. Not that Stromberg could be called warm and pulsing. He was like a fish, and it was my intent to hook that fish.

But how to hook him? I thought of poison. Traceable. A hit-and-run accident. Unpredictable—Stromberg might not die. A gun. Noisy and messy. Besides, none of these methods passed the test of simplicity. I determined to use materials and circumstances at hand.

I was evaluating the merits of a push down a stairway when Hopkinson came up to me. "I'll need two dollars from you," he said. I asked why. "Stromberg's farewell gift. He's put in for retirement. Lucky you. I hear he said you were the only man to fill his shoes." Did I hear right? Was it true?

It *was* true! Suddenly I was outside my box. I would not have to kill Stromberg. Matter of fact, he began to look quite human to me. I realized with remorse that what I thought were constraints on me were, in reality, his way of testing me, of training me. That good fellow really had my best interests at heart. At his retirement bash we posed for a parting photo, smiling, each with an arm about the other's shoulder.

I've been chief now for almost five years. But don't think it's been all fun. By no means. When you become a supervisor, you take on something called responsibility. Something only you have. It's up to you to see that the job gets done, that your section functions smoothly.

I swear, though, there are times I throw up my hands in despair. I'm pressured to produce, but with what must I produce? A bunch of incompetents who'd rather hang around the water cooler than do an honest day's work.

The worst is Hopkinson. He said a strange unsettling thing to me the other day. He said working for me is like being locked in a box.

Perhaps I should check with the personnel office about retirement.

The Physician and the Opium Fiend

by R. L. Stevens

The lamplights along Cavendish Square were just being lit, casting a soft pale glow across the damp London night, as Blair slipped from the court behind Dr. Lanyon's house. It had been another failure, another robbery of a physician's office that yielded him but a few shillings. He cursed silently and started across the Square, then drew back quickly as a hansom cab hurried past, the horse's hoofs clattering on the cobblestones.

At times he wished it could end this easily, with his body crushed beneath a two-wheeler. Perhaps then he might be free of the terrible craving that growled within him, forcing him to a life of housebreaking and theft.

William Blair was an opium fiend. He still remembered the first time he had eaten opium, popping the little pill of brown gum into his mouth and washing it down with coffee as de Quincey had sometimes done. He remembered the gradual creeping thrill that soon took possession of every part of his body. And he remembered too the deadly sickness of his stomach, the furred tongue and dreadful headache that followed his first experience as an opium eater.

He should have stopped the diabolical practise then, but he hadn't. In three days' time he had recourse to the drug once more, and after that his body seemed to crave it with increasing frequency. It was his frantic search for opium which now led him nightly to the offices of famous physicians, to the citadels of medicine that lined Cavendish Square. He had broken into ten of them in the past fortnight, but only two had yielded a quantity of opium sufficient to ease his terrible burthen.

And so it was in a state bordering desperation that Blair entered the quiet bystreet that ran north from the Square. He had gone some distance past the shops and homes when he chanced to note a high, two-storey building that thrust forward its windowless gable on the street. He was familiar enough with doctors' laboratories in this section of London to suspect that here might be one, hidden away behind this neglected, discoloured brick wall. But only a blistered and disdained wooden door gave entry into the building from this street, and the door was equipped with neither bell nor knocker.

Hurriedly he retraced his steps to the corner, avoiding a helmeted bobby who was crossing the street in the opposite direction. He waited until the police-officer had disappeared from view, his hand ready on the dagger in his pocket. As he moved on, a few drops of water struck his forehead. It was beginning to rain.

Round the corner he came upon a square of ancient, handsome houses. Though many were beginning to show the unmistakable signs of age, the second house from the corner still wore a great air of wealth and comfort. It was all in darkness except for the fanlight, but the glow from this was sufficient for him to decipher the lettering on the brass name-plate. He had guessed correctly. It was indeed a doctor's residence. He set to work at once as the rain increased.

It took him only a few moments of skillful probing with the dagger to prize open one of the shuttered windows. Then he was through it and into a flagged hall lined with costly oaken cabinets. The doctor was obviously wealthy, and Blair hoped this meant a well-stocked laboratory. He moved cautiously along the hall, fearful of any noise which might give the alarm. The house could have been empty, but it was possible the good doctor had retired early and was asleep upstairs.

Blair made his way to the rear of the first floor, heading in the direction of the windowless gable he had observed from the street. He passed into the connecting building and through a large darkened area that, by the light of his Brymay safety-matches, appeared to be an old dissecting room, strewn with crates and littered with packing straw, and dusty with disuse. Blair moved through it to a stairway at the rear. This would lead to the second floor of the windowless gable, his last hope of finding a supply of opium.

The door at the top of the stair was a heavy barrier covered with red baize, and it took him ten minutes ere he finally forced it inward with a loud screech. The disclosed room proved to be the small office-laboratory he sought—his work had not been in vain! The remains of a dying fire still glowed on the hearth, casting a pale orange glow about the room. The laboratory had been in use that very night, and in such a home the storage-shelves would be well stocked.

It took him but a brief search to discover, amidst the chemical apparatus, a large bottle labeled LAUDANUM. This was a tincture of opium, he knew, and no less an authority than de Quincey had reckoned twenty-five drops of laudanum to be the equivalent of one grain of pure opium. Yes, this would satisfy his need.

His hand was just closing over the bottle when a voice from the doorway rasped, "Who is there? Who are you?"

Blair whirled to face the man, the dagger ready in his hand. "Get back," he warned. "I am armed."

The figure in the doorway reached up to light the gas flame, and Blair saw that he was a large, well-made, smooth-faced man of perhaps fifty, with a countenance that was undeniably handsome. "What do you want here, man? This is my laboratory. There is no money here!"

"I need—" began Blair, feeling the perspiration collecting on his forehead. "I need opium."

There was a sharp intake of breath from the handsome doctor. "My God! Have conditions in London come to this? Do opium fiends now prowl the streets and break into physicians' homes in search of this devilish drug?"

"Get out of my way," returned Blair, "or I will kill you!"

"Wait! Let me—let me try to help you in some way. Let me summon the police. This craving that obsesses you will destroy you in time. You need help, medical treatment."

As he spoke, the doctor moved forward slowly, forcing Blair back towards the far wall of the room. "I don't want help," sobbed the cornered man. "It's too late to help me now."

The doctor took a step closer. "It is never too late! Don't you realize what this drug is doing to you, man? Don't you see how it releases everything that is cruel and sick and evil in you? Under the influence of opium, or any drug, you become a different person. You are no longer in command of your own will."

Blair had backed to the wall now, and he could feel its chill firmness through his coat. He raised the dagger menacingly. "Come any closer, Sawbones, and I swear I will kill you!"

The doctor hesitated a moment. He glanced at the darkened skylight above their heads, where the rain was now beating a steady tattoo upon the glass. Then he said, "The mind of man is his greatest gift. To corrupt it, to poison it with drugs, is something hateful and immoral. I hope that I am never in a position where I lose control of my free will because I have surrendered to the dark side of my nature. You, poor soul, are helpless in the grip of this opium, like the wretched folk who smoke it in the illegal dens, curled upon their bunks and oblivious of the outer world."

"I—I—" began Blair, but the words were lost in his throat. The physician was right, he knew, but he was beyond caring now, beyond distinguishing between right and wrong. He only knew that the doctor had forced him further from the bottle of laudanum.

"Let me call the police," urged the doctor, softly.

"No!"

The physician's hand moved, all in a flash, seizing one of the bottles from the shelf beside him and hurling it upwards through the skylight. There was a shattering of glass and a shower of silvery white pellets from the bottle. Then a sudden violet flame seemed to engulf the entire skylight, burning with a hissing sound that ended almost at once with a burst of explosive violence.

Terrified, Blair tried to lunge past the doctor, but the large hands were instantly upon him, fastening on his coat and wrist, forcing the dagger away.

They were still locked in a life-and-death, silent struggle when, moments later, a helmeted bobby burst into the laboratory. "What's happening here, sir? I saw the flame and heard the explosion—"

"Help me with this man," shouted the physician. "He's trying to steal opium!"

Within seconds Blair was helpless, his arms pinioned to his sides by the burly police-officer. "Take me," he mumbled. "Take me and lock me up. Help me."

Another bobby arrived on the scene, attracted by the noise and flame. "What was it?" he asked the doctor.

"I had to signal you somehow," he told them. "There were potassium pellets in the bottle and I took a risk that enough rainwater had collected on the skylight to set off a chemical reaction. Potassium reacts even more violently with water than does sodium."

"You were successful," returned the second policeman. "I heard that boom two streets away."

The doctor was busy moving some of his equipment out of the rain which was still falling through the shattered skylight. "I think with treatment this man can be saved," said he. "It is his addiction that has led him into a life of crime."

"I would not worry too much about him, sir. He could have killed you with this dagger."

"But I do worry about him, as I would about any human being. As for myself, I was much more fearful that he would wreck my laboratory. I have been engaged in some important experiments here, relating to transcendental medicine, and I feel I am on the verge of discovery."

The first police-officer pulled Blair towards the door. "Then we will leave you alone to clean up, sir. And good luck with your experiments." He was half-way out the door when he paused and said, "O, by the by, sir, I will need your name for my report. I did not have time to catch it on the brass outside."

"Certainly," replied the physician, with a smile. "The name is Jekyll. Doctor Henry Jekyll."

Over the Borderline

by Jeff Sweet

"Don't you see? He had to be stopped."

"Stopped, Mrs. Sutherland? Stopped from doing what?"

"If I hadn't acted she would have died. He would have killed her."

"Who, Mrs. Sutherland? Who would he have killed?"

"You're looking at me like you don't believe me, Lieutenant Foley. You think I'm just a batty old lady, don't you? An old lady who's lost her marbles."

"No, I don't. Really, I don't."

"Like crazy Mrs. Jessup who's always calling the police or the F.B.I. about enemy agents hiding under her bed. I'm right, aren't I? That's what you think."

"I swear, Mrs. Sutherland, I don't think that at all."

"Then why don't you believe me?"

"Well, I'll tell you, Mrs. Sutherland, it isn't that I don't believe you. It's just that I—well, I guess I really don't *understand*. I mean, I don't have the full picture."

"I've tried to answer all your questions, Lieutenant."

"Yes, and I appreciate that, Mrs. Sutherland. But still—"

"What?"

"Look, I have an idea. Why don't you tell me about it again, from start to finish? I promise you I won't interrupt."

"From start to finish? Yes, maybe that would be best, and I suppose the best place to start would be with Cora and Jim. Cora and Jim Franklin. Such a nice couple. They remind me of the late Mr. Sutherland and myself when we were young. A very nice couple, the Franklins. Of course, they have their problems. More than their share. She was pregnant when they got married, you know. That's not always the best way to start a marriage, especially since the baby wasn't Jim's. That awful Harrington Furth."

"Uh, Mrs. Sutherland—"

"Lieutenant, you promised you wouldn't interrupt."

"I know, Mrs. Sutherland, but I'm afraid I'm a little lost. Who is Harrington Furth?"

"Lieutenant, if you will hold your horses I'll get to that, I promise you. All in good time. But you mustn't interrupt."

"Yes, Mrs. Sutherland."

"Where was I?"

"Harrington Furth."

"Oh, yes, Harrington. A very rich, very irresponsible young man. His father is the president of Furth Electronics, you know—a very distinguished man. But Harrington, I'm afraid, doesn't take after his father. Or should I say Harrington *didn't* take after his father? Oh, well, you understand my meaning, I'm sure. It must have been very hard on old Mrs. Furth, having a son like Harrington. Always racing around in his fancy cars, always getting into trouble. And his father always coming to the rescue. I swear, if it had been me, I would have let that young man stew in his own juice! It might have taught him a sense of responsibility. And the way he drank!

"Anyway, there was poor Cora. She hadn't married Jim yet, you know. Jim was going with the Stanton girl then— the one with the big false eyelashes and all the teeth. What Jim saw in her I don't know. But like I say, there was poor Cora. Her mother had just died on the operating table and Cora was all alone. She was scared and vulnerable. And that awful Harrington saw this and—well, he took advantage of the situation, and when he'd gotten what he wanted he left Cora flat. Not too long after she found out she was pregnant."

"You mean with Furth's child?"

"That's what I said, didn't I? Really, Lieutenant, you must learn to listen. Anyway, around this time the Stanton girl left Jim and took up with young Harrington, which in my opinion served them both right. Meanwhile, Jim was desperate, almost suicidal, and then, one day, in came Cora. Did I tell you Jim was an obstetrician?"

"No."

"Well, he was, and all the girls on the staff at the hospital thought he was the handsomest doctor around. But he didn't pay any attention to them. And then, as I said, in came Cora and he told her she was pregnant and she just stood there, very bravely, fighting back the tears. But, of course, it wasn't any use. Before you could blink an eye she was in his arms, crying like a little girl. And he was holding her so tenderly. It was love from that first moment, I could tell. I could tell right off because it was just like that when Mr. Sutherland and I met. Except I wasn't pregnant and Mr. Sutherland wasn't an obstetrician.

"What I'm talking about is the way you—well, you know in your heart when someone's just right for you. You don't think about it, you just *know*. That's the way it was with Mr. Sutherland and me. And that's the way it was with Cora and Jim.

"I'll never forget the day Jim proposed. She was in her eighth month then and he'd been seeing a lot of her. 'Marry me,' he said. 'No,' she said, 'I couldn't do that to you. I couldn't make you part of my shame,' she said. I remember how difficult it was for me to keep from shouting out to her, 'Don't be a fool, Cora! He loves you! Don't give up this chance for happiness!'

"But I needn't have worried because that's just what he said to her himself. 'I love you,' he said. 'You give my life purpose. If you don't say yes, I don't know what I'll do.' To make a long story short, she did say yes and they were married soon after. He even delivered the baby."

"Mrs. Sutherland, what has this got to do with—"

"Lieutenant, please!"

"Sorry, Mrs. Sutherland."

"As I said, they were married and were so happy, and the baby didn't look a bit like Harrington. But I could tell they weren't over the worst of it. I knew in my bones that tragedy was going to strike, but for the longest time I didn't know how.

"To tell you the truth, I was having an awful time sleeping. I finally had to go to Dr. Sumroy and get a prescription for sleeping pills. I'd never used them before because I've heard so many stories of old people accidentally taking an overdose. And not just old people. Young people, too. It's supposed to be especially bad if you take them when you've been drinking, though in my case that was no problem. But I was having so much trouble sleeping because of all my worrying about Cora and Jim that I just *knew* something tragic was going to happen even though I didn't know what.

"Then, suddenly, it came to me. I can't tell you how it came to me because I honestly don't know how to explain such things. Call it woman's intuition, if you like, but I knew what was going to happen. *Harrington was going to kill Cora in an automobile accident!* It was inevitable. He'd just bought a new sports car—one of those fancy foreign things that makes a lot of noise, and it was common knowledge he was speeding recklessly all over town. So you see, it was logical.

"Of course, I couldn't let it happen. I remember how heartbroken I was when Mr. Sutherland died in an accident, only he wasn't killed by a foreign car. I was so miserable, I nearly died. So what was I supposed to do? I knew what would happen if something weren't done, and I couldn't just sit quiet and *let* it happen. I had to do something. But what?

"Then, today, an amazing coincidence brought me the answer. I came into the city to shop on Fifth Avenue for my nephew's birthday, and I stopped into a restaurant on Forty-Seventh Street. Not too far away from Radio City and Rockefeller Center, you know the area? And who was in the restaurant but young Harrington!

"I went up to him, and I said, 'Mr. Furth?' He smiled. I'll say that for him, he had a nice smile. 'Mr. Furth,' I said, 'I want to talk to you.' He stood up, a little woozy from all the liquor he'd been drinking, and offered me a seat, which I accepted. 'Mr. Furth,' I said, 'I'm going to speak plainly. I know what's going to happen.' 'What's going to happen?' he said, still smiling. 'I know you're going to kill Cora Franklin with that fancy foreign car,' I answered.

" 'How did you find out?' he asked, obviously surprised. 'Never you mind how I found out,' I said. 'What I'm saying is so, isn't it? You're going to kill her with your sports car, aren't you?'

" 'Yes,' he said, 'that's so.'

"He admitted it! With a smile! There wasn't a trace of

regret anywhere on his devilish face. He actually seemed happy about it! I knew I was in the presence of great evil.

"He excused himself and went to the men's room. I suddenly knew what I had to do. I opened my handbag and took out the sleeping pills I had got from Dr. Sumroy, and I dropped something like two dozen of them into his coffee. I left, waited until I was sure it was all over, then came here to turn myself in. And that, Lieutenant, is my confession."

"I see."

"Do you believe me?"

"Yes, I believe you, Mrs. Sutherland."

"One thing you have to know—I did this for them, Lieutenant. For Jim and Cora and the baby. You have to realize that it was the only way. You do understand, don't you?"

"Yes, Mrs. Sutherland, I think I do."

A few minutes later, after Mrs. Sutherland had been led away, Lieutenant Foley turned to Sergeant Warren, who was standing a few feet away. "Well, that settles that," he said.

"Lieutenant, maybe I'm some kind of an idiot," said the sergeant, "but I don't see that it settles anything. Her story about the overdose in Maxwell's coffee jibes, and she matches the waiter's description, but I'll be damned if I can figure out why she kept calling Taylor Maxwell by the name Harrington Furth."

"Sergeant, Taylor Maxwell was an actor."

"I still don't get it, sir."

"I've just been looking at his résumé. For the past few years he's been a regular on an afternoon TV soap opera called *The Will To Live*," explained the lieutenant. "The name of the character he played was Harrington Furth."

It Could Happen to You

by John Lutz

I never dreamed something like this could happen; or rather, I'd always thought something like this could happen only in a dream. But looking back on it piece by piece, it's easy to understand how it did happen. It was just a chance combination of circumstances, none of those circumstances so unbelievable by itself. It's the sort of thing that could happen to anybody; to you.

There'd been some mix-up in the flight schedule, so here I was with a six-hour layover in a city a thousand miles from home. It was a big city, and a nice summer night, so I decided to take a little walk around the downtown area, just to look things over.

That was at eleven o'clock, maybe too late for that kind of walk on a week night. And there wasn't much happening downtown, only a few night spots here and there open; or maybe I'd just picked the wrong part of town.

I strolled innocently along, my light raincoat slung over my arm against any threat of rain. I'd stopped in a few places that looked fairly respectable, staying in each for only one drink and a few words of conversation before going back outside and resuming my wandering. Walking around and sort of taking in the atmosphere of strange cities is a habit of mine. My job keeps me traveling just enough not to get bored with it, so I'm usually interested in new places. And I knew I'd probably never get back to this city.

It was almost one o'clock when I noticed my wallet was missing. I was on Nineteenth Street at the time, idly walking along and looking in the windows of the closed shops.

A lost wallet. Nothing so unusual about that. You've

probably lost your wallet at some time and felt that sudden rush of helplessness. Well, that feeling's even stronger in a strange city, in case you've never had the experience. Everything that gave me a sense of identity or security was in that wallet—my driver's license, my folding money, my credit cards . . .

For a moment I stood in bewilderment, checking my other pockets, but of course the wallet wasn't in any of them. A wallet's the sort of thing you automatically return to the right pocket. I hurried back along the almost-deserted streets toward the Posh Parrot on Twelfth Avenue, the last cocktail lounge I'd been in, all the time keeping my eyes to the ground on the off-chance I might see the wallet where it had fallen from my pocket.

The Posh Parrot was closed, the neon sign in its window dull and lifeless, the window itself throwing back a pale reflection of my worried self.

I told myself it didn't matter. If I had lost the wallet in the lounge and someone had picked it up, he'd probably taken it with him. But I distinctly remembered sliding the wallet back into my hip pocket after paying for my drink; I even remembered folding the corner of a fifty-dollar bill to mark it from the smaller denominations. I began retracing my route back to Nineteenth Street, figuring the wallet must have slipped out of my pocket somewhere along the way.

No luck. What was I going to do? What would you do?

Even the ticket for the last leg of my trip home was in that wallet. I felt suddenly like a vagrant, a trespasser. I realized what a difference a dozen credit cards and a few hundred dollars' cash make in our society.

The only thing I could do was phone Laurie, my wife, and get her to wire me some money. I felt in my other pockets, and among keys, comb, and ballpoint pen, could muster only a nickel and two pennies. So much for that inspiration.

To make me feel worse, a light drizzle began to fall. I hurriedly slipped on my raincoat and turned up the collar.

I was walking forlornly, head down, hands jammed in my coat pockets, so I didn't see the man walking the poodle toward me until we were only about a hundred feet from each other.

My awkwardness and embarrassment about trying to borrow money from a stranger, combined with the short period of time I had to come up with what I was going to say, made my throat suddenly dry. You'd feel the same way.

I stopped directly in front of the man, a little guy with wire-framed glasses and a droopy mustache, and he stood staring at me with alarm.

"Would it be possible for you to lend a stranger some money?" is what I meant to say, and then I was going to explain the reason to him. I was ill at ease, as nervous as the little man appeared, and my voice croaked so I guess he only heard the last part of my sentence, the word "money." He backed up a step, and his poodle sensed his fear and my nervousness and began to growl.

The man's droopy mustache trembled. "I don't have much . . ." he said, "honest . . ." I saw his eyes dart down to the bulge of my right hand in my raincoat pocket, and I understood.

"Wait a minute," I started to say, but I saw him glance off to his right and his eyes grew wider behind his thick glasses. I looked and saw the cop almost on us.

"Trouble?" the cop asked. He was young and rangy, built more like a cigarette-ad cowboy than a cop.

"In a way, Officer," I said.

"He was trying to hold me up!" the little man almost screamed, and his poodle started growling again.

"I thought so," the cop said. "I was watching from across the street."

I felt my heart fall like a meteor. "Hey, no, wait a minute!" I was shoved roughly so that I had to support myself against the side of a building with both hands.

"Be careful!" I heard the little man shout. "He's got a gun in his right coat pocket!"

The cop's hands searched me the way they'd been trained in the police academy, and I knew by his unsteadiness that he was nervous. All three of us were standing there frightened. Even the dog was frightened.

"He was bluffing you," the cop said. "They do that." He jerked me up straight and held onto my arm.

"Bluffing? . . . I was only trying to borrow some money! . . ."

The young cop let out a sharp laugh. "A polite mugger, huh?"

"This is insane!" I said.

The cop shrugged. "So plead that way in court."

"I'll press charges!" the little man kept saying. "You can be sure of that!"

But the cop was ignoring him now, reciting my rights in a low monotone. He was even ignoring me somewhat as he droned on about my "right to remain silent." He was really going to do it! I might really be going to jail! And even if I wasn't convicted, what would the arrest mean to my family, my friends, and my job?

I panicked then, and in what seemed at the time a lucky break, a bus turned the corner and lumbered toward us. I remember one headlight was out and the wiper blades were swinging back and forth out of rhythm. The bus was only doing ten or fifteen miles an hour, and when it was almost even with us I jerked out of the cop's grip and darted in front of it, around it. The front bumper even brushed my pants leg, but I didn't care.

Now the bus was between me and the law, and I had a few precious seconds to run for freedom. The bus driver helped me by slamming on his brakes, probably stopping the bus directly in front of the cop so he had to run around it. I was running down an alley, not looking back or even thinking back, when I heard the shot. In my state, the bark of the gun only made me run faster. I turned the corner, flashed across the rain-slick street and cut through another alley. That alley led to a parking lot, and I ran through there to the next street. I slowed then, listening, but hearing no footsteps behind me. I knew I wouldn't have much time, though. The cop was probably calling in for help right now.

I walked for three more blocks before I saw a cab. It scared me at first; I'd thought the lettering on the door signified a police car. Then I saw that the light atop the car was blue, and there was a liquor advertisement on the trunk. I waved to the cab and climbed in with deliberate casualness when it stopped to pick me up.

"Regent Hotel," I said, trying to keep my breathing level. Didn't every city have a Regent Hotel?

"Torn down," the cabby said, glancing over his shoulder. "You mean the Regency?"

"That's it," I said, and we drove on in silence.

After about ten minutes I saw an all-night drugstore ahead of us, and I had the cabby pull over.

"I'll only be a minute," I told him. "I want to see if they'll fill an out-of-town prescription for insulin."

"Sure." He settled back in his seat and stared straight ahead.

It was a big drugstore, with a few other customers in it. The pharmacist behind the counter gave me a funny look, and I smiled and nodded at him and walked over to the magazine rack. After leafing through a news magazine, I replaced it in the rack and walked over to a display of shaving cream as if it interested me. From there I walked out the side door.

I walked until I was clear of the drugstore's side display window and ran for three or four blocks. I turned a corner then and started walking at a fast pace, but slow enough so that my breathing evened out.

I must have walked over a mile, trying to think things out, trying to come up with some kind of an idea. The agonizing thing was that nothing that had happened was really my fault. You could be in this same kind of mess sometime, just like me. Anybody could.

If only I had some money, I thought, I could get a plane or bus ticket. The police didn't watch bus terminals or airports for every fleeing street-corner bandit. If I could get out of this city, get back home a thousand miles away, I'd be safe. After all, no one had my name or address. The cop hadn't gotten any identification from me when he searched me because I wasn't carrying any. It would be as if none of this had ever happened. Eventually Laurie and I would joke about it. You and your spouse joke about that kind of thing.

Right now, though, things were a far cry from a joke! If I didn't get out of town fast, I might well wind up ruined, in prison!

I was in more of a residential part of town now, wide lawns, neat ranch houses, and plenty of trees. The moon was out and it had stopped raining, and I saw the man walking toward me when he was over a block away, on the other side of the street. The desperation surged up in me, took control of me. You can understand how I felt. There was no time to make phone calls or wait for money. I had to get away fast, and to get away fast I needed money. I stooped and picked up a white grapefruit-sized rock from alongside someone's driveway.

Crossing the street diagonally toward the man, I squeezed the rock concealed in my raincoat pocket, smiling when I got close enough for the man to see my face.

He was carrying enough money for a plane ticket to a nearby city, where I had Laurie send me enough to get home. At home, though, where I'd thought I'd be safe, I still think about it all the time.

I'd never had any experience in hitting someone's head with a rock, so how was I to know? I was scared, like you'd be, scared almost out of my senses, so I struck harder than I'd intended—much harder.

Think about it and it's kind of frightening. I mean, here's this stranger, on his way home from work on the late shift, or from his girl-friend's house, or maybe from some friendly poker game. Then somebody he's never seen before walks up and for no apparent reason smashes his skull with a rock. It could happen to you.

Class Reunion

by Charles Boeckman

The banner across one wall in the Plaza Hotel banquet room welcomed "Jacksonville High, Class of '53." The crowd milling around in the room was on the rim of middle age. Temples were graying, bald spots were in evidence.

Tad Jarmon roamed through the crowd. At the bar, he found his old friend, Lowell Oliver, whom he had not seen since graduation. "Hello, Lowell," he said.

Oliver drained his glass. "Hi, ol' buddy," he said with a loose grin. He shoved his face closer in an effort to focus his eyes. Suddenly, he became oddly sober. "Tad Jarmon."

"In the flesh."

"Well . . . good to see you, Tad. You haven't changed

much." He held his glass toward the bartender for a refill. His hand was shaking slightly.

"We've all changed some, Lowell. It's been twenty years."

"Twenty years. Yeah . . . Twenty years . . ."

"Have you seen Jack and Duncan?"

"They're around here someplace," Oliver mumbled.

"We'll have to get together after the banquet and talk over old times," Tad said.

Oliver stared at him with a peculiar expression. Beads of perspiration stood out on his forehead. "Old times. Yeah . . . sure, Tad."

Tad Jarmon meandered back into the crowd. Soon he spotted Jack Harriman with a circle of friends in another corner of the room. Jack looked every inch the prosperous businessman. He was expensively dressed. His face was deeply tanned, but he was growing paunchy. He'd put on at least forty pounds since graduation.

"Hello, Jack."

Harriman turned. His smile became frozen. "Well, if it isn't Tad Jarmon." He reached out for a handshake. "You guys all remember Tad," he said, a trifle too loudly. His hand felt damp in Tad's clasp.

One of their ex-schoolmates grinned. "I remember how you two guys and Duncan Gitterhouse and Lowell Oliver were always pulling off practical jokes on the town."

"Yeah," another added. "If something weird happened, everybody figured you four guys had a hand in it. Like the time the clock in the courthouse steeple started running backward. Took them a week to figure out how to get it to run in the right direction again. Nobody could prove anything, but we all knew you four guys did it."

The group chuckled.

"I saw Lowell over at the bar," Tad said to Harriman. "I told him we should get together after the banquet and talk over old times."

"Old times . . ." Harriman repeated, a hollow note creeping into his voice. "Well . . . sure, Tad." He wiped a nervous hand across his chin. "By the way, where are you living now?"

"Still right here in Jacksonville, in the big old stuffy house on the hill. After my dad died, I just stayed on there."

Tad excused himself and went in search of Duncan Gitterhouse. He soon found him, a man turned prematurely gray, with a deeply lined face and brooding eyes.

"Well, Duncan, I guess I should call you 'Doctor' now."

"That's just for my patients," Gitterhouse replied, his deep-set eyes resting somberly on Tad. "I was pretty sure I'd be seeing you here, Tad."

"Well, you know I couldn't pass up the opportunity of talking over old times with you and Jack and Lowell. Maybe after the banquet, the four of us can get together."

The doctor's eyes appeared to sink deeper and grow more resigned. "Yes, Tad."

The banquet was followed by speeches and introductions. Each alumnus arose and told briefly what he had done since graduation. When the master of ceremonies came to Tad, he said, "Well, I'm sure you all remember this next guy. He and his three buddies sure did liven up our school years. Remember the Halloween we found old Mrs. Gifford's wheelchair on top of the school building? And the stink bombs that went off during assembly meetings? They never could prove who did any of those things, but we all knew. How about confessing now, Tad? The statute of limitations has run out."

Tad arose amid laughter and applause. He grinned and shook his head. "I won't talk. My lips are sealed . . ."

After the banquet, the four chums from high school days drifted outside and crossed the street to a small, quiet town-square park. Jack Harriman lit an expensive cigar.

"It hasn't changed, has it?" Duncan Gitterhouse said, looking up at the ancient, dome-shaped courthouse, at the Civil War monument, the heavy magnolia trees, the quiet streets. "It's as if everything stopped the night we graduated, and time stood still ever since."

"The night we graduated," Jack Harriman echoed. He pressed a finger against his cheek, which was beginning to twitch again. "Seems like a thousand years ago."

"Does it?" Tad said. "That's odd. Time is relative, though. To me it's just like last night."

"We don't have any business talking about it," Duncan Gitterhouse said harshly. "I don't know why I came here for this ridiculous class reunion. It was insanity."

"Don't know why you came back, Duncan?" Tad said softly. "I think you do. You couldn't stay away. None of you could. You had to know if anyone ever suspected what we did that night. And you wanted to find out what that night did to the rest of us, how it changed our lives. We shared something so powerful it will bind us together always. I was sure you'd all come back."

"Still the amateur psychologist, Tad?" Harriman asked sourly.

Tad shrugged.

"It was your fault what we did that night, Tad," Lowell Oliver said, beginning to blubber in a near-alcoholic crying jag. "You were always the ringleader. We followed you like sheep. Whatever crazy, sick schemes you thought up—"

"We were just kids," Gitterhouse argued angrily. "Just irresponsible kids, all of us. Nobody could be held accountable—"

"Just kids? We were old enough in this state to have been tried for murder," Tad pointed out.

There was a heavy silence. Then Tad murmured slowly, "I used to go past the place on the creek where old Pete Bonner had his house-trailer. For years you could see where the fire had been. The ground was black and the rusty framework of the house-trailer was still there. It was finally cleared away when the shopping center was built, but every time I go by that place I think about the night old Pete Bonner died there. And I think about us. A person acts; the act is over in a few minutes. But the aftermath of the act lives on in our emotions, our brains, perhaps forever. We committed an act twenty years ago. The next day, they buried what was left of old Pete. We're stuck with that for the rest of our lives."

They fell silent again, each thinking back to that night. It was true that Tad had been the ringleader of their tight little group, and the night of their graduation, it was Tad who thought of the final, monstrous prank: "Let's set Pete Bonner's trailer on fire."

"But Pete's liable to be in the trailer," one of the others had said.

"That's the whole point," Tad had grinned, then explained, "After tonight, we'll be going different directions.

Duncan is going into medical school. Lowell's going into the Army. Jack's going to business college. I'll probably stay here. We need to do something so stupendous, so important, that it will weld the four of us together forever. So, we'll roast old Pete Bonner alive."

Tad had pointed out to the rest of them that Pete was the town drunk, an old wino who had no family. It would be like putting a worthless old dog out of his misery.

Because of the hypnotic-like hold Tad had on the others, they had agreed—sweating and scared—but they'd agreed.

That night after graduation exercises, Tad led them to Pete Bonner's trailer with cans of gasoline and matches. As they ran away from the blazing funeral pyre, the screams of the dying old wino followed them.

"I can still hear that old man screaming," Duncan Gitterhouse said, his hands shaking as he chain-lit another cigarette.

"Tad, you said we're stuck with what we did for the rest of our lives," Jack Harriman sighed. "It's true. I've made a pile of money, but what good is it? I can't go to sleep without pills. I eat too much. My doctor says I'm going to have a coronary in five years if I don't quite eating so much, but I can't stop. It's an emotional thing, a compulsion. Look at poor Lowell there. He's spent the last five years in and out of alcoholic sanitariums."

Duncan Gitterhouse nodded. "My practice is a success. Compensation, I guess. I have the idea that if I save enough lives, I'll make up for the one we took. I do five, ten operations a day. But my private life is a shambles—my wife left me years ago; my kids are freaked out on drugs." He turned to Tad Jarmon. "I suspect you didn't get off any better than we did, Tad. You never married. You're stuck here, in the home you grew up in. I don't think you *can* leave . . ."

They sat in the park for a while. Then they got up and went off to their respective motel rooms—Tad to his big, old-fashioned house with white columns.

In his study, Tad took down one of his journals from a bookshelf. In his neat, precise hand, he carefully described the events of the evening, recording in detail all that Jack, Duncan, and Lowell had said. Following that entry, he added his prognostication for their future. "I would estimate that Jack will be dead within ten years, probably suicide if he doesn't have a stroke first. Lowell will become a hopeless alcoholic and spend his last years in a sanitarium. Duncan will keep on with his practice, but will have to turn to drugs to keep himself going."

He sat back for a moment. Then as an afterthought, he added, "I will continue to live out my life here in this old house, on the inheritance my father left me, eventually becoming something of a recluse. Duncan was right; I can't leave. It is a psychological prison. But I am reasonably content, keeping busy with my hobby, the study of human nature, that will fill volumes when I am through."

He put the journal away. Then he turned to another bookcase. It was lined with similar neatly bound and dated journals. He went down the line until he found one dated 1953. He opened it and flipped the pages, stopping when he came to the date of their graduation, then he started to read:

"Tonight being graduation," he had written, "I decided we must do something spectacular. A crowning achievement to top any previous prank. Early in the afternoon, I stopped by Pete Bonner's trailer. I had in mind giving him a few dollars to buy us some whiskey for the evening. Being underage, we couldn't go to the liquor store ourselves, but Pete is always ready to do anything for a small bribe. I was surprised, indeed, when I walked into Pete's trailer and found him sprawled out on the floor. He was quite dead, apparently from a heart attack. If I hadn't found him, he'd probably have stayed there for days until someone accidentally stumbled upon him as I had done. I immediately got a brilliant idea for a colossal joke and a chance to test a theory of mine. They say time is relative. If someone believes he has committed an act, it's the same to him as if he *has* committed the act. The consequences, as far as they affect him, should be the same.

"This time the joke would be on Jack, Duncan, and Lowell. They're so gullible, they'll do anything I tell them. I hurried home and swiped the wire recorder out of Dad's study. I recorded some agonized screams and put it under Pete's trailer, all hooked up so it would take only a second to turn it on. I then went over to talk to Jack, Duncan, and Lowell. I convinced them it would be a great idea to burn up Pete's trailer and roast Pete alive. Of course, they had no way of knowing Pete was already dead. Tonight, after graduation, we slipped down to Pete's trailer with gasoline and matches. I went around the other side, pretending to slosh my gasoline around, and reached under the trailer and switched on the wire recorder. As soon as the flames shot up, we began hearing some very convincing screams. It will be most interesting, in future years, to see what effect tonight's act will have on the lives of Jack Harriman, Duncan Gitterhouse, and Lowell Oliver."

Tad Jarmon closed the journal and leaned back with a cold, thoughtful smile.

The Way It Is Now

by Elaine Slater

When they were first married right after graduation from college, he had never been able to spend enough time with her. They bought a small cabin in the North Woods with no communication to the outside world, and spent every weekend there, walking hand in hand, sitting by a roaring fire, lost in each other—that is, when they weren't chopping wood or hauling water from the brook, huffing and laughing at the unaccustomed exertion.

But lately things had changed. Business commitments kept him occupied on Saturdays. He could no longer find the time to escape to the cabin. When she spoke to him, he was never quite there. His reading moved gradually from the *Partisan Review* to the *Wall Street Journal,* and endless market reports. He still sat through the arty movies— Fellini, Truffaut—but when she tried to probe their murky depths, he never contributed a word.

"Where *are* you?" she would ask in exasperation. "Am I talking to a stone?"

"I heard you," he would reply, jumping slightly as though she had caught him at the cookie jar. "Your last words were precisely 'and the dog, of course, symbolizes the eternal evil in man.'"

She would sigh. He was listening evidently, but still . . . he wasn't all there. His mind was on other things, and not all the newly acquired luxuries that his business success brought could compensate for the loss of her young, playful, loving husband. His sense of humor seemed now to be reserved for his business associates, who told her how he broke them up at the Board meetings. He worked several nights a week and came home bone-weary. How could a man that tired exercise a sense of humor, or talk, or, for that matter, make love?

Now they had a house in the suburbs and a housekeeper. She read the magazine advertisements and decided there was a ready remedy at hand. She bathed at twilight, perfumed herself, donned an expensive dressing gown, lit candles, and made a mixer of martinis. When he arrived home, his favorite Mozart concerto was playing. He looked mildly surprised at her outfit, commented that she smelled good, said he preferred a bourbon on the rocks to a martini which gave him indigestion, suggested more lighting over dinner because he couldn't see what he was eating, picked up the latest *Barrons Report,* and fell asleep on the sofa. His own snoring woke him up and he stumbled up to the bedroom.

If she had suspected another woman, she would have had a better idea of how to fight back. But how does one fight the overwhelming commitment to Business? She read Betty Freidan and decided to get a job, but even that didn't fill the gaping void in her life. She thought about taking a lover, and had lunch with one of the young men with whom she worked. He showed an extraordinary interest in her husband's stock portfolio, and shuddering at the thought of a preoccupied lover, she decided she hated all men.

She began to brood. Her friends had children on whom they could vent their frustrations. She had no one. She mulled over the idea of suicide, but her other self kept calling out rebelliously.

"Why should *I* die? *I'm* perfectly capable of laughter, of life, of love! It's *he* who is dead already and doesn't know it. It's not fair for you to kill me."

The *Evergreen Review* slipped out of her lap, and she stared for a long time at her hands.

When he came home that night, she made no attempt to share with him the boring day's activities. He didn't seem to notice the deathly silence, although the housekeeper became so nervous that she broke a rare Minton plate. When the telephone rang just as they were having their coffee, he jumped up to answer it.

His suddenly animated voice was saying, "Harry! How did it go in Toronto? I've thought of nothing else all evening."—as she walked thoughtfully upstairs.

When he came into their bedroom, he was jubilant. He caught her around the waist and shouted, "The Toronto deal is going through! Can you beat that? After two years of negotiating it's finally going through. Bigness is the only thing that talks these days, and we're going to be *BIG!* If only Harry was here right now, would I love to hear all the details. I'd—"

She interrupted him quietly. "Let's celebrate. Let's go to the cabin this weekend. We haven't been there in months. The road will soon be impassable and we won't be able to go again until spring."

"This weekend?" He looked dubious.

"Yes—we'll have a second honeymoon. We could find each other again."

"Have you lost me? Or have I lost you?" he asked in his old teasing voice. "Okay, honey, if you want a second honeymoon you'll have it. But I'll have to cancel two meetings on Saturday. How about putting it off for a week or two?"

"No," she said firmly.

He was too triumphant at the thought of the successful Toronto deal to argue; so on Friday they drove up to the cabin.

It was just as they had left it. No one ever came near the place. There was a pile of wood in the snow by the ax. The wood was not too wet and they quickly made a smoky fire to warm the little room.

She bounced on the squeaky brass bed a few times, and gazed about her happily. All the old warmth and affection began to return. Perhaps here they would find what they had lost. Perhaps here he would look *at* her again, not *through* her. Perhaps here he would once again be interested, if only for a weekend, in her, in her life, in her love—and forget the business world which consumed him. Yes, she was ready to settle for a weekend.

He gazed into the fireplace, at the crackling blue and orange flames. There was a distant, even wistful look on his face. She watched him tenderly, feeling the old love for that tired worn face. She sat opposite him in the shabby old chair that they had bought together in a country junk shop, and had loaded hysterically onto the pickup that he had driven in those days. The front seat was so loaded with their gear that she had ridden the whole day to the cabin seated on that chair in the back of the truck amid a clutter of second-hand household goods.

How funny that had been! Everyone on the road had turned to look, laugh, and wave. And when they arrived at the cabin after an unbelievably bumpy trip—over miles of isolated dirt roads with low overhanging branches that clawed at her face and battered the truck—she had jumped into his waiting arms. Happily he had carried her to the threshold, where he discovered he had to drop her unceremoniously in order to get at the key which was hanging on a rusty nail. They had laughed together until they couldn't stand up, but they had clung to each other for support. Yes, clung to each other . . .

She was deep in nostalgia. He lifted his head and gazed at her. She gazed back into his eyes, trying to guess his thoughts. Were they as far away as hers? He started to speak, and she leaned forward, a slight smile on her lips.

"You know—" he began wistfully.

"What?" she interrupted flirtatiously.

"—Central American Tobacco has just merged with Amalgamated Biscuit."

She buried the bloodstained ax in the snow and went back to sit by the fire—to lose herself in nostalgia before she had to go look for the shovel.

The Hot Rock

by James McKimmey

A sharp, chilling wind blew fog across London. The portly man, wearing a dark duster-length overcoat with a fur collar and a homburg fitted squarely on his bald head, closed the door of his small shop on Chandos Place and locked it. When he had escorted the mink-clad woman into the waiting cab, the fog had obliterated the gold lettering on the door of the shop, which read: *Henry Thornwall Esq., Jeweler.*

Henry leaned forward, patting an inside pocket to make certain that he had not, in the tension of what they were doing, forgotten his examining glass, then gave the driver an address near the Thames. He leaned back with a sigh.

Street lamps flashed against the face of his companion. She looked young from a distance, but on closer examination it was obvious that she was middle-aged, heavily made up, rich, and, right now, very excited.

She put a hand on Henry's plump wrist, squeezing fingers glittering with rings. "How dangerous is this, Henry?"

Henry shook his head, "I wish I knew, Madam. It's not my . . . ah . . . accustomed . . . well, you know."

"I know," she said softly, a waver in her voice. "But the Sional, Henry!"

"Shhh." He looked ahead at the driver.

"For twenty thousand pounds!" She tapped her large purse. "And it's worth double that!"

"Shhh, shhh," went Henry.

The cab moved ahead, the driver making his way through the murk as though by magic. Henry leaned sideways and put his mouth close to her ear. "It's all happened so quickly. Tell me again what he said on the telephone."

"He *whispered,* Henry," she said softly.

"Yes, quite," Henry nodded. "What did he whisper, then?"

"That he had the Sional Diamond and would sell it to me for twenty thousand pounds if I would meet him at the address you've given the driver—with the money."

Henry nodded again. "And that name he gave himself?"

"The Cockroach." She shuddered. "I said I'd do what he asked if I were allowed to bring you to examine the stone. But why do you suppose he has chosen me, Henry?"

Henry shrugged. "Mrs. Peter Sterling-Bahr?"

"I suppose it's obvious, isn't it? Peter would die if he knew. But he won't find out. He never pays any attention to *my* money. Unless something happens that . . ."

Henry put a hand into the right pocket of his coat and pulled out a small chrome-plated pistol. It reflected lights they were passing as he checked it.

"Henry!" the woman said.

Henry returned the pistol to his pocket. "Chaps like this . . . I don't know. They whisper so you can't get a good chance at their accent so you might know something that way. They constantly run underground like sewer rats. I, well, thought it might prove comforting."

The woman touched Henry's hand again. "I never thought of you as being so heroic, Henry. I'll make it up to you. I promise."

*"Ma*dam," Henry said gently. He smiled. Then the smile disappeared. "And we are here, I'm afraid."

They moved toward an old warehouse in the wind-driven fog as the cab's taillights abruptly disappeared.

"Shouldn't we have kept him?" Mrs. Peter Sterling-Bahr asked.

"I shouldn't think so," Henry said. "His license may already have been observed. We wouldn't want you followed to the hotel where you're going to put it, you know."

"Of course. Oh, Henry," she said, hugging his arm, "what would I do without you?"

"Let's, ah, complete the business first, Madam. Then . . ."

His voice trailed away as they stopped before a closed wooden door. Henry put his hand on the latch, paused, took a breath, then opened it. There was a yellow crack of light far across a large high-ceilinged room. Henry dug into the left-hand pocket of his coat and produced a small flashlight.

"You thought of everything, didn't you, Henry?" the woman whispered.

"I rather hope so, anyway," Henry said as they moved forward following the small beam of light.

"I'm trembling, Henry."

He squeezed her hand.

They arrived at the door where light was escaping below on the dusty wooden floor. Again Henry took a breath, then turned the handle. They looked in at a small figure seated at an old desk beneath a naked light bulb hanging from the ceiling of a small room; long and greasy-looking hair with streaks of gray hung shoulder-length; metal-rimmed glasses with tinted lenses decorated a face that looked surprisingly boyish; the suit was wide-shouldered, gray and pin-striped; delicate hands rested on either side of a wide-brimmed fedora placed on the desk.

Henry and the woman stood in absolute silence, staring.

"Madam Sterling-Bahr?" came the throaty whisper. "I am The Cockroach."

The woman managed to nod.

The Cockroach curled a slender finger and motioned them forward. They went to the desk and stood looking at the tinted glasses reflecting light from the bulb above. The Cockroach removed a small revolver from a pocket. The woman turned in alarm just in time to see that Henry had also gotten out his pistol. The two weapons pointed at each other.

"No nonsense, you understand," Henry said in a controlled voice, and adoration showed in the woman's eyes.

The Cockroach stared at the chrome pistol for some time, then drew out from a pocket a small object wrapped in velvet. The fabric was worked loose, exposing a magnificent briolette-cut diamond. The woman drew her breath in, blinking. Henry's eyes narrowed. "May I?" he asked.

The Cockroach shrugged, and Henry carefully placed his pistol in the woman's hand, saying, "Don't hesitate to pull the trigger, my dear, if he should become cute in any fashion."

"Oh, Henry," the woman breathed, but she held the pistol firmly as Henry got out his jeweler's loupe and fitted it to his eye and examined the stone at length. Finally he nodded. He returned it to the velvet and put away his examining glass. "Yes, indeed." He reclaimed his pistol from the woman.

"*Is* it?" she asked.

"Most assuredly."

"Money," The Cockroach whispered.

When the transaction had been completed and the diamond was in the woman's purse, Henry said, "Shall we, then?"

He began backing toward the door, pistol in hand, and the woman went with him. In the large outer room, they made their way through darkness. "I'd use the torch," Henry said quietly, "but I shouldn't want him to go out the back door of that room and up into the loft somewhere where he could shoot at it."

"Dear God," the woman whispered.

They finally fumbled their way outside into a shroud of cold. Then they hurried along the sidewalk. It seemed an eternity, but at last they were able to find a free cab. As they got in, Henry gave the address of a club near Piccadilly Circus. He put an arm around the woman's fur-covered shoulders, feeling her trembling.

"Foolish place to go, rather," he said. "Too many theatrical types, and worse. But I do have a membership."

"Must we go there?" she asked. "Can't I simply go straight to the hotel, then—"

He shook his head. "Beggar might be following. Best to put him off."

"Of course," she said. "I think I'm falling in love with you, Henry."

"Mr. Peter Sterling-Bahr would not like that, I suspect."

"But I shouldn't care," the woman said, holding Henry's hand tightly.

They went upstairs to an informal room which hummed with conversation as members stood and sat about. Henry ordered a gin and orange for both of them. The woman sipped hers, face looking pale.

"Henry," she said, "the Sional! In my purse!"

"Yes, Madam. We seem to have done it."

"Not madam, Henry. Not ever again. Elizabeth."

"Elizabeth," Henry nodded, testing the sound of it. He repeated it.

She had removed her coat, and it was spread on the sofa beside her. Her dress was black, her jewelry was notable, and her legs looked much younger than the rest of her as she crossed them and gave Henry that same look she'd shown in the warehouse near the river.

"You couldn't go with me to the hotel?" she asked.

"I should rather like to, certainly," he said.

"You couldn't come after I've checked in—please, dear Henry!"

"I should like that, indeed, Elizabeth. But—"

"Later, then?" she said. "Some other day or night?"

"I shall require you to remember that."

"I shall. And how do I do it at the hotel, again?"

"Ask them to put the item you have in your purse into safekeeping for the night."

"But if I went home instead—"

He shook his head. "With your husband on business in Paris—"

"But the servants," she said. "Surely—"

"Blighter may already be in with one of them. I would rather trust the Ritz, my dear," he said positively. "A formidably reliable establishment. Then, tomorrow, I shall accompany you to the vault. I think we might go now, if you've finished your drink," he suggested.

They returned to the street where Henry obtained yet another cab. He directed it to the misty glitter of Piccadilly Circus and said to the woman, "Much better if you get out and walk to the hotel rather than taking another cab. If someone should be following this one, they'll continue, I think. When we next stop with the traffic, simply get out and join the crowd on the sidewalk. I'll call you at the hotel the second I've gotten home."

"I do hate leaving you, Henry."

Henry smiled. "I hate leaving you, Elizabeth." He touched her, then said, "Now, my dear."

She got out swiftly and hurried toward the crowded sidewalk where neon cut through swirls of reflecting fog.

The cab moved on, and Henry looked through the back window just as a small figure in a pin-striped suit, wearing tinted glasses and a wide-brimmed fedora over long greasy hair, came up to Elizabeth. An arm was put around her waist, and she was drawn toward a dark doorway. Her mouth opened as though she might be screaming, but Henry, looking away and settling back in his seat, guessed that she wasn't making a sound.

When he reached his flat, the telephone was ringing. He lifted it, saying, "Henry Thornwall here."

"Oh, Henry!" Mrs. Peter Sterling-Bahr said in anguish. "How could it have happened!"

"Are you all right?" he asked with concern.

"Not hurt. Not physically. But he just came up on me on the sidewalk the minute I got out of the cab. He put his arm around me and whispered he had his gun pointed at me and made me go into a doorway where he got the stone out of my purse and ran off! What could I do! It's stolen! I couldn't . . . Oh, Henry! How could he have followed us? In the fog? Two cabs? The club? And yet be there on the sidewalk, waiting . . . Henry?"

"I don't *know* how," Henry breathed. "I rather . . . thought I'd been so clever. But I guess I'm no good at that sort of thing. Oh, damn, Elizabeth. Dreadful, altogether."

"Dreadful, yes," she said limply. "Yes, it is. What do I do now, Henry?"

"Go home, I should think. Have something to drink. Try to forget it."

"It that really all there is for me to do now?" she said wearily. "Henry, is that all?"

"I rather think," he said slowly, "that it is."

Twenty minutes later, Henry's door buzzer sounded. When he opened the door, he saw no one on the stoop. Then he looked behind the bushes and saw the small figure wearing the wide-brimmed hat and tinted glasses standing beside the wall. Henry reached out and pulled the figure in and closed the door. "And here you are, my dear," he said fondly, then kissed a boyish forehead.

The sound of the shower stopped in the bath off Henry's comfortable bedroom. Henry stood in the adjoining study by the bar mixing two Scotches with soda. When his visitor, an extraordinarily beautiful creature with thick blonde hair, came out of the bedroom, he could see the suit, hat, glasses, and wig on the bed beside the carelessly dropped currency. The girl was dressed now in a satin negligee. She smiled beautifully as she crossed to Henry and put her arms around his neck.

"Oh, darling," she said, "it was so smooth, wasn't it?"

"Practice makes perfect, doesn't it?" he said, kissing her boyish forehead again.

A Puff of Orange Smoke

by Lael J. Littke

Bill O'Connell knew all about the way his wife Alice liked to have Paul Newman in the kitchen with her when she washed the dishes. He didn't mind. After all, didn't he sometimes have Raquel Welch snuggled by *his* side as he drove home from work?

Everyone was entitled to his own private fantasies, and certainly a pretty girl like Alice must occasionally yearn for something a little more spectacular than an ordinary, slightly homely, not-very-tall guy who made an adequate but not fancy living in an insurance firm, a guy who was totally untalented except for a real flair for emptying the garbage.

Bill knew he was neither handsome nor suave, and definitely not the dashing romantic type. But Cortland Marshall was, and, confound him, he was coming through Los Angeles on his way to Washington, D.C. from his most recent diplomatic post in Thailand, an exotic spot if Bill ever heard of one. He couldn't blame Alice for being all agog over the fact that Cortland was coming to dinner. Cort had never married and liked to keep in touch with Alice, even though she had married. When he wrote that he was coming through L.A., Alice had written back insisting that he stop and visit.

So now the kids were packed off to Grandma's, the house was shining with wax and polish, the rib roast in the oven was giving off an aroma which could tempt any man to give up his bachelorhood, and Bill was cautioned to "be nice to Cort."

It wouldn't have been so bad if Cortland had been a plumber or a grocery clerk; but a man with a glamor job like his could set a girl's heart to thumping even if he was bald and hollow-chested, which Cortland was not. It had never been quite clear to Bill why Alice had married him—Bill—when she could have had Cort. But then she was the type who yearned over stray kittens and wept for starving dogs, and she said she fell in love with Bill because he looked as if he needed someone to take care of him.

The big question was, could that kind of love withstand the strain of Cortland showing up once or twice every year still obviously smitten with his old flame? Certainly Alice seemed perfectly happy—but what was it then that made her cheeks glow when she ran to open the door in answer to Cortland's knock?

"Cort!" she cried, and then giggled happily as Cortland engulfed her in a bear hug. Right in front of Bill. As if Bill did not exist.

"Alice, honey," he said. "You haven't changed a bit."

"Neither have you, Cort," Alice-honey said.

Bill had to admit she was right. He had been away almost a year this time, but his well-tailored clothes and close-cropped dark hair were as attractive as ever. And he absolutely oozed charm.

Finally Cortland noticed Bill. "Well, Bill," he said affably, "howza boy?"

Bill wanted to snap his teeth and snarl, but instead he pasted on a wide silly grin and said, "Fine, Cortland. How are you, buddy?" Immediately he felt like a clod, which was how Cortland always made him feel.

His duties to his host taken care of, Cortland turned back to Alice. "Tell me what you've been doing to stay so beautiful," he said.

Alice giggled again. "Oh, Cort, I've just been a housewife. Come on out in the kitchen and talk to me while I finish fixing dinner."

Cortland put his arm around Alice's shoulders and they walked into the kitchen, leaving Bill alone with his bad thoughts. He wished that Cortland, in the time since Alice last saw him, had lost his teeth or his hair or something so that he didn't look like every housewife's dream of romance.

Not that he was afraid Alice would run off with Cortland or anything like that. Or would she? Even if she didn't, she might start imagining it was Cortland standing by her side each time she washed the dishes. Bill could put up with Paul Newman in the kitchen. But Courtland Marshall — *NO!*"

"Oh, Bill," Alice sang out, "come on in and join us."

You bet he would join them. He'd go in there and sit and watch and if Cortland got fresh with Alice he'd poke him in the nose. Or at least he would think about it hard.

"Bill," Cortland said as he walked into the kitchen, "we've just been going over old memories."

Bill wished viciously he could wipe out those memories. Or better still, wipe out Cortland. Just a flick of the magic finger, folks, and poof, he's gone!

Bill flicked his fingers at Cortland and said aloud, "Poof, you're gone!"

There was a poof of orange smoke and Cortland was gone.

Bill stood in rigid silence for almost two minutes. Then Alice said in a matter-of-fact voice, "All right, boys, that was a nice trick. But dinner is almost ready. Come on back, Cortland."

Bill swallowed. "Alice," he said. His voice was a high squeak.

Alice went on stirring the gravy. "Bill, show Cort where he can wash his hands."

Bill tried again. "Alice," he squeaked. "I think Cortland *is* gone."

"Where'd he go?" Alice asked. "This is a fine time for him to go somewhere."

Bill collapsed on a kitchen chair. "I think I made him disappear."

"Well, make him reappear."

Bill shook his head. "I don't know how. I don't even know how I made him *dis*appear."

Alice stopped stirring the gravy. "Bill, are you sick?"

"I sure am," Bill groaned. His scalp felt tight and his eyes were so large he didn't think he could close the lids over them. "I've got to call the police," he whispered.

Officers Magee and Smithson were big, burly, and jaded. They had heard everything. Many times. Bill noticed, however, that they still had spirit enough to glance appreciatively at Alice.

"Sure," Officer Magee said when Bill had told his story. "You just flick your fingers and some guy disappears."

Bill gave them a sickly grin. "I know it sounds crazy, but that's what happened."

Officer Magee sighed. "Maybe we better search the premises," he told Smithson. "See if there are any signs of a struggle. Maybe he really did do away with this guy."

Magee looked again at Alice, who gave him a warm smile. Bill could almost hear the wheels in the officer's head grinding out, "Pretty wife, jealous husband, so goodbye, boy friend."

The two policemen conducted a thorough search of the house and back yard, poking around in the flowerbeds—for signs of digging, Bill thought.

"Okay," said Officer Magee when they returned. "Now tell us the truth. We're busy men, Mac. Our next call is a complaint about a billygoat who whistles *Yankee Doodle*."

Officer Smithson guffawed.

Bill stood up and drew himself to his full five feet seven inches. He glared straight into the eye of his own reflection in Officer Magee's shiny buttons. He slumped down again. "I did tell you the truth," he mumbled.

"Well, tell us again," boomed Officer Smithson.

Bill licked his dry lips. "You see," he began, "Cortland was standing just about where you two are now. All I did was flick my fingers like this." He flicked his fingers. "And I said, 'Poof, you're gone!'"

There was a poof of orange smoke and Officers Magee and Smithson were gone.

Bill gulped. "Aw, come on back, you guys," he said weakly.

"Bill," Alice said. "Is that *all* you do? Just flick your fingers and someone disappears?"

Bill scarcely had the strength to nod as he sank onto a chair.

"I didn't know you could do that," Alice said with admiration. "You're quite a guy. No wonder I love you so much." She kissed him on top of the head. "I think I'll put dinner on now. Or maybe I should wait until Cortland gets back. When *will* he be back?"

Bill shook his head.

"Let me know when he gets here," Alice said. "I'll go put the finishing touches on the dining room." She left.

Bill wasn't at all sure that Cortland would get back. Or the two officers, either. He found himself wondering if Magee and Smithson had families. Maybe right now several little kiddies were crying for their daddies to come home. Bill stared bleakly at the spot where the three men had stood.

"I've got to turn myself in," he said to himself. "I'll call and tell them to come get me."

He wasn't sure just what he would say. As he waited for his call to be transferred to the police lieutenant, he tried to formulate something that wouldn't brand him immediately as an absolute nut. What could he say? "See, I've got these magic fingers—"

"Lieutenant Hargrove," said a gruff voice on the wire. There was a pause.

"Lieutenant Hargrove," repeated Bill. There was another pause.

"I'm Lieutenant Hargrove," the voice said, a wary note coming into it, as if Lieutenant Hargrove were girding himself to deal with an addled brain.

Bill cleared his throat and considered hanging up. "Well, you see, Lieutenant Hargrove," he said, "these two officers came to my house to investigate a strange occurrence, and I don't know what happened to them."

Lieutenant Hargrove asked quickly, "Which two officers was that?"

"I believe their names were Magee and Smithson."

"Oh, those two loonies," said Lieutenant Hargrove.

"They just called from Palm Springs. Said they didn't know how they got there. Couple of nincompoops. Get lost crossing the street."

Bill clutched the phone. "Palm Springs, you say? Are they all right?"

"Sure," said Lieutenant Hargrove. "Physically, at least. Say, did you get that strange occurrence taken care of?"

"Yes," Bill said hastily. "Yes. Oh, yes. Thanks." He hung up quickly. No reason to be thought a nut if everyone was all right. Of course there was still Cortland. But he would undoubtedly show up somewhere. San Francisco, maybe. Probably figure the State Department sent him on a rush mission or something.

Bill started to whistle. He walked to the mirror that Alice kept on the wall just inside the kitchen door. He *was* quite a guy, he thought, peering at his reflection. But he didn't look any different. He sort of thought he might, considering his newly discovered talent. And what a talent! Just let Alice's old boy friends come nosing around now. Just a flick of the fingers, and away they'd go. Even Paul Newman couldn't do that.

Bill smiled at himself in the mirror. Just let them come. He could take care of them. He flicked his fingers at his reflected image. "Poof," he said, "you're gone!"

"Bill," Alice said, coming in from the dining room. "I think we'd better go ahead and eat before the roast dries out."

She looked around the empty kitchen. "Bill?" she said. "Bill? Where are you?"

The Chicken Player

by Joe L. Hensley

Jamie pulled the dusty, black T-bird onto the shoulder of the road he'd been cruising and sat there waiting. The radio was off because on a still day he could hear a car from further away than he could see it.

In that hour of cruising he'd checked the road carefully. It wasn't in top condition, but it was all right, better than many he'd played the game on, and it had the advantage of sparse traffic, perhaps too sparse. The only other car he'd seen during that hour of driving was an old Chevy, worn out, down at the springs, driven by a man with white hair. Not very good prey, but a possible. The old man had driven by without a glance, moving very slowly. Jamie was still debating with himself whether to follow when he'd seen a child's curious face appear in the rear window of the old car.

That had ruined it. He was superstitious about kids and there'd been enough bad luck recently. Thursday, he'd almost been arrested by a State Trooper, but had managed to outrun him. Friday, the transmission had gone out of the T-bird and he'd been dismounted the whole weekend. Now, deep inside, he felt he'd about worn out this part of the country and it was time to move on. People were starting to look familiar to him, remind him of people he'd known before in other places and at other times. It was kooky how so many faces reminded him of Mr. Kelly. Mr. Kelly was thousands of miles away, back in New York State. Mr. Kelly was five years before in time.

Jamie remembered with narcissistic nostalgia that he'd been an amateur then, just learning the game. Then it had been a game of half-grown kids, played on deserted roads, with sentries out to warn if police came near. The Chicken Game. God, it had grabbed him even then.

The run at Mr. Kelly's car had been a lark, an impulse, a broadening of the game to include the world around Jamie. He'd have gotten away if he hadn't blown a tire at the critical moment. That had thrown him into the Kelly car when he thought himself safely past and it had jumbled his hopped up Ford into a junk pile, but he'd scrambled out unhurt.

He would not have thought that a kid could scream as much or as long as the Kelly boy had. Mr. Kelly had been thrown clear and he was unconscious, so only Jamie had to listen to the screams from the burning Kelly car. He had listened and felt strange inside and when the screams stopped he'd giggled a little.

After awhile there'd been lots of police and questions.

"I lost control," he told them. "The tire blew and I lost control." He repeated it and repeated it, and stubbornness and the good lawyer his Aunt hired made the difference. The jury turned him loose.

Only Mr. Kelly knew. Jamie remembered the eyes that had burned right through him during the trial.

When it was done and Jamie was free, he moved on. It was an act of protection, not fear. By that time he'd played again and again and without the game there was nothing. No angry, vengeful man was going to take the game away.

So now he was twenty-three years old and he'd been playing the game for a long time. It was now a professional thing, done carefully, accomplished at rare, safe intervals when the desire became overpowering. The game was more than anything else, more than the sum total of all the rest. It was more than love, greater than sex, better than drugs, and stronger than the fear of death.

Sometimes when Jamie was around other people who were his age, he could have screamed. The talk was mundane, the pleasures crude, and there was an eternal sameness to each scene. Sometimes he was sure that the only time he was really alive was when he was behind the wheel of the T-bird, alone, hunting. The rest of it was just the scene, all papery and fragile.

The game was simple, but there were rules. The other car was the mark. You passed it and accelerated away, making sure the highway was clear. A mile or so ahead you turned and came back at the mark, twisting right lane to left lane until the mark saw you. Then you took his lane, going straight for him, foot deep in the accelerator, forcing the mark to turn away, to chicken.

The rest of the game was of his own variation. When the mark turned away, Jamie followed, while the brutal, delicious fear rose within him.

Sometimes other drivers froze and stopped dead in the road, and that filled Jamie with contempt. More often they came on erratically until he forced them from the road. Two months back, he'd run a lone, male driver down a steep hill and seen him roll, metal shrieking, against rocks and trees until all sound stopped. That had been a very good one.

The game took nerve and a sure knowledge of the condition of the highway and an instinctive feel for what a car would do, but the shuddery exultation was worth all of it.

He'd not played the game for two weeks now and the last time had been a washout. He leaned back in the T-bird's bucket seat and thought and let the heat of anticipation wash over him. Vaguely he remembered his mother and father. They'd died when he was ten years old. It had been an accident on the Turnpike. A truck had smashed their car to nothingness. In a way he was a child of speed. The insurance had made him nearly rich and he lived frugally now, except for cars. An indulgent, adoring Aunt had raised him, given him his first car, protected him first from angry neighbors and, later, the police.

A sound brought him back to awareness. He heard a faraway motor, and then he saw the tiny, fast-moving car in his rear-view mirror. He started the T-bird and listened to the sweet motor, the best that money could buy. He fastened his seat belt. Once he would have snarled at the idea of wearing a seat belt, but now the game was so precious that he took no chances and the belt held him firmly as he twisted back and forth.

He waited the other car out and it came past, moving fast, on the borderline of speeding. He caught a furtive glimpse of a lone, male driver who sat stiffly upright, appearing to be almost drawn back against the seat.

He gunned the T-bird out behind and passed the other car and was elated when it speeded up as he went around it. He could almost envision the other driver cursing him as he cut in sharply and pressed the accelerator down. There was no riding passenger in the other car. There was only the driver.

A perfect mark. *Oh, Heat that lives within me: Make this one of the good ones.*

Jamie made his turn when the distance was right. There was no car behind the mark and nothing in his own rear-view mirror. The heat began to build.

He let the engine wind up until the speedometer read ninety, and he eased, right lane, then left lane.

He saw dust puff from the rear tires of the other car and something inside him screamed: *No! Don't quit on me!* The other car came on and Jamie smiled.

At three hundred feet away he slid the T-bird into the left lane, dead at the other car, anticipating what would happen. The other driver would panic now, move out of the path of Jamie's hurtling car. Then the variation. Jamie would follow, forcing the other driver away from the traveled road, onto the tricky shoulder.

At this moment Jamie liked to see the oncoming driver's face. He lifted his eyes, and the face he saw seemed vaguely familiar and smiling, but that was impossible. Savagely, with hate, Jamie floorboarded the T-bird.

At fifty feet the other car cut sharply left and Jamie corrected happily, for this was as anticipated, but then the other car cut right again and there was no time to recover. The T-bird was caught slightly broadside. Jamie heard the thunder of the crash and fought the wheel and got the T-bird straightened as his wheels bounced on the shoulder, but one of the wheels hit a rut and he felt the T-bird going. He bent desperately into the seat, felt the top hit on the parched ground, heard the renewed tearing of metal and then it was a roll that seemed endless. The door came away beside him, but the belt held him firmly until all of the crazy, loud motion stopped and there was silence. Jamie reached then very quickly for the ignition, smelling the gasoline smell, breathing as hard as if he'd run a mile.

He could see the other car out of his starred windshield.

Its right front end was smashed. The driver had the door open and he was unhooking a complicated safety harness that ran from a roll bar in the car over his shoulders and waist. It was the harness that had given him the stiff look, Jamie calculated.

Jamie unhooked his own seat belt, but the steering wheel was still in the way and his left leg was caught somewhere. He felt the beginning of pain, and the warmth of blood running down his injured leg brought a leaping panic.

"Help," he called.

The other man came slowly up to the jumbled T-bird.

"Hello, Jamie."

"I remember you," Jamie said incredulously. "You're Mr. Kelly."

"Can you make it out?" Mr. Kelly asked.

Jamie shook his head. "It's my leg."

Mr. Kelly's eyes sparkled.

Jamie looked at the other man, unable to read him, fighting away fear. "You like the game?"

Mr. Kelly smiled. "Enough to learn to play it. I trained in sports cars and drove dirt track for awhile after my boy died and before I came after you."

"Maybe . . ."

Mr. Kelly held up his hand. "If they put you away you'd be back." He nodded. "There isn't any way to break you, Jamie."

"We could play again," Jamie said. "I've never had anyone before who could really play." He searched within. "It was better than it's ever been." And it had been.

"Not ever again, Jamie," Mr. Kelly said gently.

The fear came up in waves. "If you do anything they'll find out somehow. You prosecuted me once. They'll catch you."

"Not about us," Mr. Kelly said. "You've changed your name too many times."

Jamie laughed and the fear went away and he was exultant with triumph. "My fingerprints haven't changed. They took them then. They'll take them again. They'll use them and find out."

Mr. Kelly smiled a curious smile and sniffed at the gasoline fumes.

"I thought about that, too."

He lit a match.

When the screaming was all over, Mr. Kelly giggled.

Nothing But Bad News

by Henry Slesar

Dillon whirled and shot the bully for the fifth time. Pauline clenched her teeth and said *Miss, you bastard,* but the marshal didn't, his accuracy guaranteed by rerun inexorability. Arnold Summerly breathed a fifth sigh of relief, and Pauline said, "For God's sake, Arnold, didn't you *know* how it was going to turn out?" but Arnold was narcotized now by the commercial following the shoot-out.

Pauline reached out to tune in the seven o'clock news, but Arnold's hand beat her to the dial and spun it to the local channel; it was their own shoot-out, re-enacted every night.

"Arnold, please!" Pauline said. "Let's watch the news for once, just *once*. Anything could be happening. Greenland could have declared war on us. The world may be coming to an end. Anything!"

"If it happens, we'll hear about it," Arnold said.

"How? How? You never watch the news. You never read a paper. You care so little about the world, what difference would it make if it *did* come to an end?"

"This beer is warm," Arnold said. "You've been putting the beer in the refrigerator door again. How many times do I have to tell you to put the beer inside?" The screen divided itself into the shape of a heart, and Arnold forgot his pique. The prospect of Lucy in the twentieth year of her pregnancy erased all rancor.

"You're a vegetable," Pauline said. "Do you know that, Arnold? You're an office machine in the daytime and a vegetable at night. A head of lettuce sticking out of a shirt collar."

At least he had the decency to get angry.

"All right! All right! You want to know why I don't watch the news? Why I don't read the paper? Because it's all *bad* news. Nothing but *bad* news. That's the reason so many people turn mean and rotten, they get to hear nothing but *bad* news from morning till night. There's not one nice, decent, cheerful thing you ever hear about, not one thing you can feel *good* about. That's why!"

"It's not true," Pauline said. "Maybe it seems that way, but it isn't."

"Yeah? Yeah? You want to bet? You want to bet, like, that new fur coat you want so bad? You want to bet that, Pauline, huh?"

"What do you mean, bet?"

"You heard me. Put your money where your big mouth is. You turn on the news, go ahead. And you hear one real *good* piece of news, you can quit saving for that fur coat, I'll buy it for you. Tomorrow. You won't have to wait another year, I'll put it on your back right now!"

The coat was an ebony mink. Pauline's Holy Grail.

"And if there *isn't* any good news?"

Arnold grinned.

"You give me that money you been saving and we take the fishing trip."

Pauline hated fishing trips. So she hesitated.

Arnold chuckled, both at her and at Lucy. Lucy thought the baby was coming. Desi was panicked. Pauline was simultaneously sickened at the thought of dead fish and exhilarated at the thought of mink.

"All right," she said. "OK, Arnold. Turn on the news."

Arnold gave Lucy a regretful smile and wrenched the dial.

Jensen looked so grim that Pauline's heart wrenched, too.

"The prospect for a major conflict in the Middle East intensified tonight, after an Israeli commando raid into Lebanon followed a series of bombings in Tel Aviv that claimed ten lives. . . ."

Arnold sucked loudly on his beer bottle.

"A new threat to the Vietnam truce was posed tonight as reports of a buildup. . . ."

Arnold burped and chuckled and chortled.

"And now, here's a film report on the fire that destroyed the ocean liner Marianna and cost the lives of thirty passengers and crewmen. . . ."

Arnold enjoyed the account of the disaster almost as much as *I Love Lucy*.

"The strike of longshoremen, now in its third week, may cripple the economy of the entire Eastern Seaboard, according to a new study. . . ."

Arnold basked in the blue light of the set.

"Another charge of corruption in Government came today from a high-placed official in the Justice Department. . . ."

"After a week-long search, the mutilated body of seven-year-old Sharon Snyder was discovered in an abandoned tenement. . . ."

"A tax rise forecast by both Federal and state economists brutally slain in apartment-house elevator the highest increase in food prices in ten years accident total now five hundred but expected to rise as floods sweep tornadoes struck hurricane winds rising to thirteen children dead twenty injured as train strikes school bus and protesters arrested on steps of mugging victim dies as new strain of flu virus thousands homeless as assassin forecasts rain for holiday weekend. . . ."

Arnold was having a very good time.

"Well, how about it, how about it?" he said. "How's about the news, Mrs. Current Events, you enjoying the show? And how's about that fishing trip, you going to throw up again, like you did the last time, when I bring home the catch?"

"It's still on," Pauline said gratingly. "The news is still on, Arnold; will you at least let the man finish?"

"Sure," said Arnold, smiling.

"And now," said Jensen, not smiling, "repeating our first item, the state health authorities have issued an urgent warning concerning the danger of botulism in the canned mixed vegetables packed by Happy Lad Foods. Any can of Happy Lad mixed vegetables marked five-L-three is known to contain these deadly bacteria and should be destroyed immediately or returned to the place of purchase. . . ."

The credits were beginning to roll and Pauline couldn't bear Arnold's chuckling noises a moment longer. Tears blurred her path between living room and kitchen. In the center of the tiled floor, she fought a wave of nausea (smell of dead fish, nonsmell of mink), and then she went to the cupboard and looked through her canned-food inventory, searching the labels for a can of Happy Lad mixed vegetables, series 5L3. Suddenly, she realized that all the news wasn't bad that night. She had one.

The Quick and the Dead

by Helen McCloy

She was a remarkable woman. Basil Willing recognized that the moment he saw her.

She opened the door of his beach cottage without knocking. Behind her a jagged streak of lightning split the night and vanished. Thunder roared above the steady drumming of the surf. An edge of white foam thrust its way up the sand; beyond, the ocean was a blackness—as void as if nothing were there, and never had been. Thunderstorms were rare in California, but when they came they were, like most things California, larger than life.

She was like a storm herself, all darkness and suddenness, all flash and tumult. Basil remembered that the words hurricane and houri have the same root.

"Sorry to bother you." Her voice was rich, deep, warm. "My telephone is dead. May I use yours? I live next door."

"Of course. Over there by the stairway."

She wore a silk sheath, shrill yellow like a flame in the dimly lighted room. Her sandals were gilt; her only jewel was a big round brooch on one shoulder, bits of coral and turquoise pieced together to form the image of a Nepalese god. An artful woman to combine yellow-pink and yellow-blue with yellow.

"Damn! Your phone is dead too! What am I going to do now?"

"What's the trouble?"

"I'm Moira Shiel."

"The singer? Max and Moira?"

The team specialized in folk songs and satirical sketches. They were famous for their quickness in picking up each other's cues when they ad-libbed, as they often did, even on television. Moira was the better actor; Max, the better musician—he had perfect pitch.

She nodded. "I just had a phone call from the Santa Barbara police. Max's father was found dead there an hour ago, at nine o'clock. He lived alone. A neighbor heard his dog barking and called the police. They said he had died of a heart attack about eight thirty.

"They called me because they couldn't locate Max. They had tried the studio in Burbank first, but the night staff said that Max had left there alone, in his car, at six, telling everyone that he was driving to Santa Barbara to have dinner with his father. The police had also tried to call Max's house in Santa Cristina, a hundred miles south of Burbank, but there was no answer. His wife should have been there, but she wasn't.

"I don't want Max to hear this news suddenly, on his car radio. He adored his father. The shock would prostrate him for weeks, perhaps months. I got the Santa Barbara police to promise they would not release the news until I found Max, but they can't hold it back indefinitely. What shall I do? If your phone is also not working it means the line is down all along Malibu Beach. I may not be able to reach him for hours."

Basil glanced at his watch. "Ten after ten now. If he left Burbank at six, he should certainly be in Santa Barbara by this time. I suppose you could drive to Burbank, or to Los Angeles, and find a telephone that's working and—"

"I wouldn't dare leave my house for so long. The line may be fixed at any moment. A call might come through from Max and I'd miss it."

"Then why don't I take you home and drive to Los Angeles myself? I can give Max the message, if you'll tell me the most likely numbers to call."

There was a fire already burning on the hearth in her living room. She stood before it turning the pages of a small black address book. "First, his home number. That's one I always forget—I suppose, because I so rarely have occasion to use it."

"I always assumed you and Max were married," said Basil.

"Oh, no. He was married when we teamed up. Katie, his wife, is nice, but—"

She stopped at the sound of a car on the road that runs above the beach houses at Malibu. In a few moments footfalls were noisy on the wooden steps that led down to her house. She ran to the front door.

"Miss Shiel?" The man in the doorway was stocky and curt. The police. How could you always tell, even without the uniform?

"I'm Carson Dawes, Lieutenant, Los Angeles Police." He smiled at Basil. "Good evening, Dr. Willing. You probably don't remember me, but I've been attending your lectures on forensic psychiatry at the University."

"Dr. Willing?" Moira whirled to look at Basil. "You're a sort of policeman, too!"

"Sort of. I'm really a psychiatrist."

"Sorry to trouble you, Miss Shiel," Dawes went on. "But I couldn't reach you by phone from Los Angeles, so I came out to the beach."

"My line is down. The storm."

"I'm looking for your partner, Max Weber. Do you know where he is?"

"No, I was trying to reach him myself when the line went down. His father, Abraham Weber, died suddenly of a heart attack this evening in Santa Barbara."

"I know," Dawes said. "When I called Mr. Weber's number, trying to find Max, a Santa Barbara policeman answered the phone and told me all about it. They were trying to locate Max, too, he said. They had just talked to you and promised you they'd not release the news until he was found. That was when I tried to call you and discovered your line was down. The studio people in Burbank had told me Max was in Santa Barbara with his father. But he wasn't. Interesting. If he had been, it would have given him an alibi."

"An alibi? For what?" asked Moira.

"His wife, Katie, was murdered this evening."

"But who would want to kill poor Katie?"

"Who but Max? They were on the verge of divorce—as you probably know."

"I didn't."

"The Santa Cristina police called us a little while ago and asked us to bring Max in for questioning. Under California community property law, Katie would get half of everything if there were a divorce. That seems to be very inconvenient for Max just now—as I understand it, he wants to start his own recording company and needs all his capital. Don't tell me you didn't know about that?"

"Of course I knew. That's business. We're partners."

"Katie Weber was in the Santa Cristina house this evening, sitting beside a picture window. According to medical evidence it was about eight thirty when someone fired a shot through the window and killed her instantly. No one heard the shot. Her body was found by her housekeeper, who had left the house at eight, when Katie was still alive, and returned at nine to find her dead. Where was Max at eight thirty?"

"I don't know, but he would never kill Katie."

Dawes looked at her skeptically. "Tough luck for a murderer to have his only alibi-witness die a natural death while he's committing murder and so blow his carefully planned alibi sky-high."

"How dare you assume that Max and his father would plan a cold-blooded murder together?"

"Before Abraham Weber retired, he was a lawyer for the racketeers. He never committed a crime himself, but he was not exactly punctilious about the letter of the law. And he loved his son. The heart attack suggests that the old man knew what was going on tonight and the excitement was too much for him. If I'm right—if Max did plan to use his father as an alibi-witness—the Lord hath delivered him into our hands."

"What do you mean?"

"You asked the Santa Barbara police not to release the news of Weber's death until Max was found, so Max cannot possibly know his father is dead. When we pick him up, he'll undoubtedly claim he was in Santa Barbara with his father at eight thirty, the time of the murder, never suspecting that his father was already dead at eight thirty. That will prove that Max was not at his father's house at all tonight. We'll hardly have to question him. We can just sit back and let him talk himself into the gas chamber."

"That's horrible!" cried Moira. "You're setting a trap for him!"

Again there was the sound of a car on the road above the beach. Moira was already at the door. Dawes drew her back, almost roughly.

"That may be Max Weber now. I left word with the highway police to bring him here if they picked him up within an hour of the time I left Burbank. Miss Shiel, if you try to warn him in any way, I'll have you charged as an accessory after the fact. You must not speak to him at all—not a single word. Understand?"

"Yes." She moved like a sleepwalker to the piano bench and sat down. Basil offered her a cigarette. She took it with trembling fingers. It was Dawes who opened the door when the knock came.

The first man to enter was slender, frail, shy. Basil had an impression of intelligence and sensitivity but without strength—always a dangerous constellation. He was followed by a uniformed highway policeman, who spoke to Dawes.

"We picked him up on the grass verge beside the freeway, Lieutenant. He was just outside Burbank, headed south. He said he was on his way home to Santa Cristina."

Basil knew what the Lieutenant was thinking: Max could have driven to Santa Cristina instead of Santa Barbara when he left the Burbank studio, shot his wife, and then returned to Burbank, so he would re-enter Santa Cristina from the north, as if he had driven south from Santa Barbara. He'd find some witness on the road between Burbank and Santa Cristina to confirm his driving south at that hour—possibly a filling station man, whom he'd talk to when he stopped for gas.

"Moira!" Max ignored the others. "Have you heard the radio? Katie is dead—murdered—"

He started toward Moira, but Dawes put a hand on his arm.

"You are Max Weber?"

"Yes, but—"

"I'm Lieutenant Dawes, Los Angeles Police, and I must talk to you before anyone else does. Where have you been?"

Moira crushed her cigarette in an ashtray on top of the piano. Her restless fingers strayed across the keyboard.

"Miss Shiel, I know you're nervous, but this is no time for playing the piano. Mr. Weber, where have you been?"

"Santa Barbara. I had intended to dine with my father but—"

"But you didn't? Why not?"

"My poor father." Max dropped into a chair and covered his face with his hands. "Dad died all alone. He must have died just before I got there at eight thirty. He was still warm."

"You called his doctor?"

"No. I should have, shouldn't I? But I didn't. It was such a shock, I went kind of crazy. I drove around for a while, trying to realize what it would be like to live in a world without Dad. At last, I headed for home."

"Still without notifying a doctor?"

"I was going to do that as soon as I got home. It didn't seem to matter, really. Dad was gone. The—the thing lying there had nothing to do with him now . . . I was on the freeway, just south of Burbank, when I heard about Katie on the radio. It was just too much, coming on top of Dad's death. I couldn't drive. I pulled off onto the grass and a few minutes later the cops picked me up and brought me here."

"I guess that lets you out." Dawes couldn't hide his disappointment. "I must apologize for—"

"Apologize?" Basil's voice was sharp. "Lieutenant, are you assuming Max Weber was in Santa Barbara tonight solely because he knows his father is dead?'

"Yes. No one knew about Mr. Weber's death except the neighbor who called the police and the police themselves and Miss Shiel and you. It wasn't on the air, because Miss Shiel made the police promise they wouldn't release the news until Max was found. She couldn't have telephoned Max about his father's death, because her line went down right after the Santa Barbara police called her and told her the news. I know, because it was then I tried to reach her myself. Obviously, she had no opportunity to tell Max that his father was dead before I arrived."

"True, but Miss Shiel did have an opportunity to tell Max Weber that his father was dead after you arrived."

"What do you mean? She didn't say a single word to him!"

"Words are not the only means of communication."

"You're thinking of some sort of code?"

"I suppose it could be called a code." Basil stepped over to the piano. Slowly he played seven notes. "Do you recognize those notes?"

Dawes looked blank, but the young highway policeman gazed at Basil with awe. "Well, I'll be damned! Key of C natural. It would have to be. You must have perfect pitch, too."

"No, I was watching her hands, as you were watching mine just now."

"What are you two talking about?" demanded Dawes.

"These are the seven notes Miss Shiel struck on the piano: A B E D E A D. *Abe dead.*"

"I hate you!" Moira screamed at Basil. "What business is it of yours? Why didn't you leave it alone?

"It's all right, Moira," said Max gently. "I might as well give myself up—I haven't a chance without Dad to alibi me. The police will dig and dig until they trace the gun back to me."

"Then ... you did do it?" Moira's voice was now a whisper.

"Yes, I killed Katie. For you as much as for the money. Moira, I love you so much . . ."

"Why the key of C natural?" Dawes asked Basil, later that evening.

"The enharmonic factor. On the keyboard, B sharp is also C natural, C flat is also B natural, E sharp is also F natural and F flat is also E natural. You can't tell which note of these pairs is indicated unless the notes are written and the key indicated. C natural is the one exception—the one key that has no sharps or flats.

"Max Weber was quick to realize that if Moira's playing was a message in code, it would have to be in the key of C natural—otherwise, he would have no way of identifying the notes—that is, the letters. Because he had perfect pitch, not just relative pitch, he was able to do what few people can do—identify a single note, or a small group of notes, played alone.

"Moira took advantage of Max's gift on the spur of the moment. She was quick, but he was even quicker. They were quite a team, justly famous for picking up each other's cues at an instant's notice . . . I hope you're not going to charge her as accessory?"

"I should," said Dawes slowly. "But I won't. Max's punishment will be punishment enough for her . . . But I'm glad you were here, Dr. Willing—she fooled me completely."

An Exercise in Insurance

by James Holding

When three masked men walked into the bank with sawed-off shotguns that afternoon and calmly began to clean out the tellers' cash drawers, I wasn't even nervous. I was sure they weren't going to get away with it. I was perfectly certain that five straight-shooting policemen, strategically placed, would be waiting for the robbers outside the bank door when they emerged.

That's the way it would have happened, too, if it hadn't been for Miss Coe, Robbsville's leading milliner.

As proprietress and sole employee of a hat shop, just around the corner from the bank and felicitously called *Miss Coe's Chapeux,* Miss Coe fabricated fetching hats for many of the town's discriminating ladies. She was an excellent designer, whose products exhibited a fashionable flare, faintly French, that more than justified her use of the French word in her shop name.

Miss Coe was middle-aged, sweet, pretty, methodical, and utterly reliable. Indeed, her dependability was often the subject of admiring comment from local ladies who had become somewhat disillusioned by the unreliability of other tradesmen. "You can always count on Miss Coe," they frequently told each other. "If she says she'll have the hat ready on Tuesday at eleven, she'll have it ready. She'll be putting in the last stitch as you come in the door." I had even heard remarks of this kind at my own dinner table, since my wife was one of Miss Coe's steady customers.

But perhaps you are wondering what Miss Coe, a milliner—reliable and methodical as she undoubtedly was—could possibly have to do with the robbery of our bank?

Well, you may remember that some years ago, several of the companies that insured banks against robbery agreed to reduce the premium rates on such insurance if the insured bank was willing to conform to a certain security arrangement.

This meant, simply, that to win the lower insurance rate, a bank must maintain a robbery alarm system somewhere *outside* the bank itself; that in the event of a robbery, a warning bell or buzzer must sound elsewhere so that police could be instantly alerted without interference, and arrive on the scene in time to prevent the robbery and even, hopefully, to capture the bandits in the act.

In those days of rather primitive electrical wiring, the insurance companies did not insist that, to meet this security requirement, the outside alarm be necessarily installed in the police station itself. Any other location where the ringing of the alarm would unfailingly initiate instant action would serve as well.

The potential savings on insurance premiums made possible in this way were quite substantial. Our bank accordingly decided to take advantage of them. As Cashier, I was entrusted with the job of selecting a suitable outside alarm site, preferably somewhere near the bank, since the installation charges would thus be minimal.

After some thought, and with the memory of my wife's recent words to a bridge partner, "You'll find Miss Coe utterly dependable," fresh in mind, I went around to see the milliner on my lunch hour one day.

After introducing myself, I explained to her that the bank intended to install an alarm buzzer somewhere in the neighborhood. I explained the alarm's purpose. Then I went on diplomatically, "Miss Coe, I have never heard you referred to among the ladies of my acquaintance without some warm testimonial to your complete reliability, to your calm, methodical turn of mind."

"How nice," she murmured, pleased. "I do try to be precise and methodical about things, it's true. I find life less complicated that way."

"Yes. And that's exactly why I am going to ask you to permit us to install our alarm buzzer in your shop."

"Here?"

"Right here. You are always in your shop during banking hours, are you not?"

"Of course. I carry my lunch, so I'm not even away at lunch time."

"Good. With your penchant for doing exactly what is needed at exactly the right time, I am certain that our alarm buzzer, although placing a new responsibility on your shoulders in the unlikely event of a bank robbery, will in no way discommode or harm you. And I might add that the bank will naturally expect to pay you a small stipend for your cooperation."

She flushed with pleasure. "What would I have to do?" she asked.

"If the alarm buzzer should ever ring, you merely go at once to your telephone there, Miss Coe . . . ," I indicated her telephone on a counter at the back of the shop, ". . . and place an emergency call to the police, giving them a prearranged signal. That is all. Your responsibility then ceases. You see, it's very simple."

"I'm sure I could do that, if that's all there is to it," Miss Coe said, glancing at her wall clock a little guiltily, as though she feared she were three stitches late on a hat promised a customer one minute from then. "And I won't say that a bit of extra income won't be more than welcome."

By the end of the week the buzzer was installed in her shop. The system was thoroughly tested, and it worked perfectly. On our first "dry run", the squad of police arrived at the bank just four minutes from the time they received their telephone call from Miss Coe. The insurance people, satisfied with their inspection of the system and my recommendation of Miss Coe, granted us the lower insurance rate forthwith.

Since a daily test of the wiring circuit, to assure its constant readiness, was specified in our insurance agreement, I arranged with Miss Coe that at exactly three o'clock each day, I would press the button under my desk at the bank and ring the buzzer in her shop. That was as far as the daily test needed to go; it was expected that Miss Coe's telephone would always be operative but if, in the event it were out of order or in use when the buzzer should ring, Miss Coe could merely nip into the shop next door and telephone the police from there.

For two years it seemed that Miss Coe would never be called upon to display her reliability in behalf of the bank's depositors. We had no bank robbery, nor even an attempted one. I tested the alarm buzzer each day at three; Miss Coe continued to make fetching hats for Robbsville's ladies undisturbed; and each month I mailed her a small check for her participation in the bank's alarm system.

You can readily see now, I am sure, why I had no qualms whatever when our bank robbery finally did occur. This was the event for which the police, Miss Coe, and I had so carefully prepared. This was the actual happening that our rehearsals had merely simulated. I knew that our outside robbery alarm was in perfect working order. I knew that Miss Coe was in her shop, ready to act, as dependable and unfailing as the stars in the heavens.

So, far from being startled or apprehensive, I really felt a certain pleasurable excitement when I looked up from my desk, just before closing time that afternoon, and saw the three masked bandits presenting their weapons to our staff and terrified patrons. In common with the other occupants of the banking room, I slowly raised my hands over my head at the robbers' command. Simultaneously and unnoticed, however, I also pressed my knee against the alarm button under my desk.

I could picture clearly the exact sequence of events that would be set in train by that movement of my knee. Miss Coe's buzzer would sound. She would perhaps sit immobile for a shocked second at her work table. She would drop the hat she was working on and cross speedily to her telephone. She would place her emergency call to the police with splendid calm. And then she would wait confidently for the news from me that our bank robbers had been circumvented or captured.

Unfortunately, as I found out later, Miss Coe did none of these things.

What she did do, when the alarm buzzer sounded in her shop, was merely to glance at the clock on her wall, rise impatiently from her sewing stool and cross the room, and there (bless her methodical heart!) push the minute hand of the wall clock ahead ten minutes so that it pointed to exactly three o'clock.

The Old Heap

by Alvin S. Fick

August 8, 1975

Acme Parking Plaza
2135 Congress St.
Akron, O.

To whom it may concern:

This afternoon when I picked up my car at your parking garage I discovered that all four hubcaps were missing. Obviously they were stolen during the day, because I'm sure all of them were on the car when I left it on C level, the one you reach from the Orville Avenue ramp.

I spoke to one of the attendants about this, but all he did was shrug his shoulders and say probably the hubcaps fell off on the way in this morning and I didn't notice. Impossible—not all four, anyway. He said the office was closed and wouldn't even give me his name, so I am writing this letter expecting a reply which will enable me to get an adjustment on this.

Yours truly,
Dennis Daggett
14 Pepper Lane
Chatham, O.

August 12, 1975

Mr. Dennis Daggett
14 Pepper Lane
Chatham, O.

Dear Mr. Daggett:
Your letter of August 8 has been brought to my attention. On behalf of Acme Parking Plaza, I express sincere regret for the loss of hubcaps from your car which occurred, you say, while your vehicle was parked at our facility. In view of the activity in the garage section of our Plaza, I find it difficult to believe this could have happened on C level, or anywhere else on our premises, to be quite candid. We employ an ample staff of trained, dependable and reputable attendants who constantly monitor all areas.

We trust you will have no problem in obtaining reimbursement from your insurance carrier under the terms of your comprehensive coverage.

Again, sorry you incurred a loss.

Cordially,
Elroy R. Kent
Customer Relations
Acme Parking Plaza

August 15, 1975

Mr. Elroy R. Kent
Customer Relations
Acme Parking Plaza
2135 Congress St.
Akron, O.

Dear Mr. Kent:
I have your letter, and I don't like your Doubting Thomas attitude. I have been parking at Acme Plaza for three years,

and I don't like the way you imply I am lying about this matter.

I only use my car going back and forth to work. It never sits on the street. It is parked in my garage—locked, by the way—when I am home. I have always used your indoor parking area instead of the big outdoor lot on the Congress St. side. I do this because I take great pride in the way I take care of my car. I have never left it outdoors in the weather.

Don't talk to me about comprehensive insurance. The money that would cost I have been putting into the cash register of Acme Parking Plaza, just so I wouldn't need comprehensive. Why do you think I paid your outrageous indoor fee if not to protect my property?

I am checking on the cost of replacement hubcaps. I will be sending you the bill.

> Yours truly,
> Dennis Daggett
> 14 Pepper Lane
> Chatham, O.

August 19, 1975

Mr. Dennis Daggett
14 Pepper Lane
Chatham, O.

Dear Mr. Daggett:

In view of the low cost of comprehensive insurance, it seems a little foolish of you not to have it. But that is your business, shortsighted though it may be. It would be pointless for you to send us a bill for your replacement hubcaps, which I doubt you will be able to obtain anyway in view of the age of your car. I spoke to the C level attendant to whom you complained on August 8. He tells me you drive a 1949 Kaiser.

Really, Mr. Daggett, you can't hope to find hubcaps for *that!*

> Cordially,
> Elroy R. Kent
> for Acme Parking Plaza

August 20, 1975

Mr. Kent:
   You are damned right that it is *my* business whether or
not I carry comprehensive insurance, and it certainly is
none of *your* business to call me foolish because I don't.
And just what the hell do you mean, "It would be pointless
for you to send us a bill"?
   You have a responsibility in this matter, and I aim to see
that you fulfill it.
   The tone of your letter of August 19 makes me madder
than spit. Who in blazes are you to call me shortsighted?
How many shortsighted people do you know who have
nursed along, loved and cared for a single automobile for
twenty-five years? Let me assure you I can and will find
hubcaps. They will cost you a pretty penny, because I am
going to charge you for the time I spend searching, and
when I find them I expect they may be dented and rusty.
Repair, including re-chroming, will be part of the bill.
   On August 19 I stopped in at your office to discuss this
matter in person, but your secretary said you were out, and
she said she didn't know when you would be back. Bull! Or
were you too busy writing that goddamned letter dated the
19th to see me? There's no need for me to ask why I got the
same answer from her every time I tried to reach you by
phone.
   I expect an immediate reply by return mail that you will
honor the bill for my new hubcaps. Don't phone about this.
I want it in writing. I don't trust you.

Dennis Daggett

P.S. Needless to say, I have found another place to park my
car.

August 22, 1975

Mr. Dennis Daggett
14 Pepper Lane
Chatham, O.

Dear Mr. Daggett:
   It pains me that I find it necessary to warn you about the

intemperate language you are using in your letters. I understand perfectly well the circumstances surrounding the loss of hubcaps from your old car.

It strikes me that, for a person who parked in our facility for three years, you were remarkably unobservant, even singularly inattentive to the prominently posted stipulations regarding vehicles left on our premises. There was not a day you parked at Acme when we at Acme Parking Plaza carried a single iota of responsibility for your vehicle or, for that matter, your person.

It's as simple as that. We have no responsibility. Period.

Cordially,
Elroy R. Kent
for Acme Parking Plaza

P.S. If your vision is so bad you couldn't see the three-by-four-foot signs stating in letters two inches high THE MANAGEMENT IS NOT RESPONSIBLE FOR LOSS OR DAMAGE FROM ANY CAUSE TO VEHICLES, CONTENTS, DRIVERS OR PASSENGERS—well, in that case you shouldn't even be on the road with your old heap.

August 25, 1975

Kent:

There is only one way you can avoid a lawsuit. I stated in my letter of August 20 that I do not trust you. Double that. Prove to me that you and the rest of your crew at Acme are not a bunch of crooks and I may even forgive your insult to my fine old Kaiser. I'll have you know it is a choice and carefully preserved part of automobile Americana. I can accept anything in the way of insults, but you went too far when you called my Kaiser an old heap.

If you wish to prove your point, take down one of those "prominent" signs next Tuesday and bring it to Rose's Cafe across from your Congress St. entrance. Be there at 6:15 P.M. Don't make me wait, because I have lost my patience. If this keeps you from your 9-to-5 routine, count it as small cost to get me to drop this affair without other courses of action.

I don't recall seeing the signs you mention. You better not bring a freshly painted, trumped-up version, and you know damned well I'd never set foot on Acme property to see one.

Don't forget: September 2 at 6:15 sharp.

Dennis Daggett

P.S. Confirm our appointment in writing, and don't be late.

August 28, 1975

Mr. Dennis Daggett
14 Pepper Lane
Chatham, O.

Dear Mr. Daggett:

Your request of August 25 is ridiculous, but I am going to humor you just so I can see the silly look on your face when you read the sign. I will bring one from the open parking lot rather than one from the inside area. That way you will be able to see the weathering for yourself.

I say I will show up to humor you. Closer to the truth is my desire to get a look at the priceless pile of old tin and rust you call auto Americana.

Aside from the fact I will be carrying a big sign, you will have no problem identifying me. I will be the one who is laughing—probably uncontrollably after seeing the Kaiser at the curb.

See you on the 2nd, Dennis.

Cordially,
Elroy R. Kent
for Acme Parking Plaza

September 17, 1975

Mr. Dennis Daggett
14 Pepper Lane
Chatham, O.

Dear Mr. Daggett:

Just this morning I reviewed for the first time the correspondence of Elroy R. Kent. I note that you and he exchanged letters during the month of August. Obviously, there was a strong disagreement between you and Acme Parking Plaza regarding the loss of hubcaps from your car while it was parked on C level of our garage.

To the regrets expressed by Mr. Kent I wish to add my own. Further than that, I think it might be in order for me to apologize on behalf of Mr. Kent for his failure to keep the appointment he had with you on September 2. I do not know if you read the Akron papers, since you are a resident of Chatham, but Mr. Kent met with a tragic accident which kept him from meeting you. As you already know, he was planning to bring with him one of the signs from the parking area—a rather unusual agreement on his part, but perhaps in keeping with the strange nature of the correspondence the two of you conducted.

As he was crossing the street, Mr. Kent was struck by a hit-and-run car. I add with personal sorrow that he died on the way to the hospital without regaining consciousness.

The police have theorized that the sign obscured Mr. Kent's vision, and that he stepped in front of the car which hit him. However, there is so little traffic on Congress St. at that hour I cannot understand how the driver missed seeing Mr. Kent. How could he have missed seeing a man carrying a three-by-four-foot sign? I devoutly hope the police find him.

No one in the cafe saw the accident, and apparently no pedestrians or other drivers witnessed it. As I said above, the street is not very busy at 6:15 of a summer evening.

Perhaps you wondered why Mr. Kent failed to keep the appointment. The police interviewed everyone in the cafe, and took names. Since you were not on that list, I can only assume you were late for the meeting in spite of your insistence on Mr. Kent's punctuality.

My primary reason for writing this letter is to settle the disagreement which culminated in Mr. Kent's untimely death. I must apologize for the manner in which your loss was handled. I cannot say for sure until I read some of his old files, but I do not believe it was customary for Mr. Kent to be quite so caustic. I'm sure you understand, however, that he had to be firm in his capacity as arbiter in customer problems.

Mr. Daggett, Acme Parking Plaza wishes to make full

financial restitution for your loss. We will do so, although I am obliged to reiterate that Mr. Kent was accurate in his assessment that we are devoid of responsibility. Please stop in to see me with your bill, and I will personally hand you a check to cover it.

Sincerely yours,
Robert Winsett
Vice President
Acme Parking Plaza

September 19, 1975

Mr. Robert Winsett
Acme Parking Plaza
2135 Congress St.
Akron, O.

Dear Mr. Winsett:

Isn't that a shame about Mr. Kent!

Thanks for the offer to buy my hubcaps, but that won't be necessary. I had a little accident with my Kaiser several days ago, and you know how hard it is to get parts for an old heap like that—especially such things as grills, lamps and so on.

I figured the best thing to do was get rid of it, so I drove it to an auto junkyard. They would only give me $20!

A couple of days ago I stopped to see if I could check the glove compartment for a pen I think I missed when I emptied the car. One of the guys in the yard said they had put my car through the crusher and shipped it out for scrap the day before.

I suppose it's on the way to Japan already.

Yours truly,
Dennis Daggett
14 Pepper Lane
Chatham, O.

P.S. Seeing you are in the automobile business in a manner of speaking, I sure would appreciate your dropping me a line if you ever learn of anyone with a 1956 Hudson Hornet for sale—in nice shape, that is.

As the Wheel Turns

by Jane Speed

Paula Thorpe drank three cups of coffee, slowly, without being interrupted by so much as a glance from her two breakfast companions. There they sat, the pair of them: Howard, her husband of six months, poring over *Art Treaures of Ancient Syria;* and his mother, a fat little mountain of a woman squeezed into a wheel chair, applying herself assiduously to the one pursuit which fully engaged her interest—eating.

Paula slammed her empty cup down into its saucer. Mother Thorpe lifted her head at the sound like a startled rabbit and hastily snatched the last blueberry muffin from the bun warmer. Howard merely shifted in his chair and murmured, without looking up, "Excellent breakfast, my dear."

Paula sighed, gathered up a stack of dishes, and carried them out to the kitchen.

From earliest memory Paula had yearned for the company of artists. She had not been able to coax forth any noticeable talent of her own, so she had set her sights on what seemed the next best means of entry into the charmed circle—to be the guiding genius of some creative spirit.

And then, at a cocktail party last fall, she met Howard Thorpe. His gaunt, tousle-haired good looks and his habit of protracted, brooding silences made him appear a romantic figure of Byronic proportions. And when Paula learned that his field was art (he "earned his bread and butter" by teaching art at a small New England college) and that he was in New York to discuss the possible publication of a book he was working on, she could hardly be blamed for feeling that here indeed was the embodiment of the chance she'd been looking for.

They were married quietly in New York the day after Thanksgiving and set out immediately for his home in Vermont. Howard's teaching schedule and his modest Assistant Professor's salary precluded any honeymoon, but Paula didn't mind in the least. She had embarked on this marriage willing, even eager, to starve in a garret (or the small college-town equivalent) for the sake of her very own struggling artist.

She had plunged with fanatical zeal into her new role. His mother's welfare seemed a matter of prime importance with Howard, therefore it became so with Paula, too. Great plans were afoot for the celebration of the good lady's sixty-fifth birthday which was to occur late in the spring, and Paula fell in with these plans enthusiastically, adding many small refinements of her own to make the occasion more festive.

And every clear day since the first real thaw she had dutifully pushed Mother Thorpe in her rickety wheel chair to the fat little woman's favorite spot, the top of a steep rise which commanded an impressive view of the neat, stone-walled campus. Here, beneath the shade of an ancient elm, Paula, who didn't trust the brake on the venerable contraption, carefully settled one wheel of the chair into a rut. Then she sat patiently while the old woman droned on and on until she finally talked herself into her morning nap.

Mother Thorpe was touched by Paula's devotion and often in her rambling monologues she reiterated her regret that she couldn't do more for her dear Howard and his dear wife. Howard's father, she would explain vaguely, though a dear man, had been a bit of an eccentric and had tied up his sizeable fortune in a complicated trust fund which she herself didn't altogether understand.

"But never you mind, dear," went her favorite refrain as she patted Paula's shoulder with her pudgy hand, "you shall have it all one day, and soon."

But the days dragged into weeks and the weeks into months, and Paula found herself pinning her hopes increasingly on her mother-in-law's words. For the harsh truth was, there was very little else to pin them on.

It had by this time become painfully clear that the

perpetual frown which drew Howard's brows down at his nose in such a devilishly attractive way was not a sign of the outrage of a gifted rebel but of a mildly fussy disposition; he was essentially a silent man for the simple reason that he had very little to say; and his teaching of art history at this small college was not a means to the end of being recognized in his field, but rather an end in itself. In short, Howard was not an artist, but a schoolmaster.

And the book? Paula had clung to this long after her other illusions about Howard were dashed. True, it was to be a scholarly text, hardly destined for a place on the best-seller lists. Still, Paula had rather counted on being able to refer casually to "Howard's book" when she wrote to her friends back in New York. But just yesterday had come a letter from the publisher informing Howard that another house was bringing out a work on substantially the same subject and therefore it would be inadvisable to go ahead with the tentatively proposed publication. So even that satisfaction was to be denied her.

"Well, dear," said Howard, appearing at the kitchen door, "I'm off to the wars." Paula offered her cheek for his husbandly peck—and waited. Without fail, he added, "Lovely day." And then, as though a bright new thought had just occurred to him, "Why don't you take Mother up to the hill this morning?"

But you know I take her every day, Paula opened her mouth to protest. Then she closed it. What was the use? He'd say the same thing tomorrow anyhow. She merely nodded silently and went on with the dishes.

Half an hour later she was trundling the old lady up the hill. She settled the chair into its accustomed place and flung herself down on the ground nearby. The view of the well-trimmed campus surrounded by its stone wall seemed to Paula like nothing so much as a neat, orderly trap. She paid even less attention than usual to her mother-in-law's monotonous prattle, catching only, "You shall have it all one day, and soon."

The familiar words made Paula ache with restless longing. If only "soon" could be right now. Money, she had always piously maintained, wasn't important; and yet, when one had nothing else—

With enough money she could pry Howard out of his

narrow little life; a year in Paris, then perhaps Rome; maybe they could finally live in Switzerland as so many people were doing. It just might make all the difference. There might still be some hidden spark to be struck in Howard if only he could be freed from the deadening influence of this dismal town and its suffocating college.

A gentle snoring from the wheel chair brought Paula rudely back to reality. Not a chance, she thought bitterly. The famous sixty-fifth birthday was only a week away, and the old woman, sleeping peacefully in the shade, looked fit for another fifteen years at least. Oh, it just wasn't fair!

Paula yanked her sleep-numbed leg out from under her and extended it sharply. Her foot accidentally struck the wheel of the chair. She gasped as the chair, loosened from its place, rolled forward a few feet and came to a stop precariously near the beginning of the long downward slope.

For a few seconds Paula sat rigid, hardly able to breathe. And through it all, like an idiotically benign counterpoint, the snoring continued unbroken. The old woman apparently slept as wholeheartedly as she ate. Paula relaxed at last, exhausted from fear. What a close call!

And then, insidiously, a second thought crept into her consciousness. How *easy* it had been. Almost before she realized what was happening, Paula found herself sliding forward along the ground. She stretched her leg out cautiously, and with her foot gave the chair another shove. It moved only a few inches this time and then held, caught by a rut at the very edge.

Again Paula waited, her heart pounding. And again there was no sound except the snoring, and no movement from the woman in the wheel chair.

Paula rose silently. She seemed to have lost all sense of what it was she was trying to do and was filled only with a determination to accomplish it. She grasped the back of the chair with both hands. Gently she eased the front wheels and then the back ones over the obstructing spot. Then with a strong thrust she sent the chair forward.

It started down the grade slowly, then gained momentum. The fat little woman, squeezed in so tightly, didn't even waken fully enough to cry out. There was scarcely any sound at all till the distant, splintering thud as the chair with its heavy passenger crashed into the solid stone wall . . .

It was more than three hours later when Howard finally came out of his mother's room. Paula, sitting in the hall outside, knew by his face that the old woman was dead. The tension in which Paula had spent the intervening hours broke suddenly and she gave way to hysterical sobbing.

"Oh, dear," murmured Howard, distressed. He came to her quickly and sat beside her. "Paula, you mustn't . . . Don't blame yourself, my dear. It was a dreadful accident, that's all." Then, as her sobbing continued unabated, he went on nervously. "Please, dear, try to look at it this way. These last few months have been the happiest Mother has ever known, thanks largely to you. Really, she remarked many times about your great kindness to her."

Paula buried her face even deeper in her hands to hide the blush that flared up in her cheeks. It was several painful minutes before she could control her sobs enough to mumble, "She didn't even get to have her birthday party."

"That's true," said Howard with a sad smile. "Poor Mother. That would be her only regret, I think. She had so counted on being able to turn over Father's money to us."

Paula lifted her head at this and stared at Howard through a blur of tears. "What do you mean?" she asked finally.

"Why—didn't Mother explain to you about Father's will?"

"Not—very clearly," Paula managed to say. Her mouth felt dry.

"Well," Howard began, settling comfortably into his classroom manner, "although Father became quite a wealthy man in his lifetime, he always retained a strong Yankee fear of the corrupting influence of money not earned. He felt that Mother spoiled me and that if he left the money to her outright she'd turn it over to me immediately and I'd become a wastrel. And he may have been right, you know. Dear Mother, she found it very hard to deny me anything. At any rate, Father made out a will leaving the money in trust, allowing Mother only a monthly income until she should reach the age of sixty-five."

"Sixty-five?" Paula echoed stupidly.

"I don't know why sixty-five exactly. Perhaps he felt that by that time I'd be forty and have acquired the habit of earning my own keep."

"But—" Paula was struggling to make sense of Howard's words. "But how could he be sure she'd live to be sixty-five?"

"He couldn't, of course. And," he added with a sigh, "as it turned out, she didn't."

Paula closed her eyes. She could hardly bring herself to ask it. "What—what happens to the money now?"

"Oh—that." Howard frowned in an effort to recall the exact wording. "In the event of her death before attaining the age of sixty-five," he recited with maddening accuracy, "the money automatically goes to the college." Here he permitted himself a dignified chuckle. "Like so many people with very little formal schooling, Father had the greatest respect for institutions of higher learning."

Up to this point Howard had fastidiously avoided looking directly at his wife, on the charitable assumption that her initial excessive outburst had been as embarrassing to her as it was to him. As he turned to face her now, he was shocked to see the crushing effect his words had been having on her.

"Oh, my dear Paula," he hastened to reassure her. "Surely you don't think I mind about the money? How can I miss something I've never had? We lived very frugally even when Father was alive. Why, I have my work, a good wife, our little home—what more could I possibly want? You'll see, my dear, our life will go on quite as usual. Except that poor Mother is no longer with us, nothing has changed at all."

Knit One, Purl Two . . .

by Thomasina Weber

Flo Connelly put her lunch wrappings in the large tote bag beside her camp stool. "You'd think they would have a garbage can here," she said to her new acquaintance of the morning.

"I don't think they encourage eating in the courthouse corridors," replied Mrs. Frisbee.

"Tough. I've attended every hearing held in this courthouse, and if you're not up front when they unlock the doors after lunch, you don't get a seat."

"I had no idea so many people attended preliminary hearings," said Mrs. Frisbee.

"They don't always. But for one like this, where the sweet innocent broad knocks off her husband, they come to hear the dirt."

Mrs. Frisbee moved slightly away from the smaller woman. "They don't know for sure that Delcey Clark killed her husband," she said.

Flo Connelly laughed as she extracted from her bag a pair of knitting needles with five inches of a blue, unidentifiable something on them. "All you gotta do is look at that wide-eyed baby face and that shiny red hair, and you can see it right off. What would she want with a sick, crabby old husband other than his money?"

"How could a young girl like that kill a sick old man?"

Flo's knitting needles moved swiftly. "How could a young girl like that *marry* a sick old man in the first place?"

"Some people are dedicated to helping others."

"Horsefeathers."

Mrs. Frisbee clucked. "You seem to lack compassion, my dear."

Flo looked at the woman scornfully. "And you seem to be the kind who judges a book by its cover."

"A capacity for love can never be concealed."

Amen, thought Flo, returning to her knitting. The corridor was beginning to fill up. The people were forming a line along the wall, but new arrivals were congregating in little knots of two or three beside the line and although they seemed engrossed in conversation, their feet were edging toward the doors. Pointed looks, like poisoned darts, were directed at them by those in line, but no one challenged them.

Flo was interestedly watching the approach of one, a sweating man in dark trousers, dirty white shirt, gaping shoes minus laces and no socks. By the time he had inched up to Flo, she was ready for him.

"Where do you think you're going?" she demanded loudly.

"I'm in line, just like you," he said.

"Oh, no, you're not. You got here seventeen minutes ago and you belong twelfth from the end of the line, which is about fifty feet south of here."

"Who died and made you boss, sister?"

She stood up, her eyes on a level with his third shirt button. Shielded from the others by his broad body, Flo lightly pressed the point of her knitting needle against his abdomen. "If I were you, mister, I'd go to the end of the line." He went to the end of the line.

Twenty minutes before opening time, Flo packed her knitting and her camp stool in the tote bag and turned to face the doors. As if an invisible whistle had sounded, the mob began to move forward until it was a solid unit pushing ahead with nowhere to go.

"Mercy's sakes," gasped Mrs. Frisbee, dismayed at the crush, "you'd think they were giving away something free!"

When the doors were finally opened, Flo made good use of her elbows, netting herself and Mrs. Frisbee seats in the third of the four rows of chairs.

"Were you here this morning?" asked the woman on Flo's other side. She was fat with kinky white hair, wearing a straining green shift with a huge yellow daisy blooming obscenely on her stomach.

"Yes," replied Flo, mentally dubbing the woman Daisy. "Were you?"

"You bet. You don't think I'm going to sit in my hot little

trailer and read magazines when I can sit with air-conditioning and watch the real thing, do you?"

Flo took out her knitting. "What do you think of the pharmacist?"

"Oh, he's cute. Reminds me of my son when he was that age."

"They make a cozy couple."

"You got it all wrong. The whole thing was her idea. He didn't have anything to do with it."

"Don't be ridiculous," said Flo. "They're lovers, and he's the one who got her the drug to give the old man."

"You can't make me believe that. Why, my son used to look just like him, except that his hair is brown instead of blond."

"That's a stupid thing to base an opinion on," said Flo.

"Everybody rise!"

There was a unified surge upward as the judge entered. He was slightly built and his dark-rimmed glasses seemed too large for his handsome face. "Be seated," he said.

Delcey Clark, red-eyed and ghostly without make-up, sat at the table with her attorney, a well-built man in his early forties, at ease in his faultlessly tailored suit. His arm, across the back of her chair, rested so that his hand touched her white nylon shoulder.

"She's got her attorney right where she wants him," Flo whispered to Mrs. Frisbee.

"What's that you're saying?" asked Daisy.

"I must warn the spectators to refrain from making audible comments," said the judge, looking directly at Flo. She held his eyes until he turned to the business at hand, whereupon Flo resumed her knitting.

"Isn't that judge a doll?" said Daisy.

"I'd hardly call him that," said Flo.

"He's the one who will decide whether there's enough of a case to try her for murder," said Daisy.

"He's still a man," said Flo. "All she has to do is hike her skirt up a little and he'll be chewing on his gavel."

"Sh-h," said Mrs. Frisbee. "The judge is looking at you again."

"He's always looking at me," said Flo. "He's used to me by now."

The prosecutor called his first witness of the afternoon, a

neighbor who testified to seeing Delcey and the pharmacist together in a car in front of her house on one occasion. Under cross-examination by the defense, he admitted he had seen no embrace between them. The defense subsequently established the fact that Delcey had been in the drugstore picking up her husband's medicine when it began to rain. Since it was closing time, the pharmacist had driven her home. The pharmacist readily admitted that he was in love with Delcey Clark but insisted he was willing to wait until she was free, "even if it's years until your husband dies," he had told her.

"There are still some good people left in the world," murmured Mrs. Frisbee.

Flo laughed. People turned in their seats to see who had interrupted the proceedings. The judge frowned at Flo. "If the spectators cannot control themselves," he said, "I will be forced to clear the court."

"Hmph!" said Flo under her breath, her knitting needles flying faster than ever. "Young smart aleck! Just because he's sitting up there in a black robe, he thinks he's God Almighty."

"This judge is highly respected," said Mrs. Frisbee.

"He hasn't made a right decision yet, as far as I'm concerned," said Flo. "I don't see how one man can make so many wrong moves."

"Just because you don't agree with his decisions doesn't mean they are wrong," said Mrs. Frisbee gently.

"What's that you said?" asked Daisy, leaning across Flo.

"I said they ought to have women judges if they want justice done," said Flo.

William Clark's physician took the stand and testified that he had been in South America when he learned of the death of his patient and the arrest of Delcey Clark. He had caught the first plane back. While he respected the confidential relationship between doctor and patient, he said the patient was now dead and another life was at stake. Since Dr. Fleischman took very seriously his oath to preserve human life, he felt that his responsibility was to the living, the living in question being Delcey Clark.

The doctor further testified that William Clark, knowing he had less than a year to live, an increasingly pain-ridden year, had insisted this information be kept from his wife. The doctor said he was convinced Clark had hoarded his pain-killing drug to use in one fatal overdose. The doctor then produced his notes taken during consultations with William Clark confirming the deceased's statement that he would take his own life rather than be a burden to anyone else.

The courtroom began to buzz. The prosecutor was out of his chair, the judge was pounding his gavel.

"Very neatly done," said Flo acidly. "Anything to make it look good when they free her."

"Order, order," said the judge in a calm voice which was somehow heard above the clamor. A hush fell immediately, letting Flo's words ring out, "—the usual whitewash." She looked up to meet the cold blue eyes of the judge. He gazed at her for a long moment, then struck his gavel one more time.

"Will counsel please approach the bench," he said. There followed a sotto voce conference and finally the judge said, "In view of the testimony and supporting evidence presented by Dr. Fleischman, a witness for the defense, the case against Delcey Clark is dismissed." He rose and left the courtroom.

Flo stuffed her knitting into the tote bag and pushed her way out the door, ignoring Mrs. Frisbee and Daisy, who were left to talk to each other. She walked determinedly down the corridor to the judge's office, opened the door and stepped inside.

The judge looked up as she entered. "What are you doing in here?"

"I am here as a taxpayer and a citizen of this community, to tell you what I think of you."

"Didn't you cause enough disturbance in the courtroom?"

"It is a taxpayer's right to attend public hearings, isn't it?"

"Of course."

"And there is such a thing as freedom of speech, isn't there?"

"Yes."

"So that means I can attend all the hearings I want and say anything I please. Isn't that a fact?"

"No, it is *not* a fact. There is also such a thing as contempt of court, with which you flirt every time you come into my courtroom."

Flo was standing in front of him now, holding her knitting bag between them. He was not much taller than she.

"Do you understand what I am saying?" he asked.

"I hear you," she replied, reaching into the bag and taking out her knitting, her eyes never leaving his face.

"Of course, you hear me," he said, "but do you understand me?"

"Certainly. I may not have had a college education like you, but I'm not stupid." She unfurled the knitting from its core of needles and raised a needle to his shoulder, the work dangling free.

"You are not listening to me," he said. "Let me tell you this. If I see you in my courtroom one more time, I am going to have you forcibly evicted, taxpayer or no taxpayer."

"Well!" she said, jamming the knitting back in her bag. "Just see if I finish this sweater for you!" She marched toward the door, put her hand on the knob, and turned back to look at the judge. "Such a way to talk to your own mother!"

The Paternal Instinct

by Al Nussbaum

Big Ben came up to me near the side entrance to Leavenworth Penitentiary's B-cellhouse. Everyone calls him Big Ben because he tips the scales at 250 pounds and his first name is Benny. The nickname has nothing to do with time, or the famous London clock, despite the long sentence—thirty years—he's serving.

"Hey, Bill, ya know anythin' about boids?" Ben asked.

"What kind?" I answered, as if it made a difference. "Sparrows."

"No, sorry." I looked around to make sure no guards were close. "You have one?"

"Yeah, look."

I'd noticed that he had his right hand cupped. Now he held it out to me and opened it. There on his palm huddled the most ugly little creature I'd ever seen. It was about an inch and a half of naked flesh and the head was all beak. There were no feathers.

"*That's* a bird?" I asked.

"Sure. He's just a baby. What d'ya think I should feed him?"

"Where'd you get it?"

"Found him outside. A nest was blew down an' all busted up. I waited a while, but there wasn't no mama boids around, so I picked him up."

Hearing Big Ben say "mama boids" was comical. I almost smiled—but I didn't. I didn't want to take the chance of having him think I was laughing at him. "Birds eat worms; bread, too. Guess you could feed it bread and worms," I offered.

That was on Friday afternoon. I didn't see Ben again until the following Monday. We both were assigned to the Education Building—Ben as an orderly, and I as a helper in the library—and I met him on the way to work. "Still got the bird?" I asked.

"Yeah—see?" He opened a cigar box he was carrying and thrust it proudly under my nose. He had lined the inside with soft rags and the tiny bird was nestled in the center of them.

"You taking it to work?" I asked incredulously.

"Yeah, sure. Can't leave him in my cell. I gotta feed him. 'Sides, they might shake-down and find him. Pets ain't allowed, ya know."

"What're you going to do with it?"

"Gonna put the box on one of the windowsills of A-cellhouse. He'll get lotsa sun an' air, an' I can come out an' feed him every chance I get."

And that's just what he did. Several times that day I looked from a side window of the Education Building. Once

I saw only the cigar box on a window ledge of the building thirty feet away; the other times Ben was out there feeding the bird and whispering to it.

The next day I noticed that two pieces of corrugated cardboard about eighteen inches square were lying on the grass plot between the Education Building and A-cellhouse. This was unusual because trash doesn't get a chance to accumulate at Leavenworth. You seldom see an empty cigarette package, let alone large pieces of paper. I was wondering how they had been left there when Big Ben appeared.

He knelt, lifted a corner of one of the squares, and quickly reached under it. He got to his feet with a pink worm dangling from between his thumb and index finger and went to the cigar box.

I went outside to see what was going on. I heard Ben say, "Ya wants another woim, Baby?" as I approached, but he stopped talking to the bird when he saw me.

"I saw you get a worm from under the cardboard," I said. "How d'you do it?"

"Tore a couple of pieces from a box, soaked 'em in water, an' put 'em on the grass," he said. "Woims come outta the groun' under the paper last night. They didn't go back into the groun' when it got light. They don't move fast an' I can catch 'em."

I stood there watching. Ben fed three large worms to the bird, and it continued to open its beak and scream for more. When there were no more worms to catch, Ben took small pieces of bread, dipped them in water, rolled them into little balls, and then dropped them into the bird's open mouth. The bird would be quiet for a few seconds while it swallowed the bread, then it would open its beak and yell: "Cheep! Cheep!"

"He sure likes to eat," Ben observed fondly.

After that it seemed as though every time I looked out of the window I saw Ben feeding Baby. It wasn't difficult to see why Leavenworth or any prison would outlaw pets. If they were all as demanding and insatiable as Baby, no work would ever get done. Pets would quickly disrupt all order and discipline.

But they would fill a need, too.

It became clear to me that just as woman has a maternal instinct, man has a need to care for and protect a fellow creature. I could see proof of this every time I looked out the window. Big Ben, who wouldn't hesitate to break your jaw if he suspected you were slighting him, thought nothing of gently nursing a tiny bird. I suddenly realized that the empty feeling in my stomach wasn't hunger; I wished I had a skinny, ugly bird to nurse, too.

No one in prison pays much attention to time unless scheduled to get out soon. A week or two, or a month or two, passed. Then I looked out one morning and spotted Ben near the walk at the front of the building. He was on one knee in the classic crapshooter's pose. He opened his hand and released a small, mud-colored bird.

It was hard to believe that this was Baby; he had grown so. He wasn't as big as an adult bird, but no one would have any trouble recognizing him as a bird. The little guy beat his wings frantically and fluttered from side to side, then landed on the soft grass about twenty feet from where he'd been launched. Big Ben lumbered over to where the bird lay on the grass and scooped him into his hand. I could see his lips moving and I knew he was muttering praise and encouragement to the bird.

I watched a few more flights from the window. Baby kept flying increasingly greater distances but wasn't getting much altitude. Several officers entered and left A-cellhouse through its side door. Each glanced at Big Ben and his bird, then quickly looked away. None wanted to enforce the regulation against pets, so they pretended not to notice. After a while Ben stopped giving the bird flying lessons, and I left the window and went back to work.

I looked out the window several times in the next few days, but I must've picked the wrong times because I didn't see Ben. Other guys kept telling me about Big Ben and his bird and how well it could fly and how it came to him when he whistled for it. Baby became the chief topic of conversation around the Education Building. A couple of men joked that they wished Big Ben would teach them to fly—they wanted to see what's on the other side of the prison's thirty-five foot wall.

Then one day I saw Big Ben sitting alone on the steps of

A-cellhouse. I sensed that something was wrong and went over to him. "How's Baby?" I asked.

"He's gone," Ben said. "Flew away. Sat up there," he motioned vaguely toward the wall, "and looked back once, then flew away."

"Maybe he'll come back."

"Naw, he won't come back." His voice held notes of both pain and anger. "Boids is like people. When they don't need ya no more, they forgets ya."

I remembered that someone had once told me Big Ben hadn't received a letter in two years. "Maybe Baby just decided to look around," I said as cheerfully as I could. "Birds do that all the time. It wouldn't surprise me if he came back. The swallows *always* return to Capistrano."

Ben gave me a cold look, then ignored me, so I went inside; but I was a little worried and kept going to the window to keep an eye on him. That's how I happened to be around when the bird returned a few hours later and perched on his shoulder. He cupped it in his huge hands and sat talking to it for a long time. Tears ran down his cheeks, and his back shook. I watched as he touched the bird gently with his lips, then squeezed the life from it.

What Kind of Person Are You?
by Bill Pronzini and Barry N. Malzberg

I arrived at Quality Supermarkets' Fairfield branch promptly at nine o'clock Monday morning and went immediately into the office to check the weekend receipts. A roving district manager with twelve stores and nearly one hundred employees to monitor cannot afford to waste time; I work on a very tight schedule.

At 9:40 I stood and walked quickly into the store proper, to where Franklin was working at Register Three, his regular post. I waited until he finished serving a customer and then motioned him to close down and join me. When he had done that, I took him back into the office and told him to sit down.

He sat poised on the edge of the chair, hands picking nervously at each other; he was about twenty-four, red-haired and gangly, and he reminded me somewhat of my son Ronald. I did not say anything for a time, watching him. He fidgeted under my scrutiny, eyes touching mine, flicking away, flicking back. But he always seemed to be nervous in my presence; I had a reputation as a somewhat stern and uncompromising supervisor.

"I'll get directly to the point," I said. "I have just been over the weekend receipts and register slips, and you're seventy dollars short, Franklin—fifty on Saturday and twenty on Sunday."

His eyes grew wide and his face paled visibly. "Seventy dollars?" he said.

"Exactly seventy dollars. That is a considerable amount, Franklin, as I'm sure you realize."

"Are you *certain*, Mr. Adams? I mean, couldn't you have made a mistake. . ."

"I do not make mistakes," I said stiffly. "The mistake here, if that is what it is, rests squarely on your shoulders."

"I . . . I don't know what to say. I've never been short before, I'm always careful—"

"Indeed?"

"I haven't been off a penny in the two months I've been working here," Franklin said. "You know that, sir."

"I do know it, yes," I said, "but the fact remains that you are seventy dollars short for this past weekend—exactly seventy dollars, not a cent more or less. The question now is what kind of person are you, Franklin?"

"Sir?"

"What kind of person are you?" I repeated. "An honest and fallible one, whose only crime is making careless errors in mathematics? Or a foolish and culpable one who succumbed to the obvious temptation?"

His mouth opened, as though in shock, and he blinked rapidly several times. "Mr. Adams, you don't think I *stole* that money?"

"Did you?"

"No. No!"

I held up a hand. "I am not accusing you of anything, Franklin. I am merely trying to ascertain the truth of the situation here."

"I'm not a thief," he said desperately. "You've got to believe that, Mr. Adams. I don't know how I could have made a seventy-dollar mistake, but that's all it was—a mistake. I swear it."

"I would like to believe that."

"You've *got* to believe it," he said, "it's the truth."

I picked up my pencil and tapped the eraser on the sheaf of papers spread out in front of me. "Embezzlement of funds is a serious offense, you know. I could have you arrested, or at the very least summarily fired."

"Please, Mr. Adams—I didn't steal that money!"

"Have you ever been in trouble before? Any kind of trouble?"

"No, sir, never. Never."

I sighed. "Very well, then. I am not a harsh man, and I have a son about your age; I see no reason not to give you the benefit of the doubt, particularly in view of your prior work record. If you're willing to replace the seventy dollars, and assuming something like this does not happen again, I suppose I am willing to drop the matter entirely."

Relief made him slump on the chair. "I'll replace the money, sure," he said eagerly, "I know I'm responsible for it. I don't have seventy dollars with me, but I can have it by tomorrow; I'll borrow it from my father—"

"That won't be necessary, Franklin. I will accept ten dollars now and ten dollars per week for the next six weeks, assuming again that there are no further shortages and you continue to do your job properly."

"I will, Mr. Adams, I'll be extra-careful. It'll never happen again, I promise you that."

"For your sake," I said, "see that you keep that promise."

He nodded and produced his wallet and handed me a ten-dollar bill. I took it and laid it carefully on the desk. "You can go back to work now," I said.

"Yes, sir. Thank you, Mr. Adams."

When he was gone I sat for a moment looking at the register receipts, the branch ledger-books. Then I finished my work, closed everything into the safe, put Franklin's ten-dollar bill into my own wallet, and left the store to continue my rounds. . .

I arrived at the Essex branch at precisely noon and spent nearly an hour checking the weekend receipts. At 12:50 I went out into the store proper and brought Trowbridge—another young man in his early twenties, tall and thin like Ronald—back to the office and told him to sit down.

"I have just been going over the weekend receipts," I said, "and you're seventy dollars short—fifty on Saturday and twenty on Sunday."

He stared at me incredulously.

"The question now is," I said, "what kind of person are you?"

At eight the following Friday night, I arrived at the Dunes Motel on the outskirts of the city, knocked on the door of Unit Eight, and was admitted.

"Right on time," Cobb said.

"I am always punctual." I opened my wallet and laid two hundred and fifty dollars on the bed.

He picked it up and counted it twice. "O.K., Adams," he said. "That takes care of the first installment. Six more weeks and Ronnie and I will be square." He chuckled. "Unless he decides to borrow another thousand to pay off some more of his gambling debts."

"Ronald will never borrow another dime from you," I said, "I'll see to that. And he is not gambling any more."

Cobb smiled wisely. "Sure—whatever you say, Adams. Just make sure you're here with the second installment next Friday. I'd hate to have to send one of my boys out to pay Ronnie a little visit."

A sudden rush of anger made me clench my fists. "What kind of person are you to prey on decent people this way?" I said. "What kind of *monster* are you?"

Cobb's laughter rang in my ears all the way out to the car and all the way home to my son.

Shatter Proof

by Jack Ritchie

He was a soft-faced man wearing rimless glasses, but he handled the automatic with unmistakable competence.

I was rather surprised at my calmness when I learned the reason for his presence. "It's a pity to die in ignorance," I said. "Who hired you to kill me?"

His voice was mild. "I could be an enemy in my own right."

I had been making a drink in my study when I had heard him and turned. Now I finished pouring from the decanter. "I know the enemies I've made and you are a stranger. Was it my wife?"

He smiled. "Quite correct. Her motive must be obvious."

"Yes," I said. "I have money and apparently she wants it. All of it."

He regarded me objectively. "Your age is?"

"Fifty-three."

"And your wife is?"

"Twenty-two."

He clicked his tongue. "You were foolish to expect anything permanent, Mr. Williams."

I sipped the whiskey. "I expected a divorce after a year or two and a painful settlement. But not death."

"Your wife is a beautiful woman, but greedy, Mr. Williams. I'm surprised that you never noticed."

My eyes went to the gun. "I assume you have killed before?"

"Yes."

"And obviously you enjoy it."

He nodded. "A morbid pleasure, I admit. But I do."

I watched him and waited. Finally I said, "You have been here more than two minutes and I am still alive."

"There is no hurry, Mr. Williams," he said softly.

"Ah, then the actual killing is not your greatest joy. You must savor the preceding moments."

"You have insight, Mr. Williams."

"And as long as I keep you entertained, in one manner or another, I remain alive?"

"Within a time limit, of course."

"Naturally. A drink, Mr. . . . .?"

"Smith requires no strain on the memory. Yes, thank you. But please allow me to see what you are doing when you prepare it."

"It's hardly likely that I would have poison conveniently at hand for just such an occasion."

"Hardly likely, but still possible."

He watched me while I made his drink and then took an easy chair.

I sat on the davenport. "Where would my wife be at this moment?"

"At a party, Mr. Williams. There will be a dozen people to swear that she never left their sight during the time of your murder."

"I will be shot by a burglar? An intruder?"

He put his drink on the cocktail table in front of him. "Yes. After I shoot you, I shall, of course, wash this glass and return it to your liquor cabinet. And when I leave I shall wipe all fingerprints from the doorknobs I've touched."

"You will take a few trifles with you? To make the burglar-intruder story more authentic?"

"That will not be necessary, Mr. Williams. The police will assume that the burglar panicked after he killed you and fled empty-handed."

"That picture on the east wall," I said. "It's worth thirty thousand."

His eyes went to it for a moment and then quickly returned to me. "It is tempting, Mr. Williams. But I desire to possess nothing that will even remotely link me to you. I appreciate art, and especially its monetary value, but not to the extent where I will risk the electric chair." Then he smiled. "Or were you perhaps offering me the painting? In exchange for your life?"

"It was a thought."

He shook his head. "I'm sorry, Mr. Williams. Once I accept a commission, I am not dissuaded. It is a matter of professional pride."

I put my drink on the table. "Are you waiting for me to show fear, Mr. Smith?"

"You will show it."

"And then you will kill me?"

His eyes flickered. "It is a strain, isn't it, Mr. Williams? To be afraid and not to dare show it."

"Do you expect your victims to beg?" I asked.

"They do. In one manner or another."

"They appeal to your humanity? And that is hopeless?"

"It is hopeless."

"They offer you money?"

"Very often."

"Is that hopeless too?"

"So far it has been, Mr. Williams."

"Behind the picture I pointed out to you, Mr. Smith, there is a wall safe."

He gave the painting another brief glance. "Yes."

"It contains five thousand dollars."

"That is a lot of money, Mr. Williams."

I picked up my glass and went to the painting. I opened the safe, selected a brown envelope, and then finished my drink. I put the empty glass in the safe and twirled the knob.

Smith's eyes were drawn to the envelope. "Bring that here, please."

I put the envelope on the cocktail table in front of him.

He looked at it for a few moments and then up at me. "Did you actually think you could buy your life?"

I lit a cigarette. "No. You are, shall we say, incorruptible."

He frowned slightly. "But still you brought me the five thousand?"

I picked up the envelope and tapped its contents out on the table. "Old receipts. All completely valueless to you."

He showed the color of irritation. "What do you think this has possibly gained you?"

"The opportunity to go to the safe and put your glass inside it."

His eyes flicked to the glass in front of him. "That was yours. Not mine."

I smiled. "It was your glass, Mr. Smith. And I imagine that the police will wonder what an empty glass is doing in my safe. I rather think, especially since this will be a case of murder, that they will have the intelligence to take finger-prints."

His eyes narrowed. "I haven't taken my eyes off you for a moment. You couldn't have switched our glasses."

"No? I seem to recall that at least twice you looked at the painting."

Automatically he looked in that direction again. "Only for a second or two."

"It was enough."

He was perspiring faintly. "I say it was impossible."

"Then I'm afraid you will be greatly surprised when the police come for you. And after a little time you will have the delightful opportunity of facing death in the electric chair. You will share your victims' anticipation of death with the addition of a great deal more time in which to let your imagination play with the topic. I'm sure you've read accounts of executions in the electric chair?"

His finger seemed to tighten on the trigger.

"I wonder how you'll go," I said. "You've probably pictured yourself meeting death with calmness and for-titude. But that is a common comforting delusion, Mr. Smith. You will more likely have to be dragged. . . ."

His voice was level. "Open that safe or I'll kill you."

I laughed. "Really now, Mr. Smith, we both know that obviously you will kill me if I *do* open the safe."

A half a minute went by before he spoke. "What do you intend to do with the glass?"

"If you don't murder me—and I rather think you won't now—I will take it to a private detective agency and have your fingerprints reproduced. I will put them, along with a note containing pertinent information, inside a sealed envelope. And I will leave instructions that in the event I die violently, even if the occurrence appears accidental, the envelope be forwarded to the police."

Smith stared at me and then he took a breath. "All that won't be necessary. I will leave now and you will never see me again."

I shook my head. "I prefer my plan. It provides protection for my future."

He was thoughtful. "Why don't you go direct to the police?"

"I have my reasons."

His eyes went down to his gun and then slowly he put it in his pocket. An idea came to him. "Your wife could very easily hire someone else to kill you."

"Yes. She could do that."

"I would be accused of your death. I could go to the electric chair."

"I imagine so. Unless. . . ."

Smith waited.

"Unless, of course, she were unable to hire anyone."

"But there are probably a half a dozen other. . . ." He stopped.

I smiled. "Did my wife tell you where she is now?"

"Just that she'd be at a place called the Petersons. She will leave at eleven."

"Eleven? A good time. It will be very dark tonight. Do you know the Petersons' address?"

He stared at me. "No."

"In Bridgehampton," I said, and I gave him the house number.

Our eyes held for half a minute.

"It's something you must do," I said softly. "For your own protection."

He buttoned his coat slowly. "And where will you be at eleven, Mr. Williams?"

"At my club, probably playing cards with five or six friends. They will no doubt commiserate with me when I receive word that my wife has been . . . shot?"

"It all depends on the circumstances and the opportunity." He smiled thinly. "Did you ever love her?"

I picked up a jade figurine and examined it. "I was extremely fond of this piece when I first bought it. Now it bores me. I will replace it with another."

When he was gone there was just enough time to take the glass to a detective agency before I went on to the club.

Not the glass in the safe, of course. It held nothing but my own fingerprints.

I took the one that Mr. Smith left on the cocktail table when he departed.

The prints of Mr. Smith's fingers developed quite clearly.

Out of Order

by Carl Henry Rathjen

The kid got it in the back at seven-thirty that evening.

He'd answered the service station's inside phone, listened, then covered the mouthpiece and said to Jim Daly, "Duck! It's The Sniper. I'm going to call his bluff."

"Don't," Jim had warned, feeling exposed with glass on four sides of the office.

But the kid ran out to call the police from the phone booth near the driveway. A customer, driving in, made him swerve, slipping on a glob of grease. So there was no telling whether the slug got him before or after he began twisting down. No telling from which direction it came. And no sound of a shot either.

Jim Daly, with hair as black as the grease on big knuckles he kept rubbing into a palm, told all that to Whitehead, the squat, blond detective who came in the second police car while the ambulance guys were covering the kid with a canvas.

"So that's an out for you, I suppose," Daly added.

This was the seventh such robbery of a service station. Somebody phoned and said, "You're covered with a gun, every move. Put a clip or rubber band on the bills from the till. Drop them over the wall behind the air hose, then go on with your work. Don't get nosey or call the police. You'll be covered every moment." Seven of them, and the police, as usual, said they were working on it. Now the kid was dead. The first killing.

Whitehead's square face got a little white, then he spoke quietly. "Seeing anybody killed is hard to take, but was he something special to you?"

Jim Daly looked toward the canvas, a hub for a ring of morbid stares being held out of the station by uniformed police.

"He tried to hold me up once," said Daly. "I talked him out of it and gave him a job."

Whitehead stared. "Instead of calling us."

"All he needed was a break," snapped Daly.

"That's all we need too," Whitehead murmured. His partner, a thin man with razor-sharp gaze, said nothing.

"In other words," Daly charged, "you haven't done a damn thing. Now a good kid's dead, murdered. He never had a chance."

Whitehead seemed to sort words before he spoke. "You'd know better than I would how many service stations there are in the metropolitan area. Close to a couple thousand, isn't it?"

"All right," said Daly. "You can't stake out every one of them. But you guys are supposed to know how to run down these killers."

"It takes time," Whitehead began.

"I can't get away with that in my business," Daly declared. "I'm expected to trouble-shoot a customer's car in five minutes."

Whitehead nodded, staring around at apartments across the avenue, store windows facing the sidestreet with a slice of night sky showing in the alley.

"And the customer," he said with a slight smile, "expects it because he thinks it's easy, doesn't know the problems of your job. That works two ways, Daly. If you were a policeman, you'd know."

"I tried to know once." Daly pressed his lips.

Whitehead faced him curiously.

"Why'd they turn you down?"

Daly answered defiantly, staring at a fist making his thumbnail white as the blood squeezed back. "I did time once when I was a kid."

Whitehead studied him. "That's why you gave this one a break."

Daly nodded. "That's why I'm sore, damn sore. A guy

sees he's made a mistake and more than makes up for it. Then someone louses it up for him, and you hand me the usual hogwash alibi. Save it for somebody else. I'll find who got him."

"Take it easy," Whitehead began.

"That's the trouble. I have, waiting for you to do something."

Daly pulled off his coveralls.

But he was still in the station at midnight, though not open for business, when Whitehead drove in with his partner.

"Got it solved, Daly?" he asked, neither sarcastic nor hopeful as he leaned against the desk, hands in the pockets of his topcoat.

Daly poked a thick finger in a cigarette pack that looked as though it had been sat on. "It's like tracking down a miss in a car. I've found out where it can't be from."

"I know what you mean," said Whitehead. He waited. Daly carefully straightened out a bent cigarette, then thumbnailed a wooden match. He waited too. Whitehead sighed, and smiled. "All right, I'll tell you. We know where it couldn't have come from too, but being police, we had to check it out anyway. The shot couldn't have come from the apartments or stores. They've all been occupied a long time. No stick-up artist is going to have friends living in the vicinity of every place he plans to knock over. He wouldn't be on a roof either. Couldn't watch his victim at the phone. We know that from other jobs that have been pulled where he mentioned what the victim was doing while being warned."

Daly blew smoke toward the door. "You don't have to be a cop to figure that out."

Whitehead looked at the No Smoking sign, glanced at the locked gasoline pumps, then got out his own cigarettes.

"And it doesn't take a police officer to figure it took two of them to pull these jobs. One to make the phone call, the other to watch from a dark parked car."

Daly took a long drag, then gestured with his thumb toward the side street. "My guess is the car was parked up there."

Whitehead's partner shifted to peer in that direction,

then turned to look where the kid's body had been. Whitehead just leaned against the desk.

"Police officers have one advantage over citizens who think we're not doing our job. Take the chip off your shoulder and listen, Daly. We looked up records. When the kid tried to hold you up, it wasn't the first job he'd pulled, nor the last."

Daly closed his eyes and took another long drag. "I wish you hadn't told me." He looked up suddenly. "You think he was in on these sniper jobs?"

Whitehead nodded. "And he wanted a larger split. That's why he was shot."

Daly frowned. "But they tried to hold me up."

"That's what doesn't fit," said Whitehead. "They hit only stations doing a good business. We've checked on gasoline purchases with the wholesaler. You haven't been doing so well here since the freeway pulled traffic away. A lot of nights it's not even been worth staying open."

"It was a phony stick-up then," Daly growled. "Just to get the kid."

"A phony, sure," Whitehead agreed, "because we figure the kid was shot in the back, dying out there while he staggered, running to get away from *you!*"

Daly straightened. Whitehead's partner suddenly had a gun in his hand. Whitehead took his hands out of his pockets. One of them held handcuffs.

"You overplayed it, Daly. Too positive we were going to be dumb cops. Too dumb to wonder what happened to the supposed customer who made the kid swerve so you couldn't tell where the shot came from. Too dumb to thoroughly check everything out, records of all kinds, the possible and the impossible. We were even so dumb we tried the phone company, even though we figured the call couldn't be traced. It couldn't, because the kid forgot to tell you—or didn't have time to—that he'd reported earlier this evening the phone was out of order."

Daly expelled smoke. "What does that prove? I might have been confused by the shock of his being killed. I guess he took the call on the outside phone."

"The same as you were so confused," Whitehead suggested, "you forgot to rub grease on your thumbnails when we arrived. So confused you told us yourself that we had killers, not just one man, to run down on these hold-ups. You also thought we were too dumb to have men watching you while you pretended to begin tracking down the kid's killer. There's a crew opening the sewer now to retrieve your silenced gun."

He put the cuffs on Daly and guided him toward the car.

"You know," he said, "it doesn't bother us that people think we're dumb. It takes time, but we find in the long run that we meet plenty who are dumber. You'll have a lot in common with them, Daly . . . in prison."

The Handy Man

by Marion M. Markham

"I am so lucky to have a handy man like you living on the island," Thelma Norburton cooed. Thelma always cooed when she wanted someone to do something for her. She cooed at Arthur frequently. It was cheaper than paying a repair man to fix her vacuum cleaner switch, or her television set, or her toilet valve.

"I just don't *know* what I'd do *without* you. Ever since *poor* Henry passed on I've been *so lost*. You don't *know* how *difficult* it is to be a widow. *Everyone* tries to take *advantage* of me and *cheat* me."

Arthur heard only half of the cooing, as his head was under Thelma's pink kitchen sink. It was the third time in a month that his head had been under Thelma Norburton's kitchen sink. First it was a leak in the pipe leading to the dishwasher—then the garbage disposal jammed—now the diamond ring in the drain. Today he was under there longer than usual, and his back was aching badly. In addition, he had twice bumped his head against the garbage disposal unit.

"Since *you* and Millie moved in next door my *life* has

so much *easier*. You can't *think* how *relieved* I was. The house was empty for *so long*, while the will was being contested. And sometimes I saw *strange* lights at *night*. But, *of course*, the police never paid any *attention* to my calls. And then *you* moved in, and I felt so much *safer*.

"I wasn't scared to *death* that I'd be *murdered* in my bed after *you* came. And to find out that you can fix *absolutely* anything. I mean, I certainly am the *luckiest* widow in Florida. I *told* Millie that *just* yesterday. Millie, I said, I am *absolutely* the *luckiest* widow on the Gold Coast to have two of the *cleverest* people in south Florida for neighbors."

Arthur had heard all about that conversation from Millie before.

"Now she wants you to re-upholster a bedroom chair for her," Millie recounted. "And she'd like me to make new drapes to match. Is this what retirement is all about, Arthur? Making drapes for my neighbor? I made my own for years, and hung my own wallpaper, and re-covered our dining room chairs myself just so we could save enough money to retire. I don't want to spend that retirement making Thelma Norburton's drapes.

"Tell her you won't do it."

"Arthur, you know how she is. So forceful and pathetic at the same time. She can afford to have an interior designer make new drapes every month, but she still manages to make me feel guilty if I say no to her. I think it's the neighborhood. We don't belong with all these wealthy people. And Thelma knows how I feel and uses it to make me feel like a servant."

"You're not Thelma's servant. You're my wonderful wife, and you belong here as much as she does. Two million is hardly poverty."

"But it shows—all the years I washed my own dishes and made my own clothes. It shows in my hands and the way my shoulders are bent. It shows, too, that you used to wind your own condensers—or whatever those things were you worked on every night when Alice was a baby and the business just starting.

"It doesn't show. We're as good as anyone else on this island."

"Then why did Thelma ask you to put up a new shelf in her garage just two days after we moved in?"

"I'll speak to Thelma tomorrow and tell her you won't make her drapes and I won't re-cover her chair. I won't have her making my wife feel like a servant." He kissed her gently. "I promise you, I'll take care of it tomorrow."

Arthur tried to speak to Thelma the next morning. When he opened his mouth, Thelma cooed at him about how her *diamond* ring that *dear* Henry had given to her on their *last* Christmas *together* had gone down the kitchen drain, and would Arthur mind *terribly* getting it out for her?

So Arthur lay on his back under the pink sink, while Thelma sat at the glass-topped wrought iron kitchen table —also pink. She sipped grasshoppers, never offering anything to Arthur, and cooed.

"My *goodness*, Arthur. I never thought it would take *this* long to get a little old diamond ring out of a little old *sink* drain. I'm playing *bridge* at two. I mean, you fixed the *washing machine* in an hour, and you had to take it *all* apart. Remember how I bet you *wouldn't* get it all back *together* again? But you *did*. You really are so *marvellous* with your *hands*. I don't believe there's *anything* you can't do.

"Does Millie *appreciate* you? *Really* appreciate you, I mean. If she ever gets tired of you, you just come *right* over here. You *understand*? Henry Bejaman Norburton may have inherited *twenty million* dollars. But he couldn't hold a *candle* to you when it comes to *electricity* and *plumbing*. I really *am* the *luckiest* woman to have a *strong, intelligent, clever* man like *you* around.

"Almost finished," Arthur said, giving a last twist to the thin copper wire he was working with. He handed out the diamond ring that looked too small for Thelma's pudgy fingers.

"You still have time to make your bridge game." He slid out from under the sink and began gathering up the wire cutters, voltage tester, and other tools.

"I just don't *know* how to *thank* you, Arthur. Would you like a glass of *water*?"

"No, thanks, Thelma. It's almost two, and Millie will wonder what's become of me."

"Well, I do *appreciate* it. You really *are* the *cleverest* man. Is there *anything* you can't do?"

"Not once I set my mind to it, Thelma" he said proudl*

Arthur felt real pride later that evening, when he s?

sudden eerie glow in the kitchen next door, and then total darkness. He'd never wired a garbage disposal before.

Continuous feed disposal units were dangerous, he had always said, what with water running and women pushing things through the metal sink ring with wet hands. If ever the fuse on the unit didn't cut off right, if something happened to short the motor and send an electric current up to that metal ring. . .

Of course, it was probably a one-in-five-hundred-million chance—unless a handy man knew how to fix it just right.

Nightmare

by Elaine Slater

One minute the sun was out, and the next it got all gray and dark. I saw lightning 'way far off in the direction we were going, but I couldn't hear any thunder yet. A wind came up from nowhere and all the leaves on the bushes and trees did a belly-flop.

I looked at Mom, but she was driving perfectly calmly as if nothing was happening. She looked too young to be my mother, and for a second I felt sorry for her, but then I hated her again.

She was taking me to this summer vacation camp, and I didn't want to go. Cripes, how I didn't want to go! She'd showed me this brochure and it had a picture of the Director and all the campers posed outside of bunks with their Counsellors. The Director was a bald, beefy guy with a silver tooth, smiling something awful. The Counsellors were great big jerks in white ducks and open shirts. They all looked too damn proud of themselves.

But the kids! I tell you it was the kids who tipped me off. There they were, standing in front of their bunks, their

shorts hanging down, their shirts out, their hair practically
growing over their eyes. And I'm telling you there was a
look of such dumb misery on their faces, it'd give anyone
the shakes. One kid in particular—Bunk 9, I think he
was—was practically screaming a warning at me out of that
picture. "Stay away from here, kid," he was saying, "this is
Hell."

But my Mom was determined that I got to go to camp.
And when Mom makes up her mind!

I begged Dad. I said, "Just look at those faces in the
brochure. You can tell it's a crumby place."

My Dad has a fierce temper, but still he's an easier mark
than Mom. But this time all he said was, "Your Mother and I
have talked about this and you must trust us to do what we
think is right for you."

He couldn't see those faces like I could, and I was
ashamed to tell him the truth. I was scared. Cripes, I was
scared!

I tried everything. First I tried persuasion. I argued with
them all the time. I told them it was no good sending me
there because I wouldn't stay. I told them they couldn't
make me go if I didn't want to. Finally I got sent from the
table so many times, I decided to go on a hunger strike. I
had nothing to lose, I wasn't getting much to eat anyway.
But that didn't last long.

Next I ran away. I didn't get far—my bike blew a tire.
Then I tried to be as good as I knew how to be, so they'd
want me around all summer. I must admit that worked the
best. I helped Mom with everything, and when Dad came
home I helped him wash the car and mow the lawn. I never
even mentioned camp, but I could tell as the time grew
closer that they were beginning to look at each other and
then at me. They thought I wasn't looking, but I sure was.

Then the whole idea blew. We had a bang-up fight about
my fingernails of all things! I don't know what happened to
me. I guess all that helping was getting on my nerves.
Anyway, I started yelling and fighting, and boy, two days
later I was packed into the car with Mom and was headed
for camp.

We'd just reached this rickety sign, "Happy Days Camp,"
when I heard the first thunder rumbling in the distance.

The storm was coming fast. A few drops hit the windshield as we bumped down this long dirt road, and I thought, "My God! She's really going to do it. She's going to leave me here"—and suddenly I knew as sure as shooting I was gonna die here. I was screaming inside, but my Mom was still perfectly calm, concentrating on this lousy dirt road.

The Director was there waiting for us with one of the Counsellors. He grinned at me just like in the photograph, and I swear behind his fat face and sweaty glasses, I could see a death's-head. He took my hand to lead me over to the Counsellor, but I grabbed it away. His hand was like ice even though the rest of him was all sweaty. I looked up at this big Counsellor and I almost dropped right there.

"This is Archie," the Director said, "Counsellor of Bunk Nine. Your bunk."

I sidled up to that big jerk and I whispered, I think I whispered, "I'm gonna kick you in the head."

Cripes! He only smiled down at me, a smile that said, "Anything you can do I can do better, and harder, and *MORE*."

Then there was this huge clap of thunder, and rain began to fall in buckets as we stood there on this weedy parking lot.

I began to shake all over. I couldn't stop shaking. I was gonna die if I stayed here—I knew it. But nobody would believe me, most of all the people I loved best and the ones who were supposed to love me best.

I was shaking all over and had my eyes screwed shut . . . Then there was this sound like a bell screaming in my ears. I awoke shaking with cold. It was dark with just a thin edge of light coming over a distant freezing horizon, but the alarm clock was jangling insistently.

"Turn that damn thing off," my wife's voice said thickly. She was lying in the other bed in a stupor, her eyes closed, her mouth hanging open like a dead fish, and her hair in those great big curlers.

I looked at her in sudden revulsion and my trembling stopped. By God! She looked like my Mother in the dream. I pulled myself around and got out of bed. I picked up my pillow and stood over my snoring wife.

When I was finished she still looked like a dead fish, only this time she really was. Dead, that is. Then I smashed the goddam alarm clock and climbed back to bed. This was one morning I wasn't going to appear at her beefy father's plant or take any more goddam orders from her lousy brother, Archie.

Recipe for Revenge

by Jane Speed

It was a recipe for heartbreak: her love was forever, his only for a while.

She knew this, of course. She was not a fool. But forewarned is forearmed, she told herself.

Brave words, false words. His goodbye, as lightly given as his love, left her stunned and desolate.

Outwardly all went on as before. Her husband, who never suspected, continued to invite business associates to dinner to show off her charming skills; she was an excellent cook and an impeccable hostess. And she did not once fail him, though it seemed to her now a daily act of courage just to stay alive.

Why did she bother? What was she waiting for?

"By the way, my dear," her husband said one evening, "there'll be two guests for dinner on Saturday. Remember that pleasant young man who came here so often last year? Couldn't seem to get enough of your cooking. Well, he's just back from his honeymoon, so I've invited the newlyweds over for dinner. I didn't think you'd mind. You do that sort of thing well."

"Not at all," she assured him. And, smiling a Borgia smile, she set about planning her ultimate menu.

0506556947